Modern Chess Miniatures

AJNA

Ukiyoto Publishing

All global publishing rights are held by
Ukiyoto Publishing

Published in 2021

Content Copyright © AJNA

ISBN 9789364942522

www.ukiyoto.com

Preface

The creation of the first page on the 19th day of October 2020 ignites the spark of the author's passion on the game. Since childhood, his cravings and thirst on understanding this classic sport help him to realize that the beauty doesn't come from nowhere, it is carefully made, games of which upon understanding, reveals the true beauty and work behind it. The reason under every move, the analysis of the creator, makes the game be called the "miniature". Strong analysis and deeper understanding of the game creates more and more variations in the future. That in the long run, makes the game even more complicated due to countless branches of position arises on every idea applied. This genuine sport is the most complicated and so it is called "the game of intellectuals".

This book covers fifty brilliant games with their analysis from the author. Understanding every bits of its position, move by move, can delight the reader introducing them the realization behind, enhance their critical thinking, and truly feel the essence of every idea the creator want to indicate. Nowadays, games are evolving into scripted variations due to the presence of computer analysis killing the chaotic idea of the enthusiasts and even stop the madness of the psychological factor of playing. But as stated earlier, due to countless branches of unending variations of positions, human mind still cannot grasp all its scripted rules hence, providing new ways to enjoy this classical sport. Understanding of the game still holds the most essential in improving the play and not just memorizing it according to the algorithms.

If you want to make your dreams easy,

make it small.

If you want to make your dreams big,

make it difficult.

- A.J.N.A.

Dedication

Chess is somewhat easy and at the same time difficult to master. It's easy because all of the required books and materials, chess computers and game recordings are already given in front of today's enthusiasts, but despite of these, it's hard to study and master all of those, as the variations of positions are exponentially arising every move of the game. The continuations and choices are more than the mind to think, in addition to the psychological factors of playing the game, mind stamina, wit and creative ways to hold the position. Chess is truly has its own beauty from within.

My name is Austin John N. Arnaiz, a young enthusiast with a passionate heart on the beauty of chess. Amidst the Covid-19 pandemic, I decided to implant my interest and create a little legacy in this classical sport. In this critical time, I encourage young minds to take advantage of their energy, wit, and time to create their own little legacy in life and be well equipped enough to face the future.

The passion, love, cravings, and perseverance of the author on the beauty of the game made this book possible and successful in terms of his willing sacrifices and unending time devotions making this go through the hand of every dreamer in the future as he wish.

Sincere thanks to God and to the people behind every development of the pages. This project will not be possible without their excitement and patience to wait until the publishing of this book. Special thanks to Kat who made me dedicated again after several months of taking a break. Thank you in advance for those who want to read this book despite of being unfamiliar with this sport. Hoping that this book delights you and give you interest on the beauty of this game.

May this book be your guide as you go through development as learning the game requires not just reading and playing but careful understanding with passion and concentrations at the most degree. This book didn't claims that you will be thinking like a GM but it will be worth to read. Hoping to develop your knowledge and broaden your mind on a certain positions after reading this book. Read and learn the beauty of this game, heads up! Start your stepping stones towards your more competitive future.

Table of Contents

Table of Contents

Part I
Depicting Notations

Before jumping to the real game room, it is important to know the basic rules of recording the royal game. Aside from learning the basic rules of chess, knowing how to write the moves is next to essential. This will help you to remember the games you played without reminiscing it in the actual chess board. Chess notations are so important that it preserves the games of the past, records the games of the present, and will hold the games of the future. There are thousands of preserved games made possible with the help of this invention. Through the decades of wandering our minds in this classical sport, since the era of its creation, the game evolved in the way we see today. The theories and analysis went deeper and deeper in understanding. The invention of chess notation contributed a great factor for the improvement of the theory of this intellectual sport. Knowing how to record the games is having the opportunity of studying it in the future, which is essential in the preparation for the actual tournament, or even in the preparation for a specific opponent. In this book, we will be using the modern way of writing and recording game plays; the algebraic chess notation, the only system the world is using today.

Abbreviating Names

Pieces are abbreviated for a more convenient way of recording. The first letters of their names in English are chosen except for the knight being having the same first letter as the king, chosen to be abbreviated in its second letter. Excluded on the idea, pawns are not abbreviated as "P" but recorded in the square it occupies. Hence, the rook is abbreviated as "R", the knight as "N", bishop as "B", queen as "Q" and the king as "K". The capital letters are used to depict that a certain piece was moved or captured.

Naming the Squares

A chess board is an 8 by 8 board game equally divided into 64 congruent squares, each pawns and pieces can access into. To identify which squares a piece or a pawn occupied, the squares are named differently from the other. To begin, the horizontal rows on the board are called "ranks" while the vertical columns are called "files". The nearest rank towards a player with the white pieces are named as "1" and these are subsequently succeeded as "2" for the second nearest rank and so on, until meeting the "8" rank; the nearest rank towards a player with the black pieces.

Part I
Depicting Notations

Now, the left file relative for the player with the white pieces is depicted as "a" and then subsequently succeeded as "b" for the next file and so on, until meeting the right file, called as "h". To name a square, notations are using a file-rank scheme; a combination of the letter and number of the intersection of the file and rank within the board. Hence, starting from the lowest left square, which must be black, nearest with the player with the white pieces, the square is named as "a1", and the lowest right, "h1" while his upper left side must be "a8", the upper right, "h8". For better visualization let us look at the board illustrated aside.

a8	b8	c8	d8	e8	f8	g8	h8
a7	b7	c7	d7	e7	f7	g7	h7
a6	b6	c6	d6	e6	f6	g6	h6
a5	b5	c5	d5	e5	f5	g5	h5
a4	b4	c4	d4	e4	f4	g4	h4
a3	b3	c3	d3	e3	f3	g3	h3
a2	b2	c2	d2	e2	f2	g2	h2
a1	b1	c1	d1	e1	f1	g1	h1

Illustration of how the squares are named in Algebraic Notation

Other Symbols

There are handfuls of important symbols used in chess notation. The capture of the pawn or a piece is depicted as "X", a check on the king is regarded as "+". Moreover, below are some of the several important symbols seldom used in chess notations;

1.) X --- capture
2.) + --- check
3.) e.p. --- en passant
4.) 0-0 --- kingside castle
5.) 0-0-0 --- queenside castle
6.) # --- mate
7.) = --- a promotion
8.) ? --- inaccurate move
9.) ?? --- blunder
10.) ! --- excellent move

11.) !? --- bold but unsound move
12.) (1-0) --- white wins
13.) (0-1) --- black wins
14.) (½ , ½) --- drawn game
15.) = Q --- a promotion to queen
   (or with any other piece)

Part I
Depicting Notations

Writing the Moves

Now that we have learned the abbreviation of the pieces and the name of the squares on the board, we are ready to tackle the writings on how the pieces are moved through the game. Let us see and study the board below. This match happened between Robert J. Fischer and Edwin Bhend in 1959 at Zurich, Switzerland. Here, at move 20, Bhend moved his king from g7 square to h6 square as the board illustrates. In this matter, that move is written as "Kh6", this means that the king is then moved to h6 square, regardless of where the king recently placed.

Move 20: Kh6

However, if the same piece can occupy the same square, the move is written with an indication that that specific piece is then moved. As the board illustrates both of the b and h black rooks can occupy the d8 square, therefore, the move is written as "Rbd8" indicating that the rook on b file moved to said d8 square. However, ranks had been used to specify pieces placed in the same file, for example; if the rooks are placed on d8 and d4 and can both occupy the d6 square, the move is written as "R8d6" if the d8 rook is then moved.

Move 22: Rbd8

If the capture had been made, the symbol "X" is inserted between the piece and the square it occupies after the exchange and the captured piece is not mentioned. Notations are written in a short convenient way for a faster recording in and out of the game. Moreover, learning this by hand and mind may help chess enthusiasts study several games and improve their plays.

Part II
Exploring the Nerves

Now that we had studied and learned the basic ways to depict chess notations, we can now dig and explore the beauty of the games in history, move by move, as it is shown at the following pages of this book. The author had prepared for you 50 chosen great games of chess generations, from the most classical up to hyper-modernist style of ending the game. From the best games of the classical era of Tal, Fischer, Alekhine, Lasker, Korchnoi, Taimanov, Steinitz, Chigorin, Anderssen and the like, to the middle ages we barely see today, Kasparov, Karpov, Ivanchuk, Anand etc. and up to the present nerves wandering the sport, Carlsen, Giri, So, Morozevich, Yi, Liren, Aronian, Grischuk, Nakamura, Rapport and many more. Their games which contributed to the theory of this sport will never be forgotten, and carefully being lay down to the next generations of chess players. Each game has their own description every 3rd move from both sides, to better visualize what is really happening on the match. The games are incorporated with the picture of the board almost every column providing you the best way to realize and understand the set-up of the pieces without the aid of the real chess set. Several possible variations are included on the list, hence; help readers to realize the true essence of the grandmaster's move, the reason behind it, despite being it as a blunder, inaccurate response, a typical continuation, or a demolishing trick that ended the game. Such variations are shown in italicized forms to differentiate easily from the players' move. It is being suggested to analyze the games in mind, aiding only with the pictures this book provides. This will sharpen the wit and visualization of the readers' understanding of the game. After studying and analyzing the games implanted in this book, the author is hoping that the readers are going to be more competitive in the game in the near future, not saying it will make you think like a GM, but it will be worth reading. May the following games be your guide to help decide your opening repertoire, the evaluation and continuation for a certain position, and lastly the decisions you will be facing as the game goes by. Heads up! Start your journey towards a more competitive chess career.

Game 1
Winning the Queen

Vassily Ivanchuk – Garry Kasparov
8th Euwe Memorial (1994)

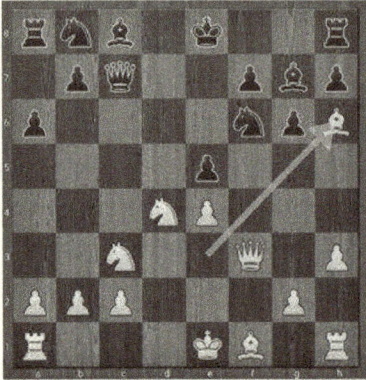

Move 11: Bh6

This game starts igniting a new way to open more variations in the Sicilian Defense. The crazy ideas of Ivanchuk left Kasparov continue the game with no queen in his hand.

1.) e4, c5

One of the most common responses against king's pawn game is playing the Sicilian Defense. Typically, white is taking the initiative to attack the kingside while the black is returning the favor to attack the queenside. This opening is always used to counter e4 as it provides better results according to statistics.

2.) Nf3, d6
3.) d4, cxd4
4.) Nxd4, Nf6

Kasparov is attacking the e4 pawn while developing his Nf6 knight. In this position, after Nxd4, e5 by black is not the best idea; white may respond Bb5+, Bd7; Bxd7, Qxd7; Nf5, g6 then Ne3. Having the position a weak pawn on d6 and white has a great control on d5 square.

5.) Nc3, a6
6.) f4, Qc7
7.) Qf3, g6

Ivanchuk defended the pawn with his c3 knight at the same time developing it. The move a6 is somehow stopping any of the white's plans by blocking the controlled square of its pieces. Followed by the move f4, opening up his kingside while his king is still in the center of its premises. The 7th move g6 by black is reasonable placing his bishop on a better square on g7 aiming to control the longer range; a1 to h8 diagonal, and making way to his king in the shortest possible time.

8.) Be3, Bg7
9.) h3, e5
10.) fxe5, dxe5

Move 10: dxe5

After 7th move upon reaching this position, black doesn't want to castle first, but wanting to take away the d4 knight by playing e5, it is then forced to move to b3 where it is more passively placed but, among else, Ivanchuk has the better response.

11.) Bh6, Bxh6
12.) Qxf6, 0-0
13.) Nd5, Qa5+

While the d4 knight is under threat, the move Bh6 stunned Kasparov for a while; here black is forced to take the bishop, destroying the black's position in an instant. At this situation, we can say that e5 is the losing move for black

Game 1
Winning the Queen

for it removed the support on f6 knight and providing a way to the queen to infiltrate the position.

> 14.) b4, Qd8
> 15.) Ne7+, Qxe7
> 16.) Qxe7, exd4

Move 16: exd4

Black now is facing a mate in one with Ne7+, and queen is the only piece who can save the game. It's the trade between the queen and the two knights forced by the situation. But there is a safer way that black should try to escape the queen sacrifice on 14th move as shown below;

> 1.) Nd5, Qa5+
> 2.) b4, Bg7
> 3.) bxa5, Bxf6
> 4.) Nxf6+, Kg7
> 5.) Nxh7, Kxh7
> 6.) Nb3, Be6

White is just a pawn up and black is not in trouble defending its position.

> 17.) Bc4, Nc6
> 18.) Qc5, Be3
> 19.) Rf1, Nd8

Now, Ivanchuk is a one-piece up but still can't completely dominate the board due to the fortress made by Kasparov; the bishop and pawn conjoined in the center. Here, the only piece available to break the fortress is the rook which if sacrificed can return the material balance. These difficulties arises new hope that the position will become equal after several moves of maneuvering.

> 20.) Rf3, Be6
> 21.) Rxe3, dxe3
> 22.) Bxe6, Nxe6

Ivanchuk now is simplifying the position knowing that a queen against the rook and knight can do better in an endgame given that the opponent king will be exposed on queen's double attack.

> 23.) Qxe3, a5
> 24.) b5, Rac8
> 25.) 0-0-0, Rc5

Move 25: Rc5

White's plan is to keep the board close until black accept the rook trade. After then, he is now willing to pawn exchanges making the black king exposed at the center in a queen vs. rook + knight endgame.

> 26.) Rd5, b6
> 27.) Qg3, Rc7
> 28.) Qd6, Rfc8

While Ivanchuk is silently killing black's position, Kasparov sets up a fortress trap by playing b6; now if white took the rook on c5, black recaptures with Nxc5; Qd4, Re8; e5, Rb8; Qd6, Rb7 then the queen has

Game 1
Winning the Queen

now difficulties destroying the position completely.

29.) Rd2, Rb7
30.) g4, Nc5
31.) Qf6, h6

Although white is a pawn up, the connected rooks are so strong that even the queen can't break its solid defenses. The c-pawn is weak giving black the opportunity to attack. It is the main reason why Kasparov played Qa5+ first before Qd8, forcing the white to move b4, weakening the c-pawn, making it the focus of black's connected rooks, preparing the endgame difficult for Ivanchuk despite of black's queen out of the board. Ivanchuk's plan now is to march his pawn toward the king to rip out and find some possibilities. Moreover, black couldn't play the fork at Nxe4 at 31st move, as it will be continued as the following;

1.) Qf6, Nxe4
2.) Rd8+, Rxd8
3.) Qxd8, Kg7
4.) Qd4+, Nf6
5.) g5, Rb8
6.) gxf6+, Kh8

And black will be on the losing position instantly.

32.) e5, Re8
33.) h4, Kh7
34.) h5, g5

Kasparov achieved the right squares for his rooks to defend the weak squares properly leaving a dead draw endgame. But the initiative is on white's hand, Ivanchuk must recognized small opportunities to sneak into white's premises.

35.) Rd6, Re6
36.) Qd8, Kg7
37.) a3, a4

Both sides are carefully maneuvering the pieces little by little. After Re6, if white chose Rxe6, black recaptures as Nxe6 and the position sits prettily drawn.

38.) Kb2, Rbe7
39.) Rxb6 (1-0)

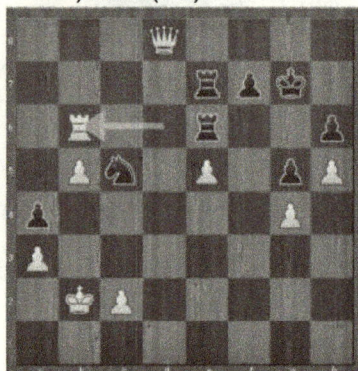

Move 39: Rxb6

Well, the weakness of fortress is zugzwang, while white is threatening Rxb6 or Rxe6 depending on the black's next move, it will create a hole in the position. After Rxb6, Rxb6; Qxb6, the b6 pawn is unstoppable, hence, Ivanchuk wins the match in a greater way possible. The game may continue as shown below;

1.) Rxb6, Rd7
2.) Qb8, Rd5
3.) Rxe6, Nxe6
4.) b6, Rb5+
5.) Ka1, Rd5
6.) Qc8, Nc5
7.) b7, Nxb7
8.) Qxb7, Rxe5

The queen against the lone rook with even pawns on the board is clearly an easy win for white.

Game 2
The Crushing French

Alexander Grischuk – Vassily Ivanchuk
World Cup (2011)

Move 4: c3

Move 9: 0-0

Typically, French Defense gives you a very aggressive game that even sometimes, keeping the king exposed behind its center pawns is a natural response. Here, Grischuk played dominantly, his unstoppable attack made Ivanchuk resigned.

    1.) e4, e6
    2.) d4, d5
    3.) e5, c5

A pawn structure genuinely from the French Opening, usually black tries to break the pawn chains to infiltrate the position, minor pieces attacks the d4 pawn while developing its way to castle the king.

    4.) c3, Nc6
    5.) Nf3, Bd7
    6.) Be2, Nge7

Black must capture the d4 pawn to develop the f8 bishop; this is the typical plan in playing the French. However, Ivanchuk tries to develop the g8 knight first; this makes his bishop passive several moves after.

    7.) 0-0, Ng6
    8.) g3, Be7
    9.) h4, 0-0

White quickly recognized the position; the black's d7 bishop is blocked and the pawn chains are covering the white's kingside. Grischuk's plan now is to march his pawns toward the king supported by his bishops eyeing a1-h6 and d1-h5 diagonals. In this position, white has the clear initiative; all of the minor pieces are aiming the kingside ready to support an attack lead by the pawn march.

    10.) h5, Nh8
    11.) dxc5, Bxc5
    12.) b4, Be7

Grischuk want to rip out the position playing dxc5. After b4, the bishop must return to e7 square in order to defend the incoming kingside attack and made the bishop passive again.

    13.) b5, Na5
    14.) h6, f5
    15.) hxg7, Kxg7

Black is starving of squares and letting the pawn exchange and advancing the f5 pawn will make some space. At this instant, black's position becomes better for the meantime.

Game 2
The Crushing French

16.) Kg2, Ng6
17.) Rh1, Rf7
18.) Bh6+, Kh8

The king is forced to move at the corner as the rook is better at f7 rather than g8 providing a square for the other rook to enter the field. However, black still has to improve as it is defending and its minor pieces are not yet coordinated.

Move 18: Kh8

19.) Nbd2, Qc7
20.) Rc1, Rg8
21.) c4, d4

After Rc1, black didn't take the e5 pawn due to the following continuation:

1.) Rc1, Nxe5
2.) Nxe5, Qxe5
3.) Bh5, Rf3
4.) Bf4,

And the queen is trapped.
And also didn't capture the c4 pawn as white will have the initiative after:

1.) c4, dxc4
2.) Nxc4, Nxc4
3.) Rxc4

But white decided to develop the rook as the f5 pawn is ready to rip the white's kingside. The position now is difficult to guess whether black or white has the advantages in hand.

22.) Bd3, b6
23.) Nxd4, Qxd4
24.) N2f3, Qc7

Move 24: Qc7

White is now preparing the queen to settle a square on h5. However, a quiet move, b6 seems to be usual but the most important, preventing the incoming c5, due to possible consequences:

1.) c5, Bxc5
2.) Bg5

And the rook must give up after a check on f6 because the bishop can't defend as it is pinned by the rook at c1.

25.) Ng5, Bxg5
26.) Bxg5, e5
27.) Qh5, Bc8

Every move of black is forced by white's attack here. Now, black king is in danger but can still hold and give counter attacks as its e and f pawn is dominant at the center.

28.) c5, exd4
29.) cxb6, Bb7+
30.) Kg1, Qe5

The most critical series of moves as white sacrificed his d4 knight to make the rook gain access on the c file, such a very complicated yet aggressive move to achieve the latter position.

Game 2
The Crushing French

Move 30: Qe5

31.) Rc7, Rxc7
32.) bxc7, Rg7
33.) Rh2, Rxc7
34.) Qxg6, Rc1+
35.) Bxc1 (1-0)

Due to countless pressure white has delivered, black cracked and made inaccurate moves. Well, instead of Rg7, Bxh1 looks better picking first one of the most important attacking piece of white's mating threat. Rg7, on the other hand, clearly defending the h7 square, making the black's position more crimped but looks acceptable as it is providing an escape square for the king.

Rxc7 was clearly a blunder, leaving the knight defenseless as the h7 pawn is pinned by the rook on h2. Better continuations are:
1.) Rh2, Qe1+
2.) Bf1, Qe6
3.) Qd1, Rd7
And will give a slightly better position.

Rc1+ looks a suicide move but there is a reasonable idea behind, black sacrificed his rook to prevent Bf6+, a brutal way to end the game. But after Bxc1 the game may continue as:

1.) Qe1+, Bf1
2.) Qe7, Bg5
3.) Qd7, Bf6#
The domination of the white's pieces from start to finish clearly wiped out the black's resources to continue the game as equal as possible.

However, after Rc1+, if white just keep his bishop waiting to give the beautiful Bf6+, and played Bf1, the game could be more complicated as before:
1.) Bf1, Rxf1+
2.) Kxf1, Qxb5+
3.) Ke1, Qb1+
4.) Ke2, Bf3+
5.) Kxf3, Qe4#

If the king moved to d2:
4.) Kd2, Nc4+
5.) Ke2, d3#

If the king doesn't take the bishop:
5.) Kd2, Qd1#

Correct sequence of moves is very essential in making combinations and attacks. Just a slight inaccurate response can give the opponent the opportunity and waste your plan. Above all, it has proven that chess has awesome possibilities. Grischuk just played very carefully and delivered a brilliant endgame finish, leaving Ivanchuk in a completely losing position.

Game 3
Destroying the Sicilian

Vassily Ivanchuk – Garry Kasparov
Linares (1991)

Move 38: Rxh4+

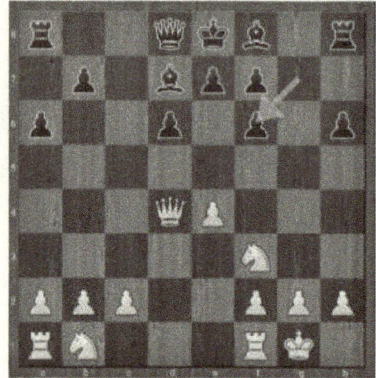

Move 09: gxf6

Sicilian Defense is one of the most aggressive yet most complicated opening choices for black. Crushing Kasparov in these broad variations require great talents and strong mind stamina. In this game, Ivanchuk not just beat Kasparov but destroyed him constantly until the end.

    1.) e4, c5
    2.) Nf3, d6
    3.) Bb5+, Nd7

White is preparing to castle putting the king to safety as soon as possible before making an attack. After Bb5+, Nc6 looks more promising as Nd7 blocks a square for the bishop although not the right time to tell which side has the advantages in hand.

    4.) d4, Nf6
    5.) 0-0, cxd4
    6.) Qxd4, a6

A typical continuation of the opening: The rapid development of white's pieces created an initiative to attack but black can easily defend several moves after. However, white must take the opportunity to sneak the black's position while the king is in the center.

    7.) Bxd7+, Bxd7
    8.) Bg5, h6
    9.) Bxf6, gxf6

If black played exf6, the d pawn would be isolated and become the center of attack so black sacrificed the kingside, saving the lone pawn. However, this is not a disadvantage to Kasparov, the four connected center pawns are solidly protecting the king and the g-file now is open giving access to the rook to directly attack the kingside.

    10.) c4, e6
    11.) Nc3, Rc8
    12.) Kh1, h5

Black doesn't need now to castle as the king is already protected at the center. Because of this, Kasparov gained a lot of tempo on developing his pieces. The position now becomes equal for both sides. On the other hand, Kasparov has the bishop pair against the twin knight of Ivanchuk ready to entangle once freed. Maneuvering the minor pieces and setting the rooks on the right square is the main factor to win this game and dominate.

Game 3
Destroying the Sicilian

13.) a4, h4
14.) h3, Be7
15.) b4, a5

White is slowly making up his dream plan, marching his pawns toward the queenside to slightly break the hard core defense of black's position. On the other hand, Kasparov found a way to use his isolated h-pawn, creeping in toward the uncomfortable white king as his king sits prettily behind his craving bishop pair waiting to unleash.

Move 15: a5

16.) b5, Qc7
17.) Nd2, Qc5
18.) Qd3, Rg8

After b5, white somehow created his weak c pawn needed to be defended unless it will be a gateway for black to infiltrate. Kasparov now has the initiative in hand using the g-file to put pressure on the white's kingside.

19.) Rae1, Qg5
20.) Rg1, Qf4
21.) Ref1, b6

The pressure executed by black is well defended by the two rooks and still waiting for the right time to free up the bishop pair. Kasparov must be very careful in moving his center pawns, once traded the king will be now open and the two knights can make their outposts on the center.

Move 24: Kf8

22.) Ne2, Qh6
23.) c5, Rxc5
24.) Nc4, Kf8

This is the critical moment of the situation. White has seen the black's weak square, the b6 pawn. The move c5 paved the way for knight to exploit it. Nc4 is the winning move here as it double attacks the b6 and d6 pawns. The rook can't defend it both due to the pawn on b5. After several moves, black's position will slowly fall. Instead of Qh6, Qe5 looks better due to the following continuation:

1.) Ne2, Qe5
2.) f4, Qc5
3.) f5, Bf8
4.) Rf3, Qb4

Both side gets compensation and hard to tell which side has the winning position.

25.) Nxb6, Be8
26.) f4, f5
27.) exf5, Rxf5

White now has created a silent queenside passed pawn. A total domination by Ivanchuk as Kasparov's bishop pair is not yet active, the white's kingside is well defended, and black's position is yet to be cracked.

Game 3
Destroying the Sicilian

28.) Rc1, Kg7
29.) g4, Rc5

The fall of the b6 pawn let white completely dominate the position. Its bishop pair can't even move to the continuous attack executed by Ivanchuk. The right timing, and clean execution, now the black king has to escape.

Move 33: Qh6

30.) Rxc5, dxc5
31.) Nc8, Bf8
32.) Qd8, Qg6
33.) f5, Qh6

Vasyl Mykhaylovych Ivanchuk also known as Vassily Ivanchuk is a leading player since 1988, and has been ranked at No. 2 on the FIDE World Rankings three times.

Black is approaching to zugzwang as white slowly blocking every bits of the white's plan. Ivanchuk is like the boa constrictor!

34.) g5, Qh5
35.) Rg4, exf5
36.) Nf4, Qh8
37.) Qf6, Kh7
38.) Rxh4 (1-0)

This is the scariest checkmate ever inflicted on Kasparov. The position sits prettily well but after c5 by white, freeing the knight to exploit the b6 pawn, starts the fire. This proved that in a close position, knights are better than bishops as they can jump into crowded places inflicting damages to the opponent. An outpost knight in a center is a threat to the observer.

13

Game 4
The Star against the Legend

Magnus Carlsen – Vassily Ivanchuk
Aerosvit (2008)

Move 32: Bf4

Magnus Carlsen sets a new style in the modern era of chess. Here, he played against Vassily Ivanchuk and gripped the position in a clean manner. His domination of the important squares leaved Ivanchuk cramped until the endgame.

1.) d4, Nf6
2.) c4, g6
3.) Nc3, Bg7

This is the set-up for the King's Indian Defense. White typically controlling the queenside while black often break his f-pawn to rip out the kingside position.

4.) e4, d6
5.) Nf3, 0-0
6.) Be2, e5

Both players are setting their kings into safety. Grabbing as many spaces as they can and developing their pieces in preparation of the middle phase of the game.

7.) 0-0, Nc6
8.) d5, Ne7
9.) b4, Nh5

Ivanchuk let Carlsen to push his knight by playing d5 and gained tempo. Black's knight is best on e7 as it

support the f-pawn in preparation of f5 to open up the position.

Move 09: Nh5

10.) Re1, f5
11.) Ng5, Nf6
12.) f3, Kh8

Black is maneuvering his pieces and opening up his kingside gaining more space. However, Ivanchuk can't keep the bishop pair as Carlsen's g5 knight is about to make an outpost on e6 square and the only pieces available to trade is the c8 bishop. The two black knights practically can't be traded as the position is slightly cramped and has no squares to maneuver it. It's a great idea on the KID variations.

13.) b5, Ne8
14.) Be3, Bf6
15.) Ne6, Bxe6

White moved his knight on e6 exactly before Bf6 to avoid Ng7 making sure that only the c8 bishop will be traded preventing Ivanchuk have the bishop pair. Black's position is still cramped and can't make any developments while white are now grabbing the queenside squares and has a plenty of space to develop his pieces.

Game 4
The Star against the Legend

16.) dxe6, Ng7
17.) Bh6, Nxe6
18.) Bxf8, Qxf8

An instructive Bh6, as black is forced again to give up his rook in return of the bishop and a pawn. In this position, Ng8 is not a good choice as the variation gives the following continuation;

1.) Bh6, Ng8
2.) Bxg7+, Bxg7
3.) Qb3, c5
4.) bxc5 e.p., bxc6
5.) c5

The queen can't stop eyeing the e6 pawn which needs several moves to capture making the black's position uncomfortable. Trading the rook with the bishop and pawn is indeed a good choice in this situation.

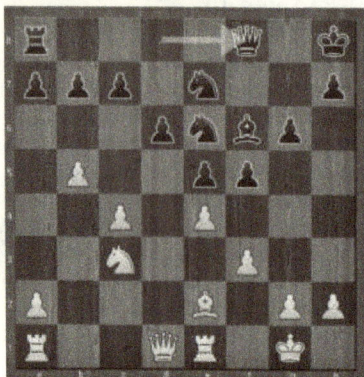

Move 18: Qxf8

19.) c5, Nxc5
20.) Bc4, Bg5
21.) Qe2, Qh6

Carlsen sacrificed his c5 pawn making a way for his bishop to control the important squares in the action.
The game now is approaching to endgame having white a two connected rooks while black is still making his way to develop his pieces to create pressures on the white wing.

22.) Rad1, Rf8
23.) a4, b6
24.) g3, Qh3

Both players are improving their position as there are no clear cut plans available. The pawns must be ripped out first to create complications thus avoiding a dead draw position.

25.) Qg2, Qh6
26.) Qe2, Qh3
27.) Kh1, Nd7

It is clear that white has the upper hand that's why Ivanchuk want to draw by making perpetual moves Carlsen didn't want to accept.

28.) Ra1, Qh6
29.) Ra2, Nf6
30.) Kg2, Nh5

Move 30: Nh5

Both continue to improve their play. Black maneuvers his pieces to attack the king while white is prepared to defend it.

31.) Nd5, Nxd5
32.) Bxd5, Bf4
33.) Qf2, fxe4

White is willing to trade pieces as he has the advantages in the endgame. Ivanchuk's plan now is to create complications with the available pieces on the board as after the

Game 4
The Star against the Legend

trades, it is now difficult to win with the game against the rook in domination.

34.) Bxe4, Qg5
35.) Rc2, d5
36.) Bxd5, Bxg3

This is a really beautiful combination sacrificing a pawn to destroy the structure of white's kingside. After several moves, the pawn will be regained. However, this is a very difficult situation for Ivanchuk, as now the two rooks are ready to infiltrate the black's kingdom and there are not enough defenses available.

37.) hxg3, Nf4+
38.) Kf1, Nxd5
39.) Rce2, Qf6

Move 39: Qf6

Carlsen attacks the isolated e-pawn and Ivanchuk can't defend it with Re8 due to the following continuation;

1.) Rce2, Re8
2.) f4, Qg3
3.) Rxe5, Rxe5
And the rook is now dominating the back rank of black's kingdom.

40.) Rxe5, Qxf3
41.) Qxf3, Rxf3+
42.) Ke2, Rf5

The only move to defend the hanging knight is to trade the only rook the

black has. And now, Ivanchuk is facing a losing continuation.

43.) Rxf5, gxf5
44.) Kd3, c5
45.) Re5, Nb4+
46.) Kd2 (1-0)

Move 44: c5

The last resort, c5, here if Carlsen plays en passant, bxc5, black recaptures with Nb4+ and take the c-pawn. In this position, black could hold longer waiting for forks, but Carlsen didn't let it happen. Now, the knight is cramped at the corner, the f-pawn is hanging, and the weak a7 pawn is exposed to rook and knight can't defend it somehow. A great game by Magnus Carlsen, gripping Vassily from the opening up to the endgame is somehow a milestone for a chess player from the modern era.

16

Game 5
So Sorry Wesley So, Says Anish

Wesley So – Anish Giri
Corus Group B (2010)

Move 31: Rh3

One of the most popular opening repertoires in the modern era of chess is the Petrov's Defense introduced by Alexander Petrov. This opening is full of sharp lines and aggressive variations which if seen and used properly can destroy nerves and stamina in a short possible time.

Here, Anish crushed Wesley So, dominating from the opening up to the staggering mating pattern ended in a rook sacrifice.

    1.) e4, e5
    2.) Nf3, Nf6
    3.) Nxe5, d6

This is the right continuation of the Petrov's Defense. Black is letting his center pawn be captured and making first his defenses by playing d6 opening a way to free up his c8 bishop which is a useful defender in this variation. To take the e4 pawn immediately is not a good choice as the continuation shows:

    1.) Nxe5, Nxe4
    2.) Qe2, Qe7
    3.) Qxe4, d6
    4.) d4, dxe5

And after white's dxe5 on move 5, white is a pawn up.

    4.) Nf3, Nxe4
    5.) d4, d5
    6.) Bd3, Nc6

This is a typical continuation of this line. Both sides are highly active in development; all the pieces are free to grab spaces to gain control of the activity on the board.

    7.) 0-0, Be7
    8.) Re1, Bg4
    9.) c3, f5

Black is willing to make his pieces active and white must be willing too, in order to avoid being behind in development. But white suddenly made a silent move, c3, permitting the black to attack continuously making white's defenses in a passive position. Instead, a better continuation after Bg4 by black is c4, keeping the fire in hand to execute the dynamics of the pieces, for it is also the typical continuation of this line.

Move 09: f5

    10.) Qb3, 0-0
    11.) Nbd2, Na5
    12.) Qc2, Nc6

It seems that black is slightly better here as white's pieces are blocked and the spaces are slightly cramped. It is a result of a passive response, c3 which gave black a tempo to develop and dominate more in the future.

Game 5
So Sorry Wesley So, Says Anish

13.) b4, a6
14.) a4, Bd6
15.) Ba3, Kh8

White now is taking the squares on the queenside but still doesn't have the concrete plans to dominate the board. Both sides have equal positions and preparing their pieces to take into action. Still difficult to tell which sides has the advantages in hand.

16.) Qb2, Ne7
17.) Ne5, Bxe5
18.) dxe5, Ng6

Move 18: Ng6

Ng6 is a powerful move by black, here it offers white to do the pawn fork, f3, attacking both the bishop and knight. But after Nxe5, black can execute a more dangerous continuation.

19.) f3, Nxe5
20.) Bf1, Qf6
21.) fxe4, fxe4

Quiet a risky move to sacrifice the knight but it gives black the initiative in hand. The rooks now can participate in the action helping to put pressures against the castled king.

This is a brilliant positional sacrifice by Anish. Now the f-file is controlled by black and white must find a way to either escape the attack or to defend.

It seems now that the black has more active pieces than white. Although Wesley has the bishop pair, he can't fully execute its mobility as the h3 bishop is trapped in the corner.

22.) Kh1, b5
23.) Nb3, Qh4
24.) Qd2, Rf5

All of the black pieces are approaching to the white king executing an attack and white must be very careful defending it. The f5 rook is aiming to go to h5 square which brought chills to white king, a deadly unstoppable pressure.

25.) Nd4, Rf5
26.) h3, Rf8
27.) Re3, Rf2

Move 27: Ng6

A total domination by Anish, all of his pieces are eyeing the white king while his own is sitting, completely fine at the corner. Can Wesley hold the position or can he find a counter attack? Can Anish execute the kill until the end?

28.) Qe1, Qf6
29.) Kg1, Rf4
30.) hxg4, Nxg4

Game 5
So Sorry Wesley So, Says Anish

Wesley has been defending it well, gaining a tempo to catch the bishop but there are still so many pieces on the board that and the initiative is still on Anish hand.

     31.) Rf3, Rxh3
     32.) gxh3, Nf2
     33.) Qe3, Qg5+

Move 33: Qg5+

Three pieces left and Anish must avoid the trades as Wesley had kept his bishop pair ready to attack once the opportunity comes. Black must stay active; any passive move is enough to control the game on white's favor.

     34.) Bg2, Nd1
     35.) Qc1, Qg3
     36.) Ne2, Rf1 (1-0)

This is almost an immortal game by Anish, sacrificing several pieces for a mating net. However, the game may end as follows;

     37.) Kxf1, Qf2# mate

Wesley might see another variation to escape the deadly threat. Instead of Qc1, he may move and continue with several pieces against the lone queen;

     1.) Bg2, Nd1
     2.) Rxd1, Rf2+
     3.) Kxf1, Qxe3
     4.) Ne2

And the game is still playable with a better position than before.

Anish Kumar Giri is a Russian-born Dutch chess player, became a grandmaster in 2009 at the age of 14, a four-time Dutch Chess Champion and won the Corus Chess B Group in 2010.

Game 6
The Unstoppable Kasparov

Garry Kasparov – Vassily Ivanchuk
Linares (1994)

Move 37: Rxf7+

Aside from Karpov, Ivanchuk is one of Kasparov's greatest nemeses in his domination in the chess world. Their games are so dynamic and tricky unlike the defensive and conservative Karpovian Style.

1.) d4, Nf6
2.) c4, c6
3.) Nc3 d5

We are entering the QGD Semi-slav variation; one of the defensive ways to battle the white's d4. But, however, after several moves the game reached a staggering complicated position.

4.) Nf3, e6
5.) Bg5, dxc4
6.) e4, b5

Center control is on white's hand but Ivanchuk want to cut it short by grabbing squares on the queenside wing. All of the pieces are open and preparing to attack. The defensive game turned into dynamic playful match.

7.) e5, h6
8.) Bh4, g5
9.) Nxg5, hxg5

The first material sacrifice occurred in this game. Kasparov gave up his knight in exchange for pawns to retain the pin on f6 which gives black an

uncomfortable position, although the knight can't escape the early capture.

10.) Bxg5, Nbd7
11.) exf6, Bb7
12.) g3, c5

Move 12: c5

Kasparov allowed Ivanchuk to play c5, opening up his bishop's diagonal attacking the h1-rook with a tempo which can easily get blocked by move d5. Right now, both sides are not willing to castle their kings into safe and just craving for dynamic play in an early manner.

13.) d5, Nxf6
14.) Bg2, Bh6
15.) Bxf6, Qxf6

Now white made his defenses solid while Ivanchuk left with open spaces for his king, a great play by Kasparov preparing his position in the endgame while attacking with his pieces, a combination of a defensive and aggressive style.

16.) 0-0, 0-0-0
17.) Nxb5, exd5
18.) Nxa7+, Kb8

Another variation may be as follows:
1.) Nxb5, a6
2.) Nc3, exd5
leads to somewhat better position.

20

Game 6
The Unstoppable Kasparov

19.) Nb5, Bg7
20.) a4, Qh6
21.) h4, Bf6

Now, black has the initiative in hand attacking white's king and want to rip out Kasparov's defenses. Ivanchuk looks safe due to his 3 passed pawns defending the center, but must be aware of the a-file that the black is in control; a fearless play by both of the players. However, playing f5 before Bf6 is better as its making use of the isolated f-pawn to add pressure and weaken the white's defense structures.

Move 21: Bf6

22.) Qe1, Bxh4
23.) Qa5, Be7
24.) Qc7+, Ka8

Kasparov didn't take the black's bait as after gxh4, Qxh4 white will be in a losing position and becomes open to rook attacks. Instead as the white's h-file is weak and black is threatening a mate in one by Qh2+, he tries to infiltrate the king provoking the black queen to remove its control in the h-file and defend his attacks. Although removing the f-rook will give the white king the escape squares after the check, it is difficult to tell after black's d4 if the white king can escape the mating threat.

25.) Qa5+, Kb8
26.) Qc7, Ka8
27.) Rfe1, Bd6

This is a great moment in chess history that Ivanchuk is willing to draw by a threefold repetition and didn't defend by Qa6, just wanting to keeps the queen providing pressure in the h-file, but somewhat somehow, Kasparov just want to resist more, confident that he can manipulate the game according to his favor. Instead he let black take down his defenses and continues the game, the combination of a pure fearless and confidence of the 13th World Champ.

28.) Qb6, Bb8
29.) a5, Rd7
30.) Re8, Qh2+

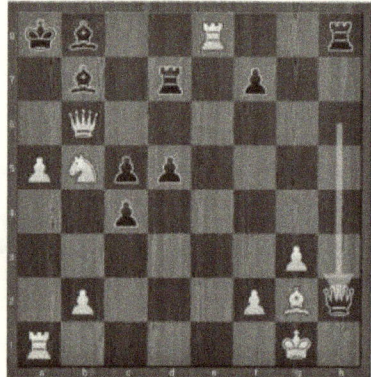
Move 30: Qh2+

In this position, a great visualization can tell which side can deliver the mating combination after several moves. White is defending with his pawns while black with his bishop pair. Can Kasparov escape the incoming attack or can Ivanchuk hold the position against the incoming a6?

31.) Kf1, Qxg2+
32.) Kxg2, d4+
33.) Qxb7+, Rxb7

Game 6
The Unstoppable Kasparov

Although taking the e8 rook first looks better, it makes black drowned in a losing position after this continuation:

1.) Kf1, Rxe8
2.) a6, Re1+
3.) Rxe1, Qxg2
4.) Kxg2, d4+
5.) axb7, Rxb7
6.) Ra1+, Ba7 (1-0)

The b7 bishop is defenseless after a6, it must be freed after d4 but taking the white bishop first on g2 makes use of that situation.

This is a brilliant queen sacrifice by Ivanchuk, thinking that after d4+ he can regain the material loss considering these following variations:

1.) Kxg2, d4+
2.) Kf1, Rxe8
3.) a6, Bf3
4.) Qf6, Bd5
5.) Qf5, Red8

A queen traded for the bishop and a rook made black position look safe after several moves, the c and d pawns in the center are protecting the black in any of the attacks white is thinking, and on the other hand Ivanchuk can now advance the pawns to promotion.

But Kasparov somehow is already preparing Ivanchuk's plan; instead he sacrificed his queen too visualizing that after several moves, he has two powerful rooks and an incoming passed pawn which itself is also a winning position.

34.) Rxh8, Rxb5
35.) a6, Ka7
36.) Rf8, Rxb2

Move 36: Rxb2

In this position black's f-pawn is hanging with a tempo of check, after the black king moves, the a6 pawn will advanced attacking the bishop, the bishop must recapture to stop the pawn from queening. Although Ivanchuk has three passed pawns in his hand, the initiative is in Kasparov, black must hold his position first to secure a win.

37.) Rxf7, Ka8
38.) a7, c3
39.) Rf8 (1-0)

The bishop is pinned and white is unstoppable on taking the bishop with check from the rook and on the queen (If Kasparov promote the pawn to queen) making the final set up a mate in one, proving that tempo can shut down material advantages, if used accordingly; a great game between players with outmost visualization and wit, indeed a true game of champions.

22

Game 7
The Immortal Rook Sacrifice

Wei Yi – Lazaro Batista
Hainan Danzhou GM (2015)

Move 22: Rxf7

Move 09: d6

Wei Yi, a youngster who happens to play chess, a young mind ready to grasp winning opportunities with tactical combinations and great visualizations in his mind. In his early career, he crushed and destroyed players with resources and ideas out of nowhere.

1.) e4, c5
2.) Nf3, e6
3.) Nc3, a6

White has two pieces already developed while black is still making his position stronger by blocking some of the knights' important squares in the Sicilian Defense; this is not a bad response for black as playing d5 to open up the position is anytime soon.

4.) Be2, Nc6
5.) d4, cxd4
6.) Nxd4, Qc7

The two knights are engaged in the play but white can't fully exploit it due to the black's control on the b5 and d5 squares in which moving the queen to c7 feels safe.

7.) 0-0, Nf6
8.) Be3, Be7
9.) f4, d6

This position arises after nine moves of maneuvering the pieces. White has already castled and controlled the central squares of the board while black haven't castled yet and need to develop his c8 bishop to gain development.

10.) Kh1, 0-0
11.) Qe1, Nxd4
12.) Bxd4, b5

It is difficult to tell which side has the initiative in hand although you can see that white put his king into safe by moving away from the a7-b8 diagonal and preparing his queen to attack on the black's kingside by moving on the e1 square exploiting its full mobility.

13.) Qg3, Bb7
14.) a3, Rad8
15.) Rae1, Rd7

Both sides are still placing their pieces into the preparation of attacks. White bishop pair is active waiting for opportunity to infiltrate while black is planning to dominate the center by moving both of the rooks to e-file. Taking on e5 by black is fatal as it will open up the d4 bishop's diagonal eyeing on g7 with a mating threat of Qxg7+.

23

Game 7
The Immortal Rook Sacrifice

16.) Bd3, Qd8
17.) Qh3, g6
18.) f5, e5

Wei Yi starts to break open the pawn chains of the black kingside and giving his two rooks a great control on the e and f files. Black's position is a little bit awkward to defend the white's incoming attack. It seems that every piece is defending but they are not on their best squares possible. The rook on d7, the clogged bishop on e7, the black's queen and the b7 bishop needs several moves to enhance their mobility to defend fully. Hence, the initiative is on the white's hand.

19.) Be3, Re8
20.) fxg6, hxg6
21.) Nd5, Nxd5

Move 21: Nxd5

Black must trade and open up the position in order to free up his pieces and trying to gain control of the game. However, white's rook has now access on the f file which can give initiative and play after several moves. Wei Yi must exploit the awkward position of the pieces to win the game in the beautiful fashion.

22.) Rxf7, Kxf7
23.) Qh7+, Ke6
24.) exd5+, Kxd5

White has sacrificed his rook forcing the black king be driven in the center and black is forced to take it due to the unstoppable Qh7+, mate, if black plays carelessly; it will be a mate after several moves of combination:

1.) Rxf7, Kxf7
2.) Qh7+, Kf8
3.) Bh6+, mate

If the king moved to f6, it can't also escape the following continuation;

1.) Rxf7+, Kxf7
2.) Qh7+, Kf6
3.) exd5, e4
4.) Rf1+, Ke5
5.) Qxg6, (1-0)

The mating threat at Qxe4+ is unstoppable.

25.) Be4+, Kxe4
26.) Qf7, Bf6
27.) Bd2+, Kd4

Move 27: Kd4

In this position, black is two pieces up which is really a winning advantage but his king is on the white's camp, exposed to mating attacks. White must continue the threat and deliver checkmate after several moves not wasting any opportunity until the end before black can sneak and defend it somehow.

Game 7
The Immortal Rook Sacrifice

28.) Be3+, Ke4
29.) Qb3, Kf5
30.) Rf1+, Kg4

This is the critical moment of the game where Wei Yi is forced to deliver a mating threat or else he will lose. He had already given up his bishop and rook for this position. If white doesn't saw the right continuation, black can gain a tempo and defend all the incoming combinations. Well, at move 22, keen visualization of the aftermath must be considered before sacrificing the rook for a pawn.

31.) Qd3, Bg2+
32.) Kxg2, Qa8+
33.) Kg1, Bg5

Move 33: Bg5

Here, black king is closed to mating threat and must do anything to prevent it. Taking on g2 sacrificing the bishop to remove one of the pawns responsible for mate is one of black's counter plans. However, it also provides a tempo with the move Qa8+ making the queen defend diagonals in front of his king but however, black can't escape the incoming mating attack.

34.) Qe2+, Kh4
35.) Bf2+, Kh3
36.) Be1 (1-0)

After several material and positional sacrifices, white finally has imposed the mating threat black can't prevent. In this position, Qd3 is unstoppable serving the black king its mating combination. However, black can hold the position but will eventually lose afterwards due to the following variations;

1.) Be1, Rf8
2.) Qd3, Rf3
3.) Rxf3+, Kg4
4.) Rg3+, Kf4
5.) Bd2+, mate (1-0)

However, if the king moved to h4, it will taste the same situation;

1.) Be1, Rf8
2.) Qd3, Rf3
3.) Rxf3+, Kh4
4.) Rg2+, Kh5
5.) Qh3+, Bh4
6.) Qxh4+, mate (1-0)

A great visualization and wit requires understanding this particular combination beforehand. This 14-move masterpiece by a young Chinese exploiting black's weaknesses and sacrificing several pieces to deliver a beautiful mating combination is a great game indeed.

Game 8
The Classic Game of Legends

Anatoly Karpov – Viktor Korchnoi
World Championship Match (1978)

Move 12: Nxe5

Anatoly Karpov is one of the finest grandmaster in his time. Here, he successfully defeated Viktor Korchnoi in a massive classical way, until at the last blow.

1.) e4, e5
2.) Nf3, Nc6
3.) Bb5, a6

Here, we are entering the Ruy Lopez Opening, one of the famous variations until the modern times. The bishop is attacking the knight which is defending the e5 pawn thus; black is kicking it by playing a6 but Karpov didn't want to enter the exchange variation and chose his prepared way. However, if bishop took the knight the board would become this after the following:

1.) Bb5, a6
2.) Bxc6, dxc6
3.) d3, Bd6

Both sides have equal positions after several moves of setting the right squares for the pieces, the position Karpov didn't chose.

4.) Ba4, Nf6
5.) 0-0, Nxe4
6.) d4, b5

Move 06: b5

Karpov has already castled and taking the initiative to sacrifice his center pawn exploiting the black king at the center with the preparation of some good combinations afterwards to make a play.

7.) Bb3, d5
8.) dxe5, Be6
9.) Nbd2, Nc5

For the meantime, Korchnoi is blocking the e-file for the safey of his king. His knights and pawns are well placed to defend some of the attacks white may imposed. Black now has up a pawn and more open spaces for mobility but his king is still at the center and needs to be in safe before white may infiltrate and exploit it afterwards.

10.) c3, g6
11.) Qe2, Bg7
12.) Nd4, Nxe5

White let black to take his pawn to clear the e-file again, exploiting continuously for the king at the center. However, placing the bishop on e7 is a more comfortable way to cover the black king and a faster way to castle.

Game 8
The Classic Game of Legends

13.) f4, Nc4
14.) f5, gxf5
15.) Nxf5, Rg8

This is a poisoned pawn indeed. Taking the e5 pawn is a blunder for black, letting white to play f4, f5, and sneak up to destroy the g-pawn preventing black to castle safely.

However, after Nd4 by white, black should play Qd7 keeping the closed e-file while defending the c-knight.

16.) Nxc4, dxc4
17.) Bc2, Nd3
18.) Bh6, Bf8

Karpov now is willing to trade the knight to free up his c-bishop to participate on the pressures. White is now successfully controlling the e and f file and the other rook is preparing to move on Re1. Black is slowly dying his two-pawn advantage after several moves after the strong move f4.

Move 18: Bf8

19.) Rad1, Qd5
20.) Bxd3, cxd3
21.) Rxd3, Qc6

Black moved his queen to make way for the long castle but white immediately stop this plan; take the knight and after the trades, the rook now controls the d-file keeping the

black king stays on the center of its kingdom.

22.) Bxf8, Qb6+
23.) Kh1, Kxf8
24.) Qf3, Re8

Move 24: Re8

White now is preparing the pieces to deliver attacking combinations but it's still unclear which move has to come. However, Karpov has found a way to forced situations and win with his resources.

25.) Nh6, Rg7
27.) Rd7, Rb8
28.) Nxf7, Bxd7
29.) Nd8 (1-0)

If the king moved his king to e7, white will move to Qf8+ and mate the king. Clearly, Karpov sees a mate in four after Re8 by black. After the move f4, white has taken all the initiative and slowly grabbing the controls of the center files, and black can't really find a way to stop this. However, if black just played Be7 instead of g6, the game would continue in a long run with black having a pawn up in a closed position.

27

Game 9
The Classical Rising Star

Daniil Dubov – Anish Giri
FIDE Grand Prix, Moscow, (2019)

Move 36: Kh8

Can you see the mate in 3 in this position? The rising star Daniil Dubov finished the game with shocking mating combination against one of the finest player in modern era, Anish Giri.

1.) d4, Nf6
2.) c4, e6
3.) Nf3, d5

This is a queen's pawn game, a conservative opening but transformed into an aggressive, complicated middle game, both enjoyed by the two classical GM's.

4.) Bg5, dxc4
5.) e4, b5
6.) a4, c6

After having just 6 moves played by both sides, their pieces are free enough and already mobilized. Although white controls the center squares, it can't really exploit the position due to the c6 and e6 pawns.

7.) Nc3, b4
8.) Nb1, Ba6
9.) e5, h6

Dubov already controls the center but Giri counter on the queenside, making two strong b4 and c4 pawns, blocking the development of the b1 knight.

It is just 9 moves that the position becomes crazier than usual. The black knight is pinned but the bishop is forced to capture the knight or move to h5, or somewhere possible. It is difficult to predict which side has the plans better than the other.

10.) Bxf6, gxf6
11.) exf6, c5
12.) Nbd2, c3

White regained the pawn as Anish doesn't chose the capture the pawn on f6, instead played the move c5, provoking the white to capture it and after dxc5, Qxd1, Kxd1, the white king sits in the center exposed to attacks.

Move 12: c3

13.) bxc3, bxc3
14.) Ne4, cxd4
15.) Bb5+, Bxb5

Giri has managed to keep his queenside pawns, and now it is approaching and blocking the white's development. But white's knight is carefully placed attacking the d4 pawn and Giri couldn't do anything stop this. Those pawns are over extended, could not make it to the last rank, and will continue to fall after several moves.

Game 9
The Classical Rising Star

16.) axb5, Qd5
17.) Qxd4, Qxb5
18.) Nxc3, Bb4

The two black center pawns have fallen, and the game now equalizes as both players has almost equal position except the passed a-pawn of Anish.

19.) 0-0-0, Qa5
20.) Nb5, Na6
21.) Qd7+, Kf8

Move 21: Kf8

A queenside castle? A somewhat aggressive move as his king became exposed and unprotected. Although castling kingside is not possible because the black queen is eyeing the a6 to f1 diagonal, a better move continuation could be the following;

1.) Nxc3, Bb4
2.) Nd2, Bxc3
3.) Qxc3, Nc6
4.) Nc4, Qb4

This is the safer continuation of the game, but Dubov feels confident at this moment and after several moves, his king just sneaks the white's incoming attacks.

22.) Kb1, Ba3
23.) Rd3, Qb4+
24.) Kc2, Qa4+

Dubov must be very careful on how to manipulate his defenses. The initiative now is in Giri's hand.

25.) Kd2, Bb4+
26.) Ke2, Kg8
27.) Ne5, Qc2+

In this position, both sides have their own advantages in hand. The pieces of white is active and his rooks will become connected several moves soon but the king is exposed and Dubov must be very careful on every attack black might impose. However, black's a8 rook must protect the last rank from the white queen, the f7 square is weak, the h8 rook is cramped, and black is in the middle of defending white's attack or continue attacking the white king.

28.) Kf3, Rf8
29.) Rhd1, h5
30.) Qd4, Rh7

Move 30: Rh7

Both problems of both players are met after several moves. The black king is now safe in the corner and the f7 square is successfully defended while white's rook now is connected and can defend black's attack as well. But Dubov's pieces are more active while Giri's rooks are passive. However, the initiative now is in Daniil's hand.

Game 9
The Classical Rising Star

31.) Qf4, Bc5
32.) Nd4, Qa2
33.) R1d2, Qd5+

Move 33: Qd5+

Anish's checks is not helping his position as white is just making the tempi in his favor. However, black couldn't impose threats but to check.

34.) Ke2, Bb4
35.) Ndc6, Qc5
36.) Ne7+, Kh8 (1-0)

After this position that white is now ready to deliver the mate in 3; a shocking combination from Dubov's mind. The mating combination being set is as follows;

1.) Ne7+, Kh8
2.) N5xf7+, Rfxf7
3.) Rd8+, Rf8
4.) Rxf8+, mate

If black took the knight with his h-rook;

1.) Ne7+, Kh8
2.) N5xf7+, Rhxf7
3.) Qh6+, Rh7
4.) Qxf8+, mate

However, there are better variations that will prolong the game but will slowly fall thereafter;

1.) Ndc6, Bxd2
2.) Qg3+, Kh8
3.) Rxd5, exd5
4.) Kxd2 (1-0)

White is one-piece up, with very strong knight pair while black has stagnant rooks defending the f7 pawn. It is an easy win for Dubov in playing this position and Anish will probably resign after the queen capture.

This is a great game for the youngster who clearly created a dynamic play from the opening to the last staggering mating pattern. The harmony of white's pieces, the coordination of its plan, with something of a risky recipe left Giri in an aimless situation, hoping to create a mating combination against the white king but the one who are getting mated after several maneuvers.

Game 10
The Match of Classical Masters

Alexander Alekhine – Emanuel Lasker
Zurich (1934)

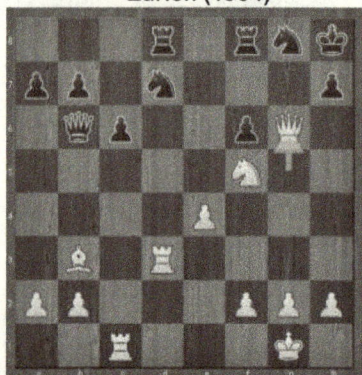

Move 26: Qxg6

This is a theoretical game between the two geniuses of the classical era of chess. It shows both sides are setting up their pieces on their planned positions and when the perfect time arises, the deadly threat of mating combination can now be imposed.

1.) d4, d5
2.) c4, e6
3.) Nc3, Nf6

This is the queen's gambit declined, a strong defensive opening avoiding the aggressive lines of king's pawn variations. But instead of making deadly draw endgames, both players had made it become dynamic that it ended into a staggering queen sacrifice.

4.) Nf3, Be7
5.) Bg5, Nbd7
6.) e3, 0-0

Lasker seems very careful in his move and made his position in a solid defensive manner while Alekhine, in his aggressive mind, first to attack with two possible moves before he can short castle.

7.) Rc1, c6
8.) Bd3, dxc4
9.) Bxc4, Nd5

Lasker want to safely trade pieces and approach the endgame early, preventing Alekhine to do combinations in the middle game, a trick that every player knew against the aggressive styles.

10.) Bxe7, Qxe7
11.) Ne4, N5f6
12.) Ng3, e5

Lasker has already put his king into safety but need first to develop his bishop and connect his rook while Alekhine is preventing the trades in his favor.

13.) 0-0, exd4
14.) Nf5, Qd8
15.) N3xd4, Ne5

Move 15: Ne5

After this position, we can tell that white has already the upper hand. The queen was forced to return to d8 square and loss a tempo, but it is not clear how white can take this minor opportunity and exploit the initiative.

16.) Bb3, Bxf5
17.) Nxf5, Qb6
18.) Qd6, Ned7

The position seems to be equal after the black's Qb6, black rooks now are connected and white can't stop this development. The game now is slowly approaching the endgame with equal

Game 10
The Match of Classical Masters

positions from both sides. It seems that Lasker succeeded his ideas against his classical opponent. The question is, is that trick well enough to beat Alekhine?

19.) Rfd1, Rad8
20.) Qg3, g6
21.) Qg5, Kh8

Move 21: Kh8

After just 3 moves of maneuvering the pieces, Alekhine achieved a dominating position against the black's defenses. The strong Qg3 that Lasker missed had made the initiative favors Alekhine greatly. However, after Qd6 by white at move 18, the best possible response is Ng6; covering squares the queen might sneak in. This prevents moving g6 and opening the square on g7 which in turn creates a weakness in black's defenses.

22.) Nd6, Kg7
23.) e4, Ng8
24.) Rd3, f6
25.) Nf5+, Kh8
26.) Qxg6 (1-0)

A shocking finish by Alekhine, black queen was made worse in the b6 square and can't defend white's mating threat. Black can't stop the Qg7+, mating the black king, if black

captures by hxg6, it's still mate after Rh3+, Nh6, Rxh6+. Moving the pawn on f6 is considered a blunder as its opening up the bishop's diagonal slicing the black's escaping squares. Instead, moving Ndf6 can hold the position and even blocks all of the white's incoming threats which Lasker didn't saw.

1.) Rd3, Ndf6
2.) Qe5, h5
3.) h3, Kh7
4.) Rcd1, Rd7

And white can't execute his attack clearly and the black can still gain initiatives after several moves.

Game 11
The Infamous Queen Sacrifice

Vassily Ivanchuk – Sergey Karjakin
   Amber Tournament (2008)

Move 14: Qxe6

It is one of the brilliant games of Ivanchuk crushing the Russian GM Karjakin and dominated the game with a tactical queen sacrifice. The talented Ivanchuk proved that it's not too old for his positional and classical skill on the board.

   1.) e4, c5
   2.) Nf3, d6
   3.) d4, cxd4

The Sicilian defense, an opening which houses the tactical shots and strategic games in town. When this opening is played by classical GM's, brilliant combinations are just waiting to unlock.

   4.) Nxd4, Nf6
   5.) Nc3, a6
   6.) Bc4, e6

Ivanchuk is preparing his pieces to participate in the middle of the board, while Karjakin is silently blocking the target squares white is aiming to, as it is the typical continuation of this opening.

   7.) Bb3, b5
   8.) Bg5, Be7
   9.) Qf3, Qc7

Move 09: Qc7

White pieces are gaining activity and are totally mobilized, ready to attack and make complications. Black is somehow under-developed but is not really losing due to the center d6 and e6 pawns defending the king plus the c8 bishop ready to aim the b7-h1 diagonal.

   10.) e5, Bb7
   11.) exd6, Bxd6
   12.) Qe3, Bc5

This position now becomes even, as Karjakin successfully opened up his bishop pair. His black bishop is pinning the knight and after Nc6 black's position is totally okay. But somewhat somehow, white seems seeing a great tactical shot.

   13.) 0-0-0, Nc6
   14.) Qxe6, fxe6
   15.) Nxe6, Qe5

A brilliant queen sac! Ivanchuk saw this engine move trading the queen for a pawn for positional advantages. I bet Karjakin was shocked after seeing this move, but somehow, playing e5, after the long castle seems to win the knight but will get into a losing

Game 11
The Infamous Queen Sacrifice

position after this continuation.

    1.) 0-0-0, e5
    2.) Bxf6, gxf6
    3.) Qg3, Bxd4
    4.) Qg7, Rf8
    5.) Rxd4, Ne2
    6.) Nd5, Bxd5

The knight is immediately regained after Rxd4, if black recaptures by exd4 the rook can be regained after the continuation;

    1.) Re1+, Kd8
    2.) Qxf8+, Kd2

And the king is forever in a chase.

    16.) Nxg7+, Kf8
    17.) Ne6+, Kf7
    18.) Rhe1, Qxe1

Move 18: Qxe1

After the queen sac, white gained so much activity on the board so trading the queen for a rook is not a bad choice to even the position but after Qxe1, white may first capture the c5 bishop with check and the game gets even in material.

    19.) Nxc5+, Kg6
    20.) Rxe1, Kxg5
    21.) Nxb7, Nd4

Another variation is better, placing the c5 bishop away from the knights' reached to gain a pawn thereafter;

    1.) Rhe1, Bxf2

    2.) Rxe5, Nxe5
    3.) Nd8+, Kg6
    4.) Bxf6, Kxf6
    5.) Nxb7, Rf8

Then black gained a pawn, and minimizes white's attack. Sacrificing the queen is forced to neutralize white's activity to dominate the board.

    22.) Nd6, Rhf8
    23.) f3, b4
    24.) Nce4+, Nxe4

Black has the connected rook, but can he diminish white's connected pawns? In this position, Karjakin first goal is to untie those pawns before coming to the promotion square which is Ivanchuk's only hope against the rook pair.

    25.) Rxe4, Nxb3+
    26.) axb3, a5
    27.) Rg4+, Kf6

Black captured the bishop to double up white's pawns making these advance slowly to the last square and to open up the file for the a-rook to infiltrate.

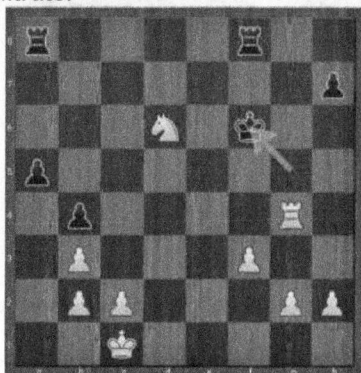

Move 27: Kf6

    28.) Ne4+, Ke5
    29.) Rh4, a4
    30.) bxa4, Rxa4

Game 11
The Infamous Queen Sacrifice

Black successfully ripped out the a-file and the white king can now be attacked. Karjakin must take this opportunity to take down the white king before the pawn swarm approaches.

> 31.) Nc5, Ra1+
> 32.) Kd2, Rg8
> 33.) g3, Rf1

The rook is threatening to steal pawns from the back rank and Ivanchuk must stop this infiltration as it is his only hope to win the game. However, the white rook stops the black king to participate the grip by defending the 4th rank as the king can't come closer. Seems Ivanchuk is prepared to this kind of endgame.

> 34.) Ke2, Rb1
> 35.) Rxb4, Kd5
> 36.) Ne4, Kc6

Move 36: Kc6

Defending the b4 pawn can't win the game, so Karjakin left this and went to the attack as white's connected pawns are slowly approaching to the last rank. However, as the b4 pawn falls, it is more difficult for the rook pair to stop the pawns.

> 37.) h4, Rh1
> 38.) Rc4+, Kb6
> 39.) b4, Rd8

The pawns are slowly advancing and the black king can't help the situation as it is cornered by the rook. This is surely the endgame which Karjakin didn't want to play.

> 40.) Rc5, Ra8
> 41.) c3, Ra2+
> 42.) Ke3, Re1+

Move 42: Re1+

Karjakin is slowly losing his hope here, as even the rook pair can't take a pawn in this position.

> 43.) Kf4, Rf1
> 44.) Rh5, Ra8
> 45.) Rh6+, Kb5

The white now is clearly winning after Kf4, because the back rank mate is now impossible to occur. It is now easy for Ivanchuk to continue this winning position.

> 46.) Nd6+, Ka4
> 47.) Rxh7, Kb3
> 48.) Rc7, Rd8
> 49.) Nf5 (1-0)

Karjakin can't help his position but to resign. The five passed pawns are all strongly connected and supported by rook and knight and slowly approaching the promotion square, a great domination from Ivanchuk, beating players in a modern era in his brilliant positional sacrifices while ignoring material values of the pieces.

35

Game 12
The French Dominated Moro

Vassily Ivanchuk – Alexander Morozevich
Amsterdam (1996)

Move 37: Bf7

This is a French game, a defensive opening against the e4, which in turn, when the white's d4 pawn was traded, creates chaos on the board as all the pieces can freely participated the attacks.

1.) e4, e6
2.) d4, d5
3.) Nc3, Nf6

This is a typical response of the French opening, black's goal is to infiltrate the queenside and white has the choices of defending it, or attack the black's kingside in return.

4.) e5, Nfd7
5.) f4, c5
6.) Nf3, Nc6

The most pressurized square in the French game is the d4, which is easily been attack by black in this position. Once the d4 pawn is traded, the c8 bishop can freely be used in the fight and the white king is slightly exposed as Ivanchuk already advanced the f4 pawn. But still, it's too early to decide which side has the initiative in hand.

7.) Be3, Be7
8.) dxc5, Nxc5
9.) Be2, 0-0

Ivanchuk didn't want to close the position and chose to rip out the center squares by trading his d4 pawn. But he must protect the b6 to g1 diagonal by his black bishop to safely continue the game.

10.) 0-0, Bd7
11.) a3, Be8
12.) Qe1, Rc8

Move 12: Rc8

As white want the dynamic play on the board, Morozevich chose the defensive manner clearly be seen as Be8 is on the board. At move 12, only a pawn is traded and all of the minor pieces are waiting to clash and fight.

13.) Rd1, Qc7
14.) b4, Nd7
15.) Nb5, Qb8

The 13th move by Morozevich lead him into a losing position as his queen is stuck in b8 square. An inaccurate move for black as it is being driven to the corner after b4-Nb5 by Ivanchuk which in turn, can't mobilize fully to defend the position.

16.) Bd3, f6
17.) Qh4, f5
18.) Qh3, Nb6

Game 12
The French Dominated Moro

Advancing the pawn to f5 is forced to block the white's bishop pair and open the black bishop's diagonal and still the black queen on b8 can't participate the action.

19.) Bxb6, axb6
20.) g4, g6
21.) gxf5, exf5

Ivanchuk seized the opportunity to capture the b6 knight as after axb6, black can't drive the b5 knight away which controls the squares of the black queen. Giving away his bishop pair makes sense as his bishops are slightly blocked by the pawns.

22.) Rf2, Nd8
23.) Nbd4, Kh8
24.) Rg2, Rc3

Move 24: Rc3

White let away the control of the squares of the black queen, instead he shift his knight to outpost the center squares which is difficult to resist as the mobility of the black bishop is blocked by the pawns.

25.) Nh4, Nc6
26.) Ne6, Rg8
27.) Nxf5, Qc8

Ivanchuk set a trap that if Morozevich recaptures by gxf5, black will be forced to sacrifice his pieces to survive the mating attack but instead

Morozevich saw this and ignore the free knight.

1.) Nxf5, gxf5
2.) Rxg8+, Kxg8
3.) Qh6, Qxe5
4.) fxe5, Bc5+
5.) bxc5, Kf7
6.) Qg7+, Kxe6

And Ivanchuk will enjoy this winning position.

28.) Rg3, h5
29.) Nh6, Rg7
30.) Bf5, Rxg3+

Move 30: Rxg3+

After h5 by black, the trap is already not effective as the queen can't go to h6 to initiate the mating pattern, but on the other hand, the black rook is trapped by the knight pair.

31.) Qxg3, Qb8
32.) Rxd5, Rh7
33.) Bxg6, Rxh6
34.) Bf7 (1-0)

Clearly Ivanchuk dominated the position here; the queen can't do anything after it had been move to b8 square. In the final position, Qg7+ and Qg8+ is the mating threat here which black can't defend both in one move possible. This is a great gripping game by the legend Ivanchuk.

Game 13
The Silent Knight Sac

Jeffery Xiong – Wesley So
US Championship (2017)

Move 21: Nxc7

This game shows how Wesley So inflicted his positional insights against Xiong. At this very position, So responded the silent Nxf2, which in turn made Xiong in a terrible losing position after several moves of surviving the game.

    1.) d4, Nf6
    2.) c4, e6
    3.) g3, d5

Xiong enters the Catalan Opening against So, providing a safe position for the king early at the game, while battling the minor pieces for the queen side domination.

    4.) Bg2, Be7
    5.) Nf3, 0-0
    6.) 0-0, dxc4

Wesley has made the first capture in this game, but it opened up the diagonal for Xiong's fianchetto bishop, creating a doubled pawn structure, and driven the pawn away from the center. It seems not accurate but it seems that Wesley already prepared this continuation against Xiong.

    7.) Qc2, a6
    8.) a4, Bd7
    9.) Rd1, Bc6

Wesley moved a6 to gain tempo after capturing the d4 pawn in this position which Xiong saw and ignored after playing a4 to block the continuation;

    1.) Qc2, a6
    2.) Qxd4, b5
    3.) Qc2, Bb7

And black will become ahead in development.

Instead of defending the d4 pawn, black maneuvers the d7 bishop to c6, seems unusual but still makes sense, placing the bishop to guard the h1-a8 diagonal against white's fianchetto making it more active and mobilized.

    10.) Nc3, Bxf3
    11.) Bxf3, Nc6
    12.) Bxc6, bxc6

Move 12: bxc6

Seems a strange move by Wesley So, letting Jeffery Xiong makes a tripled pawn and weaken his structure. But still, it's a long way to go to exploit white's advantages in this position.

Game 13
The Silent Knight Sac

13.) Bg5, Rb8
14.) e3, c5
15.) dxc5, Qe8

After gaining some positional advantages, white missed a chance to continue the initiative. Xiong has to play e4 instead of e3 to gain more space and center control; this made white's position silent and passive. However, Wesley must seize the opportunity and make his pieces active.

16.) Rd4, Nd7
17.) Bxe7, Qxe7
18.) c6, Ne5

Move 18: Ne5

In this position, black has made his rook pair connected. Black is aiming to capture the c6 pawn while white is threatening to take on c4. Xiong didn't seize the chance to dominate the board and the position sits prettily equal.

19.) Qe4, Qc5
20.) Nd5, Nd3
21.) Nxc7, Nxf2

This is the turntable of the match; Wesley sacrificed his knight to take the f2 pawn. A brilliant positional move that surprises Xiong; exploiting the defenseless 7th rank and threatens the king into a back rank mating attack.

22.) Kxf2, Rxb2+
23.) Kf1, Qh5
24.) Qg4, Qxh2

Move 24: Qxh2

Wesley is forcing Xiong to defend the multiple back ranks mating threat which luckily moving the queen on Qf3 can defend all of the possible mating combinations. But at this position, black although a piece down, gained the initiative and activity on board in which white must defend seriously to escape every mating pattern black can deliver.

However, black can simply not take the knight instead defend the b2 pawn by Qc2. This is a safe response which didn't expose the black king into checks.

1.) Nxc7, Nxf2
2.) Qc2, Nh3+
3.) Kg2, Qxc6+
4.) Kxh3, Qxc7
5.) Rxc4, Qb6

Then both position gets even after this continuation.

25.) Qf3, c3
26.) Rc1, e5
27.) Rh4, Qd2

39

Game 13
The Silent Knight Sac

White is trying to get rid of black's strong queen-rook battery that is gripping his position and threatening deadly mating patterns. The black's c3 pawn is approaching the promotion square which adds the pressure in the white's premises. However, white's only hope is the isolated c6 pawn which in turn if the back rank is successfully defended, shifting his attention on how to exploit it to the last square can make the game to swindle.

28.) Rd1, Rd8
29.) Nd5, Rxd5
30.) Rd4, Rxd4
31.) exd4, Qxd1+ (0-1)

Move 31: Qxd1+

After the 28th move of black, Xiong made a terrible blunder, sacrificing his knight for no reasons by playing Nd5, this can't help the situation as white can't recapture by Qxd5 due to the hanging mate on Qf2+. Wesley now is threatening to sacrifice his queen, capturing the rook on d1 and then followed by c2 and the pawn is unstoppable from promotion which Xiong can't stop.

If Xiong recaptures by Qxd1, white is still losing due to the following continuation;

1.) exd4, Qxd1

2.) Qxd1, c2
3.) Qd2, Rb1+
4.) Ke2, c1=Q
Then white after the queen trades, will lose the c6 pawn and loss the game.

Another variation that is important to see in this game is the following continuation;

1.) Rd1, Rd8
2.) Rxd2, Rdxd2
3.) Kg1, Rb1+
4.) Qf1, Rxf1+
5.) Kxf1, c2
6.) Rc4, Rd1+
7.) Ke2, c1=Q
8.) Rxc1, Rxc1
9.) Nxa6, Rxc6
10.) Nb8 (1-0)
Capturing the queen immediately by Rxd2 looks better but still losing after several forced situations, but the knight is still on the board unlike the latter variation.

Game 14
The Mating Pattern

Viswanathan Anand – Anatoly Karpov
FIDE World Championship Match (1998)

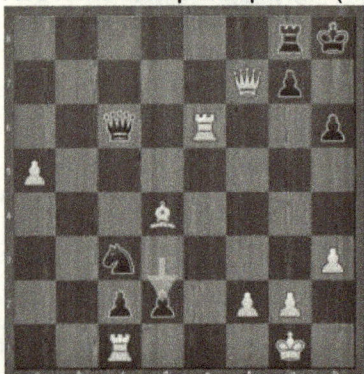

Move 39: d2

This is the game between two of the most conservative players prior the modern era where chess engines are a big part of analyzing repertoires. In the final part of the game, Vishy set up a mating pattern that Karpov hasn't been calculated.

1.) e4, e5
2.) Nf3, Nc6
3.) Bb5, a6

Vishy entered the Ruy Lopez variation, the opening always famous in its dynamic and positional manner of playing. The dominations, together with pawns are commonly occurred in the queen side in which both king is in its safe position immediately several moves after moving the pawn to e4.

4.) Ba4, Nf6
5.) 0-0, Bc5
6.) c3, b5

Both sides are claiming the activity and mobilization for their minor pieces. The bishop is attacked and at the same time, grabbing the squares for the center control. However, Karpov didn't capture the free e4 pawn, and chose to play Bc5, although white can regain the pawn thereafter.

1.) 0-0, Nxe4
2.) d4, b5
3.) Bb3, d5
4.) dxe5, Be6

Karpov didn't chose this line and prefer to play the more conservative approach possible against Vishy.

7.) Bb3, d6
8.) a4, Bg4
9.) d3, 0-0

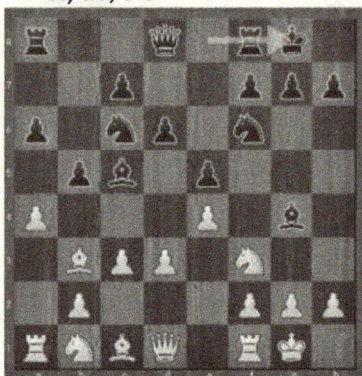

Move 9: 0-0

Karpov chose to pin the f3 knight instead of putting the bishop in the fianchetto, this made the piece more active and dynamic. Black's minor pieces are all mobilized and gaining the activity in the center but his c-pawn are blocked and needing two tempos to play c5 for full development.

10.) h3, Bxf3
11.) Qxf3, Na5
12.) Bc2, b4

Karpov captured the f3 knight instead of continuing the pin by playing Bh5. In this, white gained a tempo of developing its queen seizing the opportunity of having the bishop pair aiming at the black's kingside for possible attack.

41

Game 14
The Mating Pattern

13.) Nd2, Rb8
14.) Qe2, Re8
15.) Nf3, bxc3

Both sides are silently developing their pieces into action. While Vishy has the bishop pair, Karpov want to grab the b-file to control.

16.) bxc3, Nb3
17.) Bxb3, Rxb3
18.) d4, exd4

Move 18: exd4

Vishy is now opening up the center and seems favoring Karpov as the e4 pawn becomes the center of pressure from black's e8 rook and f6 knight and it will fall immediately after black's next moves.

19.) cxd4, Rxf3
20.) Qxf3, Bxd4
21.) Ra2, Nxe4

Karpov has sacrificed his rook for the knight and two pawns; this made black create c and d pawns strong as they are easily advanced to the promotion square. This sacrifice has made white in the difficult position.

22.) Qd3, c5
23.) Qxa6, d5
24.) a5, c4

Black now has the winning position after the rook sac. The center control and the connected pawn chains approaching the promotion favors black greatly until the endgame.

25.) Be3, Be5
26.) Bb6, Qd7
27.) Qa7, Qc6

As Karpov is avoiding the trades to secure and keep his winning advantages, Vishy tries to counter for his a-pawn. White must defend wisely to hold black's position before queening the center pawns.

28.) Bd4, Bc7
29.) Rb2, c3
30.) Rb7, Rc8

Move 30: Rc8

Vishy now is harassing the black's premises and forced Karpov to defend hoping to find some tactics to ruin black's plan. But at this position, black is so unstoppable that even the rook pair can't do nothing on the approaching pawns.

31.) Bb6, Be5
32.) Rxf7, c2
33.) Rc1, Nc3

White is in the verge of losing, as the black's bishop is carefully defending the only weak square, g7. And now threatening to fork via Ne2+, attacking the rook before promoting the c-pawn in which Vishy must consider defending.

Game 14
The Mating Pattern

34.) Rf3, h6
35.) Qf7+, Kh8
36.) Re3, d4

Vishy defended black's attack very well and found a solid defending position. Here, Karpov chose to sacrifice his bishop instead of the c2 pawn gaining the tempos to play d4, to make the pawn chain stronger. The bishop sac was forced because once one of the pawns is captured; white can easily defend and break the position using the rook pair.

37.) Rxe5, d3
38.) Bd4, Rg8
39.) Re6, d2

Move 39: d2

Vishy has sacrificed his rook for the mating pattern that he is planning to make. Although if white taking the rook first is more logical, the position will soon lose after this continuation;

1.) Re6, Qxe6
2.) Qxe6, d2
3.) Qxh6# (1-0)

Black is checkmated first before the promotion occurred.

40.) Rxc6, dxc1=Q+
41.) Kh2, Qd2
42.) Rc8 (1-0)

Now, Vishy has successfully applied his trick, and the black queen must defend the h7 square preventing Rxh6+, mate. White is threatening to capture the g8 rook then mate the king, or if the rook moves, Qxg7 is still a checkmate in which black can't defend simultaneously.

This is a great game for Vishy in which he managed to defend very well and cracked the solid center control of Karpov. The mating pattern which Karpov missed to calculate ended the game in an unstoppable mating attack, and even the promoting pawns can't help but to witness the losing continuation.

43

Game 15
Beating the Magician

Viktor Korchnoi – Mikhail Tal
USSR Championship (1962)

Move 54: d7

It's New Year's Day, and we are going to study something special; the game between the two classical legends of this sport. But at this moment, the magician loses the game in a staggering manner.

1.) d4, Nf6
2.) c4, c5
3.) d5, e6

This is the Benoni defense, a variation in which drawing the game is almost not occurring according to statistics. In this variation, the game is either wins or loses for both sides.

4.) Nc3, exd5
5.) cxd5, d6
6.) Nf3, g6

Since the move d6 is now blocking the c8 bishop's mobility, Tal want to make it in the fianchetto square eyeing the a1-h8 diagonal. The d5 pawn is gripping some of the black's developments but it is kind of over-extended and can easily be put out from the pressures black can deliver.

7.) g3, Bg7
8.) Bg2, 0-0
9.) 0-0 Na6

Both sides are developing their pieces and putting it in the best square possible. The position is now equal and still waiting for the complications to enter the board.

10.) h3, Nc7
11.) e4, Nd7
12.) Re1, Ne8

Tal is maneuvering his knights waiting for Korchnoi to enter his premises; probably preparing his pieces for the counter attack. But still it is difficult to tell which side has the upper hand.

13.) Bg5, Bf6
14.) Be3, Rb8
15.) a4, a6

Move 15: a6

It is now 15th move and still the pieces are not traded. Each side is conserving their position, keeping their pieces in their best squares waiting for the position to ripen up.

16.) Bf1, Qe7
17.) Nd2, Nc7
18.) f4, b5

Both sides now are grabbing spaces for their mobilization. Korchnoi is on the king side while Tal wants to control the queen side.

44

Game 15
Beating the Magician

19.) e5, dxe5
20.) Nde4, Qd8
21.) Nxf6+, Nxf6

Korchnoi found a way to open up the center with tempo on move Nde4, which Tal forced to return his king on d8 square. After this move, white is slowly taking up spaces and grips black mobility.

22.) d6, Ne6
23.) fxe5, b4
24.) Nd5, Nxd5

Move 24: Nxd5

In this position, white has gain the center control. The connected d and e pawn are creating a strong blockage for the black's movement. Although, it seems that, Bxc5 first before d6 is more logical, the pawns will soon fall after this possible continuation;

1.) Nxf6+, Nxf6
2.) Bxc5, Re8
3.) axb5, axb5
4.) fxe5, Nfxd5

And black destroys the solid defensive center pawns, which is white's asset for the coming endgame.

25.) Qxd5, Bb7
26.) Qd2, Qd7
27.) Kh2, b3

The pawns are scattered and every pieces can freely wander on the board. In this position, although, Korchnoi has the connected center pawn structure on black's camp, it didn't hinder black's movement whatsoever because the black bishop is already out of the board and the knight pair are sneaking in their right squares out of touch.

28.) Rac1, Qxa4
29.) Bc4, Bc8
30.) Rf1, Rb4

Move 30: Rb4

Korchnoi sacrificed a pawn for the activity of his pieces, a somewhat logical move, while Tal is starting to gain spaces and make complications on the board in his rook lift, attacking the c4 bishop but his plan is not clear enough on how he will dominate. The black queen must stay on a4 to e8 diagonal, preventing the advancing of the d-pawn from promotion.

31.) Bxe6, Bxe6
32.) Bh6, Re8
33.) Qg5, Re4

This is the most critical moment of the game. Korchnoi eliminated the e6 knight defending the g7 square providing a way for his bishop to access it after the unstoppable Bh6-Qg5-Qf6 infiltrating the position for a

45

Game 15
Beating the Magician

mating attacks. But Tal has the silent resources, moving his rook to e4 with a deadly mating trick faster than white in these following continuations;

1.) Qg5, Re4
2.) Qf6, Re2+
3.) Rf2, Rxf2
4.) Qxf2, Qd4
5.) Qf6, Qxb2+
6.) Kg1, Qd4+
7.) Kh2, Qb2+
8.) Kg1, Qd4+ (½, ½)

And the game is drawn due to repetitive moves. The king can't go to the white squares, the f1, g2, and h1 squares preventing the e6 bishop from participating into checks or the queen trade will be forced, perpetual check is unstoppable, or the king would be mated after several maneuvers.

1.) Kg1, Qd4+
2.) Kg2, Be5+
3.) Kf1, Bc4+
4.) Kg2, Be5+
5.) Kf1, Bc4+ (½, ½)

The king must not enter the e-file to prevent the move Rxe5+, making the rook add the pressure on the white's position.

However, avoiding the trades to keep the mating position is not a good idea, as white may fall to losing position as shown in this variation;

1.) Qf6, Re2+
2.) Kh1, Be5+
3.) Kg1, Rg2+
4.) Kh1, Rf2+
5.) Kg1, Rxf6 (1/0)

And white falls on black's hand, there are many variations if after Re4, white's response is Qf6, letting black to infiltrate the open spaces around

the king. There are so many variations after Qf6, and I'll bet Korchnoi doesn't want Tal to apply his creativity in this position. This move is really tempting but Korchnoi avoids the complications and go for the more conservative move, Rf2, which stops Tal from infiltrating more and forced to defend the mate in one against his king.

34.) Rf2, f5
35.) Qf6, Qd7
36.) Rxc5, Rc4

Move 36: Rc4

In this position, after white has made the safest move, black's premise seems in suffocation. The pawns are gripping the pieces' movements, and the queen and the bishop is threatening the mate in one if ever the g7 square is left unattended. Tal didn't successfully make his trick as Korchnoi didn't tempt to fall in the Qf6 Variation and made him defend in a losing position.

37.) Rxc4, Bxc4
38.) Rd2, Be6
39.) Rd1, Qa7

Tal wants to keep his queen defending the 7th rank to prevent the mating attack as his pieces are gripped and blocked by white's structures.

Game 15
Beating the Magician

40.) Rd2, Qd7
41.) Rd1, Qa7
42.) Rd4, Qd7

Drawing the game in this position is favored for Tal, as his position doesn't do any developments, just waiting for white to add pressures until black suddenly can't hold.

43.) g4, a5
44.) Kg3, Rb8
45.) Kh4, Qf7

Korchnoi is starting to use his king to participate the gripping. Well, in this position, Tal's only hope is his two isolated pawns hoping to promote in time just before his defenses are destroyed.

46.) Kg5, fxg4
47.) hxg4, Bd7
48.) Rc4, a4

Move 48: a4

Tal is trying all his might to use his pieces fully on the defenses. But after Rc7, the position gets slowly losing in time.

49.) Rc7, a3
50.) Rxd7, Qxd7
51.) e6, Qa7

Korchnoi sacrificed his bishop for the rook, paving the way for the pawns to grip black's position more. On the other hand, black's pawn is approaching the promotion square.

52.) Qe5, axb2
53.) e7, Kf7
54.) d7 (1-0)

Korchnoi prevented the possible checks by playing Qe5 blocking the black queen to sneak some repetitive moves on the king. In this position, there are so many moves that can mate the king which Tal can't defend simultaneously. However black's best move is Qxc7, which can hold the position longer but still losing in this continuation;

1.) d7, Qxc7
2.) Qf6+, Ke8
3.) Qf8+ (1-0)

Black is still mated if the king would go to g8 by playing Qg7+.

This is a great game for Viktor Korchnoi, taming the dynamic "Magician of Riga". The center connected pawns help white so much in gripping black structures for developing. However, the only complications which Tal made was Re4, a move that hides so many variations in which Korchnoi prevented easily by playing Rf2, a bad day for Tal maybe.

Game 16
Forcing a Checkmate

Mikhail Tal – Mark Taimanov
USSR Championship (1962)

Move 35: Kd2

This is the match between the two classical players of the past. The dynamic, aggressive, tactical, and positional insights from this game will give you the chills while studying the moves and the idea behind. In this very tournament, Tal showed his aggressive tactical brilliancy that forces Taimanov to kneel down, broke his position, and leave his king in a dead and losing situation.

1.) e4, c5
2.) Nf3, Nc6
3.) d4, cxd4

We are entering now the typical line of the Sicilian Defense, where variations of combinations and sacrifices are just waiting to be unlocked.

4.) Nxd4, e6
5.) Nc3, a6
6.) Be3, Qc7

This is the Taimanov Variation, where black is immediately blocking the knights controlled square by playing a6, and putting the queen early on c7, unlike other lines in which Nc3 is met with black's Nf6 dealing first with the development of the pieces,

7.) Be2, Nf6
8.) a3, Nxd4
9.) Qxd4, Bd6

We can see that Taimanov is not really engaging the complications of the middle game. He slowly trading pieces to prevent Tal comes up with the brilliant sacrifices to exploit the position. Seems the players already knew that they don't have the stand to play the crazy positions in which Tal can make.

10.) Qd2, Be5
11.) Bd4, Bxd4
12.) Qxd4, e5

Move 12: e5

Mark Taimanov is slowly killing the possibility to make things complicated here. It's just after 12 moves that this position has reached: the two minor pieces are already traded, the position doesn't call for complications, and both players have the initiative and in a defensive position. If the queen would be out of the game, black can now easily play for a draw. But after several moves, Tal found an unusual response to make things messy for Taimanov.

Game 16
Forcing a Checkmate

13.) Qb4, b6
14.) 0-0-0, Bb7
15.) Rd6, Bc6

Tal played a very uncomfortable response against Taimanov, here, after Bb7, the computer suggested that f3 is enough, supporting the center pawn and making the position solidly defending. But Tal responded Rd6, uplifting the rook, while blocking the d-pawn to advance and create a center control.

16.) Rhd1, 0-0
17.) g4, Rfc8
18.) g5, Ne8

Move 18: Ne8

Tal starts to crawl up his pawns to the black king, threatening to dominate and destroy the position. However, black too has the plan to dominate the queenside, a5 is just waiting to put away the white queen, gaining tempo, while approaching to break up the white's safe zone.

19.) R6d2, b5
20.) Bg4, a5
21.) Qe7, b4

Taimanov clearly has the initiative in this situation, white's queenside is yet to be destroyed from the pawn storm and Tal must find a way to defend and even the position.

22.) Rxd7, Bxd7
23.) Rxd7, Qc4
24.) b3, Qf1+

Tal had just found a way to escape the black's mating attack: sacrificing its rook for the bishop and pawn in order to make a play. White is threatening to mate, attacking the f7 square twice in which Taimanov must react and defend immediately. After the staggering Rxd7 by white, the position flipped and the favor goes for Tal, but still the black can sneak some good chances of repetitive checks.

25.) Nd1, Nd6
26.) Qxd6, Qg2
27.) Qd5, Kh8

Move 27: Kh8

Taimanov is forced to sacrifice his knight to escape the mating attack and still forced to play Kh8, due to the following continuation:

1.) Qd5, Rf8
2.) Rxf7, Rxf7
3.) Qxa8+, Rf8
4.) Be6+, Kh8
5.) Qxf8# (1-0)

And black is mated. Playing an early Kh8 is very important putting away the black king in the queen's diagonal preventing the incoming mating threats.

Game 16
Forcing a Checkmate

In this position, both players have the initiative to deploy their plans but the player who has the better continuation relative to their position will clearly dominate the board and win the game.

28.) Qxf7, Rg8
29.) Qh5, Qxe4
30.) Bf3, Qf4+

Move 30: Qf4+

White's goal now is to eliminate the g and f pawn covering the king while black must defend fully on the attacks of Tal. White king is still covered by its pieces and pawns in which the black queen just can't make enough noise on the white's premises. Can Taimanov do something to escape the mating threats or can he swindle the moment and find the repetition?

31.) Ne3, Ra6
32.) Bd5, Rb8
33.) Rf7, Qd4

Tal is trying to dislocate the black's pieces to easily dominate but the mating combinations are still unclear as the two pawns are covering the king and white's pieces are not fully in unison to make an attack.

34.) Qf3, Qa1+
35.) Kd2, Qc3+
36.) Ke2, Qc5

In this moment, white has the initiative while black is just defending and seeking repetitive checks in which Tal is preventing. The two rooks can't do anything to break white's position but Tal's minor pieces; the knight, and the bishop at the center, are best placed controlling and blocking some of black's line of attacks.

37.) a4, Ra7
38.) g6, Ra6
39.) Rxg7, Rxg6

Move 39: Rxg6

At the immense pressure white is delivering against black's position, Taimanov had just made a terrible inaccuracy, instead of the 38th move, Ra6, the better response is just h6, a silent move in which makes everything fine shrinking the possibility of mating combinations and sacrifices as the rook on a7 is defending very well. However, after Tal had sacrificed the rook in taking the g7 pawn, black must not recapture by Kxg7 as the continuation will be a scripted mating combination.

1.) Rxg7, Kxg7
2.) Qf7+, Kh6
3.) Qxh7+, Kg5
4.) h4+, Kf4
5.) Qh6# mate (1-0)

Game 16
Forcing a Checkmate

If Taimanov had move h6, the position will be as the following continuation:

     1.) g6, h6
     2.) Be4, Rd8
     3.) Ng4, Rxf7
     4.) gxf7, Qd6
     5.) Bd3, Rf8
     6.) Qe4, g6
     7.) Nxe5, Kg7
     8.) Qe3, Qe6
     9.) Bxg6, Qf6

Black can hold the game longer in this variation, but playing against this losing position is somewhat easy for Tal to grip more against black.

     40.) Rxg6, hxg6
     41.) Qf6+, Kh7
     42.) Bf7 (1-0)

Move 42: Bf7

Mikhail Tal, widely regarded as the creative genius and one of the best attacking players of all time, Tal played in a daring, combinational style. His play was known above all for improvisation and unpredictability.

The game finishes as black is slowly dying in the midst of the fight, craving for air. Tal brilliantly made a fortress in his premises as the white king sits prettily well covered by knight. The pawns are preventing the queen to make checks while the bishop is eyeing and waiting to attack.

In this final position, black can't defend the g6 pawn unless to sacrifice his rook and play a losing position, a better choice is to resign.

Game 17
The Classical Ruy Lopez

Wilhelm Steinitz – Mikhail Chigorin
World Championship Rematch (1892)

Move 29: g4#

Its' in the second week of the first month now, while the world is still struggling to combat the pandemic, we will study a great game from the past. This game shows that correct continuation is very important to not just gain material advantages but to jump up on mating the opponent's king which in turn gives more triumph than the latter.

1.) e4, e5
2.) Nf3, Nc6
3.) Bb5, Nf6

We are now entering the Ruy Lopez, Berlin Defense Variation. White is ready to castle anytime on its kingside while black is still needing to free up its bishop before moving his king to safe squares.

4.) d3, d6
5.) c3, g6
6.) Nbd2, Bg7

Both players are silently developing their position. White is covering much more squares, maneuvering its minor pieces to dominate the kingside while black is trying to make its position solid, trying to break open the f-file after castling.

7.) Nf1, 0-0
8.) Ba4, Nd7
9.) Ne3, Nc5

Both players are maneuvering the knights in their chosen squares. However, Ba4 seems a loss of tempo for white as a6 is not been played on the board, but Steinitz wants to also maneuver his bishop to c2 before black drives it away.

10.) Bc2, Ne6
11.) h4, Ne7
12.) h5, d5

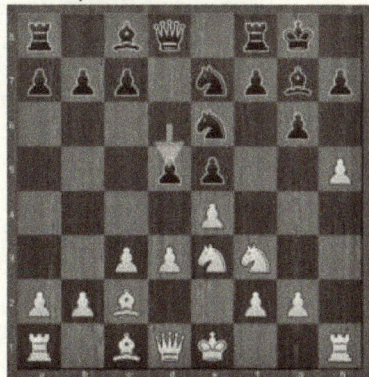

Move 12: d5

The bishop leaves the c6 knight and Chigorin can now move it to e7 supporting the f5 break but he played Ne6 first to avoid white play b4, gaining a tempo while developing the structure. In that line, white had just played h4 then h5, and the f5 break is not really a good move anymore as it is needed in recapturing the pawn after white played hxg6 to maintain a good pawn formation. Instead he played d5, which in turn after the trades isolating the e-pawn.

13.) hxg6, fxg6
14.) exd5, Nxd5
15.) Nxd5, Qxd5

52

Game 17
The Classical Ruy Lopez

Steinitz grasped the opportunity to isolate the e-pawn. In this position, although white has not yet castled, black must be careful as the h-file is already on white's control.

16.) Bb3, Qc6
17.) Qe2, Bd7
18.) Be3, Kh8

White's bishop pair are more active and in their best square for domination. Steinitz chose to castle queenside to keep its rook on the h-file and to join the other rook on the kingside attack.

19.) 0-0-0, Rae8
20.) Qf1, a5
21.) d4, exd4

Move 21: exd4

In this very position, Steinitz seems already visualized the mating combination, and if Chigorin didn't recognize this, just few inaccurate response will make the game in a losing position.

22.) Nxd4, Bxd4
23.) Rxd4, Nxd4
24.) Rxh7+, Kxh7

Black must not recapture the knight after Nxd4, a better move is Qe4 preserving black's defenses and keep the position even as shown in this variation.

1.) Nxd4, Qe4
2.) Nf3, Qc6
3.) Qd3, Rxf3
4.) gxf3, Nf8
5.) Rxh7+, Nxh7
6.) Qxd7, Qxd7
7.) Rxd7, Rc8

And the position is less difficult to play for black than before as the pins and threats are minimized.

However, Steinitz preserved the bishop pair as it slices the black king's adjacent squares sacrificing his rooks to eliminate the pawns and gain access for an attack. The moment he played Rxh7+, he knew he will mate the king and win the game.

25.) Qh1+, Kg2
26.) Bh6+, Kf6
27.) Qh4+, Ke5
28.) Qxd4+ (1-0)

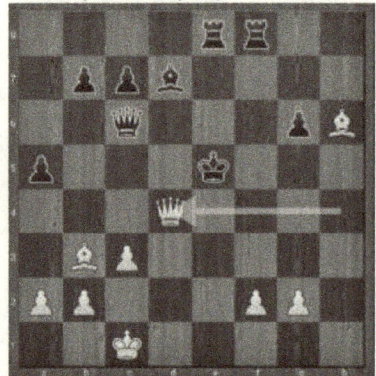

Move 28: Qxd4

White showed a very keen positional understanding of the combination. Taking the knight by Bxe5+ is not a good choice as after Rf6, Bxf6+, Qxf6, and both sides has equal position and initiative. In this position, black's only square is to go to f5 and after g4+, the king is mated. White has seen the mating threat in a surprising manner in which black didn't expected.

53

Game 18
The King's Gambit

Wilhelm Steinitz – Adolf Anderssen
World Championship Match (1866)

Move 05: Qh4

What can happen if a positional player had match against an aggressive type? This is a crazy game between two classical analysts which happen to cross roads at the World Championship Match. Steinitz chose to play one of the craziest openings against the strategic Anderssen, in which one of the nemeses of Morphy at that time. The next moves if we look at it deeply are worthy to understand.

  1.) e4, e5
  2.) f4, exf4
  3.) Nf3, g5

This is the king's gambit accepted, king's knight's gambit variation, where white is provoking black to advance the pawns toward his kingside. White doesn't care about king safety here, and just relying on the theoretical approach that anything from the black's attacks can be defended. However, black's f and g pawns are overextended and can be exploited after seizing counter attacking chances usually occurring in the center.

  4.) Bc4, g4
  5.) Ne5, Qh4+
  6.) Kf1, Nh6

This position is called "Salvio Gambit" where white is threatening the f7 pawn, but after Qh4+-Kf1- Nh6, the white king can't now take castling and the f7 pawn is defended. This is a very risky approach at the World Championship Match but seems white is ready to take his nerve on the possibilities that are waiting.

  7.) d4, d6
  8.) Nd3, f3
  9.) g3, Qe7

Move 09: Qe7

Steinitz is welcoming the black queen to take the check after g3 by Qh3+, but Anderssen is too good to sense the danger after this continuation:

  1.) g3, Qh3+
  2.) Ke1, Qg2
  3.) Nf2, Bf1 (1-0)

The queen now is trapped is forced to take the h8 rook which is not economical in material and position.

Instead of entering the losing position, black retreats the queen preserving his position and leaving white a messy kingside. But as we can see in this position, the center squares are on Steinitz in exchange for his gripped kingside which is the typical aftermath in the KGA.

Game 18
The King's Gambit

10.) Nf2, Be6
11.) Na3, Bxc4+
12.) Nxc4, Qe6

Black is planning to castle queenside, while white is rushing to develop his pieces needed to defend his structure. Steinitz has the more active pieces while Anderssen has the awkward knight on the side and still under-developed. Seems white succeeded to portray his plans as the f and g pawns are locked and can't do anything more.

13.) d5, Qg6
14.) h3, Nd7
15.) Bxh6, Bxh6

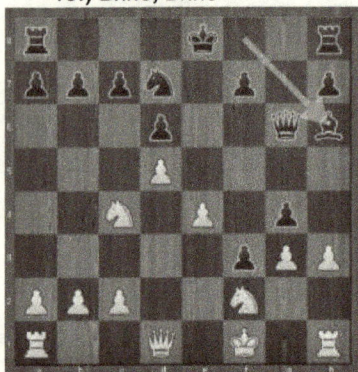

Move 15: Bxh6

White is starting to break open the pawns, eliminating first the knight in order to take the g4 pawn thereafter. But in that response, exchanging the bishop for that awkward knight seems favors the black as the bishop on h6 is immediately developed and eyeing the diagonal in the white premises.

16.) hxg4, b5
17.) Na3, Ne5
18.) Nxb5, Rb8

Anderssen had set up the fire after sacrificing the b5 pawn. Black chose to forget the queenside castling, instead, used this to spice up the game even more. In this position, each

wing has complications and the variations are rising exponentially, the whole board have now plenty of plans to make.

19.) Nd4, Be3
20.) Nxf3, Qf6
21.) Kg2, Bxf2

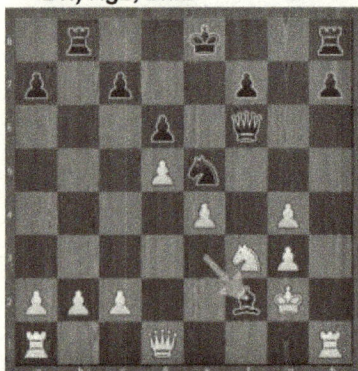

Move 21: Bxf2

The b2 and the g4 pawn is hanging now but so as the bishop. If Kxf2, black may play Nxg4+ and after the king moved, rook will take the b2 pawn and black even the position.

22.) Nxe5, Bxg3
23.) Nd3, Bh4
24.) Qe2, Qe7

Both players avoided trading their minor pieces, maybe didn't yet want to enter the rook+queen endgame, which gives more possible drawn positions. While Anderssen sneaked a pawn, Steinitz is forced to defend the b2 square to preserve his position.

25.) Raf1, Bg5
26.) Rf5, f6
27.) Rhf1, 0-0

After the trades, both position is back to developing again. White has the doubled rook on f-file but the threat is defended strongly by black's bishop and pawn combination. The bishop is placed dominantly on g5 while white's knight can outpost on c6 square.

Game 18
The King's Gambit

28.) b3, Rbe8
29.) Re1, Kh8
30.) Nf2, Bh4

Seems every little thing is carefully defended and both players are finding ways to develop more. Black is attacking the e4 pawn while white is eyeing the f6. The threats can easily been defended and neither of them has the concrete plans yet to destroy.

31.) Rh5, Bxf2
32.) Qxf2, Rg8
33.) Qf5, Rg7

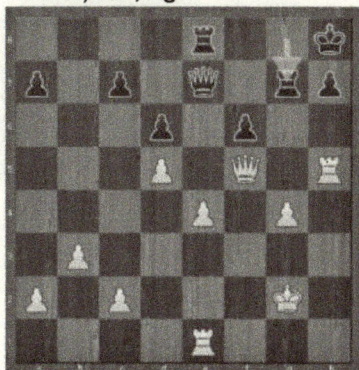

Move 33: Rg7

Anderssen had traded his bishop that seems to weaken his structures. Conservatively, the best move is Bg5, which in turn preserves black position while guarding c1 to h6 squares.

1.) Rh5, Bg5
2.) Nh3, Rg8
3.) Qf3, Rg7
The position is still strongly fixed to defend white's attacks.

34.) Rh6, Reg8
35.) Reh1, Rxg4+
36.) Kf3, Rg3+

Both players can't help to play their dynamic way even in this drawn position. Anderssen, having the classical blood, played Reg8, which

grant white to capture the f6 pawn but letting his g4 pawn fall along the way. The dead drawn endgame turns out to be dynamic one more time.

37.) Ke2, R3g7
38.) Rxf6, Rg2+
39.) Kd3, R8g3+
40.) Kc4, Re3

White has the escape squares toward the rook's attacks, its queenside. But black can't make any more rooms against white's deadly mating threat. Anderssen's instinct to fire the play instead of playing defensively is indeed an inaccuracy in this game.

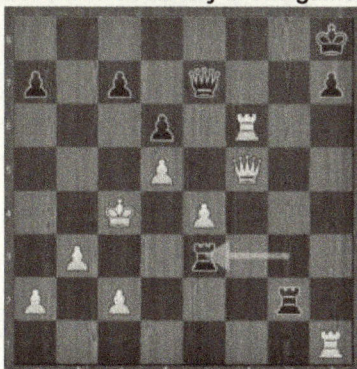

Move 40: Re3

It's white to play and mate in 5 moves. Can you see the mating combination in this position? Anderssen left the important squares to defend and made a passive move Re3 which in turn let Steinitz burn the possibility of a drawn game.

41.) Rf8+, Rg8
42.) Rxg8+, Kxg8
43.) Rg1+ (1-0)

Black already resigned after seeing the continuation after Rg1+, which is on the following:

1.) Kh8, Qc8+
2.) Qe8 or Qf8, Qxe8+ or Qxf8+
And the mate is unstoppable!

Game 18
The King's Gambit

There are possibilities that may arise if black has responded differently in the situation. If at move 40, black took the c2 pawn with check, the match will not last accordingly.

> *1.) Kc4, Rxc2+*
> *2.) Kb4, c5+*
> *3.) Ka3, Rcg2*
> *4.) Rf7 (1-0)*

And Qxh7+ is unstoppable; black must defend the h7 square, the Rf7 threat, and the Rf8+ at the same time. In this variation, taking on c2 harass the king but will not last longer after escaping to a3.

At 39th move, however, black didn't saw the opportunity to even the position. Only if he found the right move of the situation, Qg7, which defend and the same time, attack the white king from afar.

> *1.) Rxf6, Rg2+*
> *2.) Kd3, Qg7*
> *3.) Rh3, Rg5*
> *4.) Qf2, a6*
> *5.) Rg3+, Rxg3*
> *6.) Qxg3+, Qxg3*
> *7.) Rxg3+, Kd4*

And the game will continue longer than before, although black has a pawn down, it has created an isolated h-pawn which in turn a great advantage against the white. If after Qg7 by black, white risked his position and played a seemingly strong move, Rfh6, the game will swindle after this continuation:

> *1.) Kd3, Qg7*
> *2.) Qg3+, Kd4*
> *3.) Rd2+, Kc4*
> *4.) Rxc2+, Kb5*
> *5.) Rb8+, Ka4*
> *6.) Rxa2 (0-1)*

White can mate in one by Qxh7+ but black can do it against him earlier.

However, at 40th move, white's threat, Rf7, is unstoppable and Anderssen can't find a way to diminish the plan. Its rook lift to check the white king is somewhat made him lose the position as the rooks left the g7 and g8 squares unguarded from white's mating pattern. White risked his position to lit fires even if the position demands only conservative responses.

Game 19
Punishing the Inaccuracies

Magnus Carlsen – Anatoly Karpov
Tal Memorial (2008)

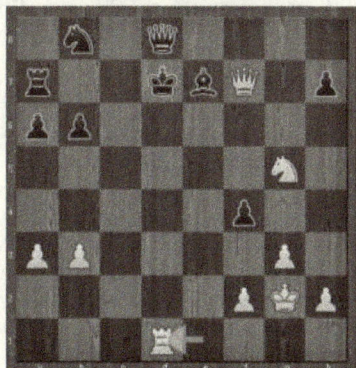

Move 27: Rd1+

In this game showcased the amazing positional skill of the present World Champion where he crushed the black pieces and drowned it into losing position. He led Karpov in a position where nobody would want to play, although black is a piece up, white's position is clearly dominating the squares throughout the game.

1.) d4, Nf6
2.) c4, e6
3.) Nf3, b6

Karpov is a classical player, here, by opening up the b7 pawn, clearly want to make his bishop in a fianchetto, he just want to improve first his position for counter attacking chances while Carlsen on the other hand, are grabbing the center squares immediately for full domination.

4.) g3, Ba6
5.) b3, Bb4+
6.) Bd2, Be7

Seems black had lost his tempo here, but it is quite logical as it displaced the bishop in the b2 square prevented Carlsen to fianchetto. Both sides are ready to castle and free up their pieces for full development.

7.) Nc3, d5
8.) cxd5, Nxd5
9.) e4, Bxf1

Carlsen let Karpov to take on f1 square and then make an artificial castle. In this position, white has better chances as the center squares are occupied by the pawns.

10.) Kxf1, Nf6
11.) Bf4, 0-0
12.) Kg2, Bb4

Move 12: Bb4

Karpov is behind in development due to the repetitive movement of his black colored bishop which loses several of his tempos and didn't get much in return while white is preserving his center dominance but although his minor pieces are well placed and developed it's still difficult to execute the winning attack.

13.) Nb5, a6
14.) Nxc7, Ra7
15.) a3, Be7

Karpov had seen the c7 square subject for attention. But instead of playing Na6, which is very typical, he had device a trap and played a6 which allows Carlsen to take the pawn, but after Ra7, the knight is nowhere to go. Now, the bishop is still supporting the c2 knight, when to capture it depends on Karpov's decision.

Game 19
Punishing the Inaccuracies

16.) d5, Nxe4
17.) dxe6, g5
18.) Nd5, gxf4

Karpov really want to eliminate the trapped knight but Carlsen can't let to leave it on his hand. Instead, white sets a trap by sacrificing his bishop to garner a better position afterwards. After several moves, the black king will be seen dragged back in the middle of the board.

19.) Re1, Nf6
20.) exf7+, Kxf7
21.) Ng5+, Ke8

Move 21: Ke8

This is a big choice for Carlsen, sacrificing his bishop to save his knight and make a better position. However, Karpov missed a chance to stop the complications, instead making his king in a worst situation. The game may continue in a peaceful way if black had just responded this variation:

1.) Re1, f5
2.) b4, fxg3
3.) hxg3, Nf6

And black stops the white's infiltration and neutralized the threats. Karpov didn't saw it and play Nf6 which in turn let Carlsen to do his plan.

However, if after the 20th move, exf7+, black traded with the rook, the position will be as good as the following:

1.) exf7+, Rxf7
2.) Nxe7+, Qxe7
3.) Rxe7, Raxe7

Black queen is forced to take the knight as it will be eliminated after with Qxd8+ by white, and from that standpoint, white is ahead of some points but black can also execute some chances due to its two connected rooks. This seems the last chance Karpov has to grab to even the position against Carlsen.

However, after exf7+, the king just moved on the corner, not taking the f7 pawn, the e7 bishop will fall as it is attacked twice by the knight and the rook. So, Karpov was forced to drag his king back in the middle supporting the bishop to maintain his material advantages which seems not a good choice to play against the World Champion.

22.) Nxf6+, Rxf6
23.) Qh5+, Kd7
24.) Rad1+, Rd6

Move 24: Rd6

Game 19
Punishing the Inaccuracies

Black had made a losing move here, after a check on Qh5, instead of Kd7, the best and more logical response is Rg6 blocking the check without further complications. It was another mishap for black, for the game may continue simply as follows:

    1.) Qh5+, Rg6
    2.) Ne6, Qd2
    3.) Rad1, f3+
    4.) Qxf3, Qh6

And black can still resist white's threats better than moving the king to d7 exposed to the rook's pins.

Black is up a piece but can't fully defend white's incoming attacks. The connected rooks are best placed to pin the king, the queen and the knight are strongholds controlling the best squares to crush black's position. White must take the opportunity and attack continuously and immediately end the game before black can rise and make a comeback.

    25.) Rxd6+, Bxd6
    26.) Qf7+, Be7
    27.) Rd1+ (1-0)

Move 27: Rd1+

Karpov can't take anymore of Carlsen domination, in this position, the king is forced to move and the queen will be taken by the rook. The black king will be forever chased and hunt down and as its minor pieces are not coordinated, it is difficult to defend white's infiltration. However, if just Karpov willing to sacrifice his rook, after the move Qf7+, he will be in a much better position shown in this continuation:

    1.) Qf7+, Kc6
    2.) Qxa7, Qxg5
    3.) Qa8, Kc7
    4.) Re8, f3+
    5.) Qxf3, Qg6

And an even continuation arises, a rook versus a bishop and a knight is better than losing the queen beforehand, a possibility that Karpov didn't chose to play.

There are many chances that Karpov didn't seized to even the position against Carlsen, instead played inaccurate moves letting white to dominate easily and crush black's position in just 27 moves. The plan of trapping the knight didn't went that far, white chose to sacrifice his bishop instead as he has more plan for the knight to outpost on black's premises and help the gripping of black's development.

Game 20
Exploiting the 7th Rank Weakness

Magnus Carlsen – Leinier D. Perez
Corus Group A (2009)

Move 39: Qh6

This game shows the amazing positional skill of Carlsen, where he managed to outplay Perez in a materially losing position. The middle game can be thought to be a draw until the finishing move ended black's hope in a staggering way.

1.) d4, Nf6
2.) c4, g6
3.) Nc3, d5

It's the Grunfeld Defense, where black is immediately preparing for the fianchetto on g7 and a kingside castling.

4.) Qb3, dxc4
5.) Qxc4, Bg7
6.) e4, 0-0

White is grabbing the center squares as a typical Carlsen style controlling the center while Perez is just waiting to counter white's attacks.

7.) Be2, Nfd7
8.) Be3, Nb6
9.) Qd3, f5

Black had made a beautiful attacking structure in his kingside while the white king is still in the center but it's not really clear which side has the upper hand.

10.) Rd1, f4
11.) Bc1, e5
12.) d5, c6

Both sides had made a good position, the pieces can freely move in both premises and therefore, develop. Black's e and f pawn are blocking white's plan to open up but black can't really infiltrate as the safety of the black king will be compromised in return.

13.) Nf3, cxd5
14.) Nxd5, Nxd5
15.) Qb3, Kh8

Move 15: Kh8

Although white's king is still in the center, its defenses are enough as black's minor pieces are not yet developed. Black was forced to move on h8, as the d5 knight is yet to be eliminated. Still at this position, its quiet difficult to tell which side has the initiative.

16.) Bc4, Nc6
17.) Bxd5, Qe7
18.) h3, Nb4

Perez can place the queen better on f6 rather than on e7, just to support the knight. On the other hand, Carlsen may just break black's pawn structure by taking the knight on c6 which he didn't make but it's an interesting variation to see.

Game 20
Exploiting the 7th Rank Weakness

19.) Bc4, b5
20.) Bxb5, Nxa2
21.) Bd2, Rb8

White didn't want to trade his bishop as it can make an outpost at the center of the board controlling squares which is a very important in the incoming middle game. But Black had found a sneaky way to trick white sacrificing a b5 pawn and after Nxa2, if the queen took the knight, the bishop on b5 will be hanged.

1.) Bxb5, Nxa2
2.) Qxa2, Qb4+
3.) Bd2, Qxb5

And the bishop will be eliminated according to black's plan.

But white saw the plan and played Bd2 immediately. But after Rb8, black is now threatening to play a6 to forcefully capture the bishop, an aggressive way indeed.

22.) Qa4, Qb7
23.) 0-0, Qxb5
24.) Qxa2, Qxb2

Move 24: Qxb2

The game continues showing a balance position. White forced to give up his bishop in exchange for the a2 knight, as it is the best choice the situation requires. Now, black has the

bishop pair and has the better chances in the endgame.

25.) Qxa7, Qb7
26.) Qc5, Be6
27.) Qd6, Bb3

In this situation, theoretically, black has the upper hand once the queens and rooks are traded. Having the bishop pair is an advantage in supporting the pawns and in breaking the pawn chains of white structures.

Carlsen must avoid such trades and continue to make complications to garner some chances in the endgame. However, after Be6 by black, the best move is just Re1, defending the defenseless e4 pawn from the black queen. Instead, white just moved Qd6, letting Perez to use the tempo in taking the e4 pawn.

28.) Rb1, Qxe4
29.) Bc3, Rbd8
30.) Qa3, Bc2

Move 30: Bc2

Now that the black has snatched a center pawn from white, the game now has material imbalances which can end the game thoroughly. Carlsen now is in the edge of losing but he can resist more against black plan. There are still many pieces on the board and the complications are waking up to unfold.

Game 20
Exploiting the 7th Rank Weakness

31.) Rb5, Qa4
32.) Qb2, Bd3
33.) Rb7, Qc2

At some extent, Carlsen can regain the pawn as the e5 pawn is attacked twice and after Qb2, it was attacked four times. White is seizing the open spaces of the black's kingside as the 7th rank is weak and exposed to rook attacks, even sacrificing a rook to break open the e file. However, if black just take the rook on f1, the game may continue as follows.

1.) Qb2, Bd3
2.) Rb7, Bxf1
3.) Bxe5, Rd7
4.) Bxg7+, Kg8
5.) Bxf8, Rxb7
6.) Qxb7, Kxf8
7.) Kxf1, Qd1+
8.) Ne1 (1-0)

White is a piece up and the black king is exposed to attacks. It is not a good choice to taste the rook compromising the safety of the black king after several moves.

34.) Qb4, Rfe8
35.) Re1, Be2
36.) Nxe5, Bxe5

Move 36: Bxe5

Carlsen had seen so much in this position, even sacrificed his knight for

a pawn to garner the perfect situation for his mating plan .In this set up, can you see the mate in few moves? The rook on b7 is a monster controlling the 7th rank in its knees. White felt that urge to exploit something from that winning perspective and delivered a deadly mating threat.

After Qb4 by white, black must secure the e7 square from white queen to infiltrate a deadly attack, and if white just ignored the threat and take the free rook, something that will end the game is shown in this variation:

1.) Qb4, Bxf1
2.) Qe7, Rg8
3.) Bxe5, Bxe5
4.) Qxh7# (1-0)

This is an unstoppable attack exploiting the weak 7th rank of black. In this position, black's e and f pawns seems to be over extended which in turn become a burden for black to support and literally made the black king exposed. Perez made a very early f break, made Carlsen gripped at some time but didn't last long to enjoy.

37.) Bxe5+, Rxe5
38.) Qxf4, Qf5
39.) Qh6 (1-0)

Now that the black bishop was eliminated, the king didn't have the security from any attacks. After Qxf4, black must defend the e5 rook and at the same time, secure the f6 square from the white queen, that move was Qf5, good defense, but still helpless after Qh6, threatening to play Qg7# or Qxh7# which black can't defend simultaneously.

Game 21
The Sicilian Najdorf

Magnus Carlsen – Alexander Grischuk
Linares (2009)

Move 35: c6

One of the most widely used variations on top level tournaments is the Sicilian Najdorf. Typically, the most complicated and waited for its aggressive lines and dynamic theories lying behind. Explore and study this game played by Carlsen against Grishuk where all of the pieces are used effectively in participation ended in a dominating pawn storm.

1.) e4, c5
2.) Nf3, d6
3.) d4, cxd4

Carlsen has two choices to recapture either by the queen like Ivanchuk did to Kasparov on Linares (1991), and made a great position after and not just won but even destroyed Kasparov in that match, or recapture by knight to continue the Najdorf.

4.) Nxd4, Nf3
5.) Nc3, a6
6.) Be2, e6

Here, we are entering the Najdorf line, where white is preparing a kingside castling and black is just making a solid defenses. As we can see, all of the minor pieces are free to move, not

gripped by any chance, but white slightly, has more squares to wander.

7.) 0-0, Be7
8.) a4, Nc6
9.) Be3, 0-0

Move 09: 0-0

Every piece now is developing and as both sides are already castled, the next several moves now are for dynamic attacks, and powerful positional defenses. It seems that black is behind in development but white has not enough resources to exploit it.

10.) f4, Qc7
11.) Kh1, Re8
12.) Bf3, Bf8

White seems planning to storm black in the middle of the board, as his bishop pair and both knights are participating, the e and f pawns are in front, and his king is now safe in the corner. White is developing easily as the spaces are safe in his premises and has achieved its ideal position, while black on the other hand, didn't have that great position, but still, can resist and hold the position against attacks.

13.) Qd2, Rb8
14.) Qf2, e5
15.) fxe5, dxe

64

Game 21
The Sicilian Najdorf

Black ignited the second trade, as white is forced to recapture. In result, his bishop pair are now opened and sits prettily well at the bank rank. Both sides are in their best positional defenses, the only difference is the unconnected rooks of the black camp.

16.) Nb3, Nb4
17.) Ba7, Ra8
18.) Bb6, Qe7

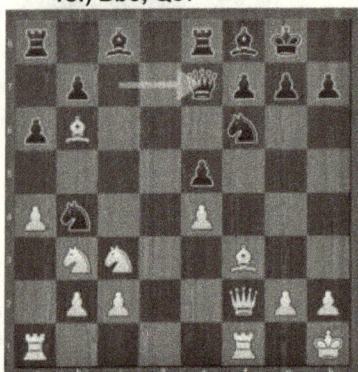

Move 18: Qe7

Here, Carlsen managed to hinder the development as white's black bishop is so strong that it controls the e3-a7 diagonal, the weak square of the black's position. Grischuk doesn't want to passive the queen on b8 square, white is threatening to play Rad1, attacking on the d-file, so he chose e7 to escape, although blocking the f8 bishop's line of fire.

19.) Rad1, Be6
20.) Nd5, Bxd5
21.) exd5, e4

Black managed to counter attack on the e-file after the exchange, as the e pawn now is supported by the queen and the rook. However, black must keep an eye on the white's passed pawn, now heading for promotion.

22.) d6, Qe6
23.) Nc5, Qf5
24.) Be2, Qxf2

As black didn't have the best square, it was forced to trade with the queen. Carlsen, saw that even after the exchange white is still better as the e pawn is isolated and heading to d8, where the b6 bishop is protecting. Black has the isolated pawn too, but didn't as much as threatening as white's.

25.) Rxf2, Nbd5
26.) a5, Nxb6
27.) axb6, Rab8

Move 27: Rab8

After Rxf2, black didn't bother to take the c2 pawn with his knight; disconnecting the support on the d6 pawn is more important and at the same time, attacking the bishop. If the bishop is then eliminated, the black rooks now can ride on d8 square to hinder the pawn from promoting.
But black instead of immediately take the bishop, can taste first the d-pawn, an interesting line shown in this variation:

1.) a5, Bxd6
2.) Rxf6, Be7
3.) Rxd5, Bxf6
4.) c3, Rb8
5.) Nd7, Rc8
6.) Nxf6, gxf6

Playable line but still losing, the bishops are monster in their

65

Game 21
The Sicilian Najdorf

respected squares and can't be driven away by rooks. The isolated pawn is now eliminated but white had garnered a better position to grip black's position, a choice in which Grischuk didn't dare to try.

28.) Rxf6, gxf6
29.) Nd7, f5
30.) c4, a5

Move 30: a5

At this moment, Carlsen had already steal the momentum and initiative, sacrificing his rook for a moment to play Nd7, forking the two rooks and threatening to play Nf6+, with again, fork. With that in mind, Grischuk had no choice but to leave one of his rooks, playing f5; preventing white to take it with check, and a5; stopping the move b4.

31.) c5, Bg7
32.) Nxb8, Rxb8
33.) Ba6, Bf6

Black now is in the losing position, the b, c and d pawns are all connected approaching the promotion square. Carlsen played the insane Ba6, intended to sacrifice a whole piece to isolate the three pawns in which Grischuk didn't dare to taste. If black took the bishop, he will face the following continuation;

1.) Ba6, bxa6
2.) c6, Rxb6
3.) c7, Rc6
4.) d7, Rxc7
5.) d8=Q+ (1-0)
The pawn storm is unstoppable.

34.) Bxb7, Rxb7
35.) c6, Rxb6
36.) Rc1, Bxb2
37.) d7 (1-0)

Move 37: d7

Carlsen really want to give way for his three pawns, sacrificing again the bishop for the pawn storm. The pawns are so strong and stopping it is inevitable. The game swindled in the favor of white starts at move 22, d6; in which white garnered a strong isolated passed pawn protected by the b6 bishop. And once the three pawns connected, Grischuk can't do anything but to counter attack which is not enough to stop the win. This showed that Carlsen really mastered his playing repertoires. His defensive and attacking styles are so conservative and precise, that there's no forms of counter attacking chances are there to sneak out. That is the style of hyper-modernists; an engine-like responses which players find difficult to beat.

Game 22
The Untouchable Knight Pair

Vassily Ivanchuk – Loek Van Wely
Tata Steel Masters (2015)

Move 37: Nb5

Vassily Ivanchuk is one of the finest players of his era. His typical opening is one of the most aggressive lines to play, the Sicilian Defense. Here, he showed the mastery in every variation, and drowned Van Wely in the losing position, with his pair of knight.

1.) e4, c5
2.) Nf3, e6
3.) d4, cxd4

We are entering the typical line of the Sicilian game, where white has the spaces and initiative and black is just making defenses, just waiting for the attack to open up.

4.) Nxd4, Nc6
5.) Nc3, d6
6.) Be3, Nf6

Both sides are continuing developing their minor pieces and improving their positions; black is solidly defending the center with his center pawns.

7.) Qe2, a6
8.) 0-0-0, Bd7
9.) f4, Rc8

Ivanchuk seemingly shut his light squared bishop into play but this move is still playable, as moving the f1 bishop is not that good in this position.

10.) Kb1, Qc7
11.) Nb3, b5
12.) g4, b4

Well, black has the initiative here, but need to be careful as white is now ready to attack the black's kingside. Which side can destroy first is really the question here.

13.) Na4, e5
14.) g5, Bg4
15.) Qg2, Bxd1

Move 15: Bxd1

White let black to capture the rook in exchange for the light squared bishop, this exchange is not really economical for black as the bishop is doing great at the center defending the king. However, after Na4 by white, black must not taste the e4 pawn as it is poisoned, shown in this variation:

1.) Na4, Nxe4
2.) Bb6, Qb7
3.) Qxe4 (1-0)

Black is one piece down, and slowly suffocating of squares to move. This is now, a losing position to play.

16.) Bxa6, Nd7
17.) Rxd1, Ra8
18.) Bb5, Be7

There are many interesting lines in this position that we may need to consider and study.

Game 22
The Untouchable Knight Pair

One variation that Van Wely didn't enter is taking the c2 pawn with check. Sneaking a pawn may reduce white's material advantages but the position calls not to as the c-file will be open for white to anticipate an attack from the rook, which is not good for black as shown in this continuation:

1.) Bxa6, Bxc2+
2.) Qxc2, Ra8
3.) Bb6, Qd7
4.) Bb5, Rc8
5.) gxf6, gxf6
6.) Bf2, Bh6

Black instantly loses its defenses as Nb6 is threatening to play, black can't stop losing the knight or the rook afterwards in which Van Wely didn't dare to try.

Another one is saving the rook instead of the knight, this opens the g-file after the trades giving a way to the other rook to participate but the idea of king safety is immediately be thrown outside the window.

1.) Bxa6, Ra8
2.) Bb6, Qd7
3.) Bb5, Nh5
4.) Rxd1, Nxf4
5.) Qf1, Be7
6.) Qc4, Rc8
7.) Na5, Bxg5
8.) Bxc6, Rxc6

And black will also a one piece down, white's minor pieces are monsters in their respected squares. It is an easy win to play for white, and a losing continuation for black.

However, if white took the rook first to ensure even materials, afterwards, the position will become prettily drawn as shown in the following continuations:

1.) Bxa6, Nd7
2.) Bxc8, Qxc8
3.) Rxd1, Qa6
4.) Qh3, Qxa4
5.) Qxd7, Kxd7
6.) Nc5+, Kc7
7.) Nxa4, h6

Ivanchuk doesn't play with materials, he play with plans. He intentionally took the bishop instead of the rook for maximum activity on the board which gave Van Wely multiple pressures to face.

Above all the logical responses, black choses to play Nd7, saving the knight which is the safest move the position calls. This is one of the keen decision from black to save his game against this classical player.

19.) f5, Qb7
20.) c4, 0-0
21.) f6, Bd8

Move 21: Bd8

Black's pieces are not so well coordinated due to a lack of squares to wander. White on the other hand, had plenty of spaces especially for the queen to attack the kingside with his pawn storm. Black didn't succeed to infiltrate the white's premises, as the minor pieces are best in their position defending the king.

Game 22
The Untouchable Knight Pair

22.) Rxd6, Ncb8
23.) Qg4, g6
24.) h4, h5

Move 24: h5

Easier said than done, why didn't Ivanchuk take the d7 knight? Let us look at this following continuation:

1.) Qg4, g6
2.) Bxd7, Nxd7
3.) Rxd7, Qa6
4.) Nbc5, Qxc4

White can regain the material but there are no other compensations, moreover, king safety is slightly compromised after the trades. As the knights are now tied with each other, their mobility are now quite limited.

25.) Qf3, Bc7
26.) Rxd7, Nxd7
27.) Bxd7, Rad8

Ivanchuk is playing positional here, instead of seizing the chances to gain a whole piece; he traded his rook for the knight pair just wanting to preserve his bishops in which are very useful in the incoming endgame.

28.) Nbc5, Qa8
29.) Qd1, Qa7
30.) Qd5, Ra8

It seems that Ivanchuk is a better handler of knight as he did to

Kasparov on their match at Linares (1991). In this match, he did again the same skill making Van Wely completely overwhelmed in his position. He let his two rooks eliminated before entering the endgame but to remain the four minor pieces is not a joke to play. After several moves, the game will end in the easiest manner possible as black is slowly suffocating of squares and plan.

31.) Bd2, Rfd8
32.) Bxb4, Ba5
33.) a3, Qc7

Move 33: Qc7

A slight inaccuracy on black for leaving the b4 pawn hanging until the bishop took it. The better response is Ba5, protecting it with no other weak squares left behind. Black now is running out of plans, the full initiative is completely in the white's hand.

34.) Nc3, Bxb4
35.) axb4, Qa7
36.) Kc2, Rac8

Black couldn't use its connected rooks to stop the dynamic activities of white's minor pieces. The three isolated pawns are so solid in defending the king and the knight are so strong in its gripping duties.

Game 22
The Untouchable Knight Pair

37.) Nb5, Qa1
38.) Nd6 (1-0)

Move 38: Nd6

It's been a long way of defending, and black is slowly creeping through, sneaking chances to infiltrate, until the final blow hit Van Wely's eyes. Here, white's Qxf7+ is inevitable unless black is willing to sacrifice his rook for the game, to continue its losing position. The most logical move to continue the variation is shown in this line:

1.) Nd6, Rxd7
2.) Nxd7, Qa4+
3.) Kc3, Qxd7
4.) Nxc8, Qxc8

With three isolated pawns in white's hand, black could not resist but to resign. The rooks being greater in material, but can't stop white's domination, making it a defending piece against the unstoppable pawn storm. It is now an easy winning position for Ivanchuk.

This showed us that in a closed position, if handled carefully, minor pieces are far stronger than the major ones. Ivanchuk's defenses are solid and at the same time dynamic, that make black just wander on the edge, while white is dominating the center.

In 2016, Vassily Ivanchuk won the World Rapid Chess Championship in Doha, Qatar, with a score of 11/15. He defeated Magnus Carlsen, among many others.

70

Game 23
Entering the Fischer Era

Robert James Fischer – Bent Larsen
Portoroz Interzonal (1958)

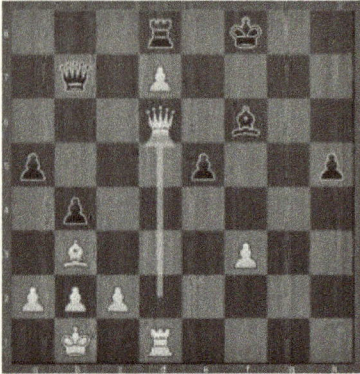

Move 31: Qd6

Bobby Fischer considered by many to be the greatest player ever, shocked the chess scene when he defeated Boris Spassky in the World Championship Match on 1972. He always has shocking resources to ignite up the game, his creative attacking style destroyed defenses of finest players in his era. His styles are so well profound that even in his younger years, had beaten some of the masters of this sport.

1.) e4, c5
2.) Nf3, d6
3.) d4, cxd4

This is a typical line of the Sicilian, in this set-up; we will witness attacks coming from both sides. The minor pieces will be free to develop, the complications will be everywhere.

4.) Nxd4, Nf6
5.) Nc3, g6
6.) Be3, Bg7

We are now heading for the Dragon Variation, a famous defense against the Sicilian in this time, giving the black king safe squares first before anything complicated arises. But throughout several games, Fischer had mastered to slay the Dragon.

7.) f3, 0-0
8.) Qd2, Nc6
9.) Bc4, Nxd4

Both players are making the typical Sicilian set ups, white's minor pieces are developing, and so as black. We will witness attacks from both sides destroying and storming each of their defenses accompanied by pawn storms after several moves.

10.) Bxd4, Be6
11.) Bb3, Qa5
12.) 0-0-0, b5

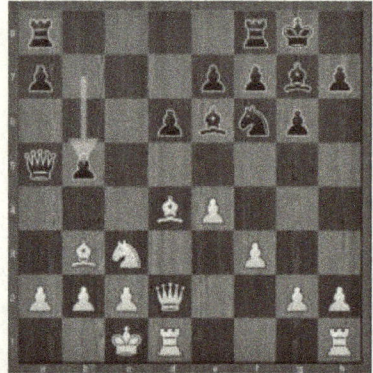

Move 12: b5

Moving the bishop to e6 seems unusual but a very good move for black's defenses, if taken, opening up the f-file for the rook and creating a doubled pawn on the center, a bit uncomfortable, but makes sense for the center control. Fischer considered it and played Bb3, and went on to continue develop his position.

13.) Kb1, b4
14.) Nd5, Bxd5
15.) Bxd5, Rac8

Not all players are feeling the urge to play Kb1. However, at top level chess, Kb1 is in need to somewhat solidify the pawn defenses being supported by the king and give rooms for the rooks to enter the c-file. With this idea behind, playing Kb1 makes sense.

Game 23
Entering the Fischer Era

There are at some sense, moves that seems to be inaccurate for white. But Fischer had his reasons behind, on the 15th move; the computer suggested that exd5 is better, instead of Bxd5. The mere reason I see why Fischer did this is to prevent the following continuation;

> *1.) Nd5, Bxd5*
> *2.) exd5, Qb5*

The light squared bishop is trapped and gripped and the e5 pawn is blocking its way to attack the kingside. Black's a-pawn is approaching the march and white must do trades to free up his bishop, but in turn weakening its defenses. In this moment in time, white is losing in position.

Meanwhile black didn't enter a simple line of taking the bishop, garnering the initiative and simplification;

> *1.) Bxd5, Nxd5*
> *2.) exd5, Qxd5*
> *3.) Qxb4, Rfb8*
> *4.) Qd2, e5*
> *5.) Bf2, Qb5*

White king is now under attack and must defend in which black's is somewhat safer in the corner, a better continuation against Fischer maybe.

> 16.) Bb3, Rc7
> 17.) h4, Qb5
> 18.) h5, Rfc8

Larsen is improving his queenside infiltrations, doubling up the rooks with the idea of a5-a4 in the future. However, white's light square bishop is doing a great way in defending the structures but it will not be enough once the two pawns connect and infiltrate. White can't just watch himself losing, thus moving his h-pawn to rip out black's kingside position.

> 19.) hxg6, hxg6
> 20.) g4, a5
> 21.) g5, Nh5

Move 21: Nh5

At this moment, both players have their initiatives and attacking chances, whoever can destroy first is difficult to see. After hxg6 by white, black is forced to recapture by his h-pawn as the f-pawn is pinned by the b3 bishop, realizing that the light squared bishop is so important in this variation, not taking it while having the chances can give regrets. Now that the h-rook controls the h-file towards the king, both sides can deliver attacks simultaneously and it will be a dynamic bloody match awaited.

> 22.) Rxh5, gxh5
> 23.) g6, e5
> 24.) gxf7, Kf8

So fast, real quick! Fischer had sneaked into black's premises. The rook sacrifice really makes sense to weaken black's kingside and the b3 bishop is still eyeing the f7 square, with just one move, a4 with tempo, returning the initiative for black, and letting him do to attack. But at this position, Fischer had the ace card, his f-pawn is just one move from promotion and the black's kingside is weak against infiltration.

Game 23
Entering the Fischer Era

25.) Be3, d5
26.) exd5, Rxf7
27.) d6, Rf6

Larsen did everything to save his rook, but it is now unstoppable. One of his rooks will be taken up in any lines you enter. White's bishop pair is so dominating and defensive at the same time. Black's king has many weak points while white's is solidly sitting on the corner. We can now say that black is losing here and just struggling to survive from Fischer's hands.

28.) Bg5, Qb7
29.) Bxf6, Bxf6
30.) d7, Rd8
31.) Qd6+ (1-0)

Move 31: Qd6+

At the peak of the attack, Larsen can't stand the pressures of the white's gripping and eventually made inaccurate moves while defending. Moving the queen to b7 doesn't make sense instead a better move, a4 awaits which can hold the position longer as shown in this variation;

1.) Bg5, a4
2.) d7, Rd8
3.) Bxf6, Rxd7
4.) Bxg7+, Ke8
5.) Bf7+, Kxf7
6.) Qxd7+, Qxd7
7.) Rxd7+ (1-0)

The end is still crushing for black, but entering many branches of this line may hold a little longer for black to continue.

However, if bishop recaptures after Bxf6, the king would be on the mating net after several moves.

1.) Bxf6, Bxf6
2.) Qh6+, Ke7
3.) Qh7+, Bg7
4.) Qxg7+ (1-0)

A mate is inevitable; the b3 bishop is the monster in this variation, guarding the b3-g8 diagonals which made the black king gripped in spaces making white mate the king in ease.

Another line is if the rook took the f7 bishop, after the white's move Bf7+. The game is eventually be adjourned in a mating pattern.

1.) Bf7+, Rxf7
2.) Qd8+ (1-0)

The black king is mate, and nowhere to go as the only escape squares is blocked by the fellow rook.

In the Dragon Variation of the Sicilian Game, we are now realizing that the light squared bishop of white can be very dangerous in the entire phase of the game if it is eyeing the b3-g8 square which in turn, the weak points of black's premises once the black's kingside was ripped out by the h and g-pawns. Fischer already knew all of these and used all of his pieces fully garnering their full potential to interact and participate on the game. The American genius of his era gives Larsen no mercy, hope and chances not just to win but to play a good game.

Game 24
A Trap to Remember

Robert J. Fischer – Samuel Reshevsky
US Championship (1958/59)

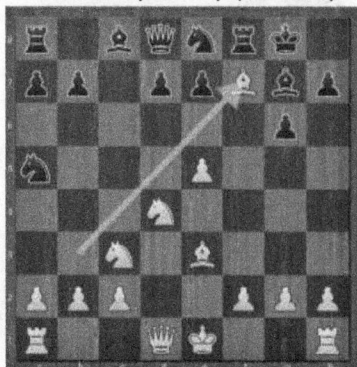

Move 10: Bxf7+

We had lots of studied games, and are now heading to analyze one of the most complicated traps in the Sicilian, popularized by Fischer after beating Reshevsky in top level match. In this game, black was shocked after being forced to give up his queen early in the opening.

1.) e4, c5
2.) Nf3, Nc6
3.) d4, cxd4

The typical formation of the Sicilian, where pieces are free to wander and develop, preparing to garner a better attacking position before infiltration.

4.) Nxd4, g6
5.) Be3, Nf6
6.) Nc3, Bg7

Black goes for the Dragon Variation that Fischer enjoys to destroy, after several continuations, black will face the crushing attack and he can't stand to endure.

7.) Bc4, 0-0
8.) Bb3, Na5
9.) e5, Ne8

This is where the shocker starts, in this position; anything has been set up in favor of white for the minor-piece sacrifice.

10.) Bxf7+, Kxf7
11.) Ne6, dxe6
12.) Qxd8, Nc6

The young Bobby sacrificed his bishop for the f7 pawn removing the defender to pave way for the knight to trap the black queen. Black recaptured with the king seemingly risking his position, as taking the bishop with the rook is a better move. However, Bb3 seems to be just a bait provoking black to move Na5, white want the a5 square occupied first before doing the trap as it is the only escape space for the queen. This trap is truly a masterpiece! However, at 11th move, if black recaptured with the king, Reshevsky will face an early mating attack.

1.) Ne6, Kxe6
2.) Qd5+, Kf5
3.) f4, h5
4.) e6+, Be5
5.) Qxe5+, Kg4
6.) Qg5+ (1-0)

The king is mate and the game is adjourned, and black is out with teary eyes.

However, black can prevent this continuation, avoiding Fischer to do his plan, shown in following variation:

1.) e5, Nxb3
2.) exf6, Nxa1
3.) fxg7, Kxg7
4.) Qxa1, e5

And the game continues longer, where the white rook is exchanged for the bishop and knight. This is a better continuation than placing the knight to e8, a variation Reshevsky didn't chose to play.

Game 24
A Trap to Remember

13.) Qd2, Bxe5
14.) 0-0, Nd6
15.) Bf4, Nc4

Now, with the queen on the white side, Fischer must reduce the black's activity by provoking the exchange of the minor pieces clearing the board to fully utilize the queen's potential.

16.) Qe2, Bxf4
17.) Qxc4, Kg7
18.) Ne4, Bc7

Move 18: Bc7

Seemingly, after the trades, the white queen is matched with the black's bishop pair which is not easy to dominate. Black is playing without the queen but has still the chances to counter attack. Its position is well defended and needing many resources to crack.

19.) Nc5, Rf6
20.) c3, e5
21.) Rad1, Nd8

White is slowly attacking the weak points on the doubled pawns but black can handle and defend it at some ways. Fischer must push the game to the end phase while black must hold its position and find chances to counter attack before the endgame.

22.) Nd7, Rc6
23.) Qh4, Re6
24.) Nc5, Rf6

As a young player who has the upper hand against the master, Fischer just not want to complicate the game even more, trying to attack the weak squares of black's structures is enough to make black defend and a trade of the minor pieces will be essential to sneak the winning chances completely.

25.) Ne4, Rf4
26.) Qxe7+, Rf7
27.) Qa3, Nc6

Move 27: Nc6

Black had established an intact defending position against white's infiltration. Sneaking a pawn would not be enough to dominate completely as it is just in a doubled pawn structure and even helps black garner some space to move.

28.) Nd6, Bxd6
29.) Rxd6, Bf5
30.) b4, Rff8

Black continues to reduce its activity and clears the board that favors the white's plan. The 30th move, Rff8 seems to be a waste of tempo, black may just continue to play a6 instead. However, white is starting to dominate squares that will grip black's movement, leading to a slightly uncomfortable endgame.

Game 24
A Trap to Remember

31.) b5, Nd8
32.) Rd5, Nf7
33.) Rc5, a6

Fischer continues to attack the slightest weak points in the black's structures, slowly grabbing the advantages of having the queen in play. Black must defend all of his pawns to hold the game even longer, before approaching the end phase.

34.) b6, Be4
35.) Re1, Bc6
36.) Rxc6, bxc6

Move 36: bxc6

Black saw an opportunity to slightly make a fortress and even make the position solid and intact using the pawn-bishop formation creating stronger defenses against white. But white didn't let the plan succeed and willing to sacrifice the rook to rattle the structures. In this moment, black is closer to balance the game materially.

37.) b7, Rab8
38.) Qxa6, Nd8
39.) Rb1, Rf7

Both sides have the ability to attack and defend with their resources. But it seems that the end is near to come and white can now fully use the queen's potential in the open position.

The young Fischer is doing great to grip Reshevsky until in this position. Since the bishop sacrifice, black had always been defending from white's attacks and slowly suffocating its resources to defend.

40.) h3, Rfxb7
41.) Rxb7+, Rxb7
42.) Qa8 (1-0)

Move 42: Qa8

Fischer had traded his pieces to settle down black's hope to win. In this position, Reshevsky can hold the game much longer and can sneak chances to dominate, the pieces are materially balanced but in open position like this, the queen has more potential to deliver the threats as long as its white king is protected by the pawns. However, to give you more insights on how the game may continue if black didn't resign immediately; we have the variation that follows;

1.) Qa8, Rd7
2.) a4, Nb7
3.) Qe8, Rf7
4.) Qxe5+, Kc8
5.) a5, Re7

The a-pawn is slowly crawling to promotion and black can't stop but to watch while defending its pieces striving to survive.

Game 25
A Chinese Specialty

Wei Yi – Alexander Areshchenko
World Cup (2015)

Move 19: Nxe6

We are now studying another game that shows the dynamics and classical styles from the modern era. The mind of a young genius, Wei Yi showed the important of not just beating your opponent, but beating them with classy combinations and positional masterpieces, breaking their thinking stamina on finding the right escape squares to hold the position from multiple incoming threats of the white's plan.

1.) e4, c5
2.) Nf3, d6
3.) d4, cxd4

The Sicilian Game, home of sacrifices and brilliant responses. At this time, we are expecting fiery and sneaking tactics, and as always been expected, crushing combinations are along the way.

4.) Nxd4, Nf6
5.) Nc3, a6
6.) Bg5, e6

A typical continuation on white's 6th move is Be3, however, Wei Yi threw his prepared line, Bg5, which changes the whole phase of the game. The position became very complicated after several moves.

7.) f4, Qb6
8.) Qd2, Qxb2
9.) Rb1, Qa3

Move 09: Qa3

At 7th move, Areshchenko is willing to retake if ever the bishop took the f6 knight, opening the g-file in favor of his h8 rook to attack white's kingside, makes sense as his king seems protected by pawns and there is no clear threat from the white. He played Qb6, attacking the defenseless b2 square, however, Wei Yi accepted the challenge, instead of defending it by Nb3, as the computer suggested, He played Qd2, provoking white to take the pawn and pushes it to the awkward square on a3, the only move after Rb1. White's idea is to dislocate the black queen to its important squares, pushing it away in defending black's position from white's incoming attack.

10.) e5, h6
11.) Bh4, dxe5
12.) fxe5, g5

After this position, the f6 knight is forced to retreat. We see that black's pieces are not improving while white is already in development, although, the position seems a little exposed to king's safety. Is the b2 pawn compensated in this continuation?

Game 25
A Chinese Specialty

13.) exf6, gxh4
14.) Be2, Qa5
15.) 0-0, Nd7

We are now starting to realize the effects of the pawn sacrifice. Black is now feeling the grip of the f6 pawn, making the black king exposed in the e8 square, castling on both sides are dangerous enough as the pawns are not covering the king. The realization of Wei Yi is so immense that since Qd2 until at this position, are somewhat difficult to see.

16.) Rbd1, h3
17.) g3, Bb4
18.) Qe3, Bxc3

Move 18: Bxc3

This is a very interesting line from the young Chinese, setting up the trap, provoking black to play Bb4 to deliver a deadly threat against the king, sacrificing his whole knight for the dreamed position, a very classical indeed.

19.) Nxe6, Qe5
20.) Nc7+, Kf8
21.) Qxe5, Bxe5

The 2nd knight sacrifice of the game, Black played Qe5 to block the pin but, he must just take the knight instead as the continuation will lead to drawn repetition. It's just Wei Yi who is willing to sac and sac in a risky manner.

The game will continue in a repetition if Areschenko is willing to enter this following line:

1.) Nxe6, fxe6
2.) Qxe6+, Kd8
3.) Qe7, Kc7
4.) Qd6+, Kd8
5.) f7, Bg7
6.) f8=Q+, Bxf8
7.) Rxf8, Rxf8
8.) Qxf8+, Kc7
9.) Qd6+, Kd8

This is the line black didn't tried to play. Black wants to hold its position and want to push more for counter attacking chances after the sacrifice.

22.) Nxa8, Nxf6
23.) Nb6, Kg7
24.) Nxc8, Rxc8

Move 24: Rxc8

White want to simplify after the combination, as at this position, Wei Yi is somewhat better but the pawn structures of black is still difficult to crack; the rook must find a way to infiltrate at the back rank. To come at this position where you have the slight edge after several piece sacrifices is very difficult to attain, it's really the skill of this young Chinese. The fire didn't end at this moment; white is still trying to push the game on madness.

Game 25
A Chinese Specialty

25.) Rf5, Bb8
26.) Rdf1, Ba7+
27.) Kh1, Bd4

It will be a long way to go before completely dismantling black's defenses. The board is quiet cleared so as the bishop is active in which gives black an edge to even the position.

28.) Bd3, Rc6
29.) g4, Rc7
30.) g5, hxg5

Move 30: hxg5

Wei Yi is trying to clear the board in his favor, for the rook to come in in all directions and even from behind. The white king is gripped but safe guarded by the rooks in that sense, both players now has the edge to win, and the position is fairly even.

31.) Rxg5+, Kf8
32.) Rg3, Nd5
33.) Rxh3, Ne3

Each player is fighting to have the edge on the incoming endgame. Literally taking pawns to that are threats for their future. The sacrifices brought by white seem to have lost its purpose and glance.

34.) Rf4, Ba7
35.) Re4, Nd1
36.) Rh8+, Kg7

Wei Yi is actively engaging his rooks in garnering domination on the board. However, Areschenko doesn't take the pawn for the following reasons:

1.) Re4, Nxc2
2.) Rh8+, Kg7
3.) Rg7+, Kxh7
4.) Re7+, Kh3
5.) Rxc7, Nb4

And white, from that simple trick, simplified the game in its favor. The rook is controlling the 7th rank, attacking the b7 and the f7 pawns which itself is winning.

37.) Rh7+, Kf8
38.) Rc4, Bc5
39.) Bg6 (1-0)

Move 39: Bg6

This is the trickiest endgame ever in this book. The brilliant Bg6 finished the game with utmost advantage against black. In this position, black is to play and there are interesting lines that we want to consider holding the game longer:

1.) Bg6, b6
2.) Rf4, Kg8
3.) Rxf7, Rxf7
4.) Bxf7+, Kg2

Black can hold longer but still in the losing position, a very classical approach in taming the Sicilian.

Game 26
The Sicilian Brilliancy

Wei Yi – Anne Haast
Tata Steel Challengers (2015)

Move 26: Qh3#

Let's look at another game by Wei Yi where he showed no mercy as he hunt the king down and mated in just 26 moves. His opponent made inaccurate continuations as early as 7th move in the opening, being exploited and punished with a series of sacrifices.

1.) e4, c5
2.) Nf3, e6
3.) d4, cxd4

Like Fischer, destroying the Sicilian is the favorite repertoire of this young talent. His classical and mastery skill in every variation in depth of his ability to visualize situations always left black with no hope of escaping his miniatures.

4.) Nxd4, Nc6
5.) Nc3, Qc7
6.) Be3, a6

Here, we are seeing the Taimanov continuation. The early Qc7 followed by Bd6 in the future threatens the h2 square. The b5-Bb7-Rc8 set up by black will be seen after a few moves. The a6 and e6 pawn are stopping the knight on attacking the black queen in its safe square. In this moment, black just wants to push for the queenside domination, cracking white's position.

7.) Qf3, Ne5
8.) Qg3, h5
9.) 0-0-0, h4

This is where the winning starts favoring white. Ne5 and h4 are just inaccurate, moving the knight twice in the opening, loses a tempo and after Qg3, there are no stronger continuations. The e5 knight will be driven away soon after f4, a move of development, and white had already castled, so all in all, white steal two tempos from black's Ne5 and h4.

10.) Qh3, b5
11.) f4, Nc4
12.) Bxc4, Qxc4

Move 12: Qxc4

Playing b5 is a little bit of being late, this is the must move, than Ne5, h5 and h4 garnering spaces and mobility for the bishop to enter the field and at the same time, attacking the white king.

13.) f5, Bb7
14.) Rhf1, e5
15.) Nb3, Qc7

There are interesting lines that we need to see that black had move instead of playing e5 as it's just weakened the e-file the white rook had already in control.

Game 26
The Sicilian Brilliancy

Instead of e5, playing b4 seems a logical response; driving away the knight to make the e4 pawn undefended but the complications arises exponentially in interesting lines shown in these variations:

1.) Rhf1, b4
2.) fxe6, bxc3
3.) exd7+, Kd8
4.) Ne6+, Qxe6
5.) Qxe6, fxe6
6.) Rf7, cxb2+
7.) Kb1, Bd6
8.) Rxd6, (1-0)

Black's Bb6+ is unstoppable and white instantly loses almost all of his materials to defend the mating technique.

However, if the king went to e7, the faster threat is inevitable:

1.) exd7+, Ke7
2.) Nf5+, Kd8
3.) Bb6+, Qc7

Putting the king on d8 is better than on e7, as Nf5+ steals a tempo to attack and garner a dominating position.

But however, black must recapture first the e6 pawn before taking down the knight to safely continue the game with ease. The game would be as the following:

1.) Rhf1, b4
2.) fxe6, dxe6
3.) Qf3, Nf6
4.) Nd5, exd5
5.) e5, 0-0-0
6.) exf6, g6

Both sides are even in position and in material and maintain the complications and dynamics of the pieces but black didn't enter this line instead played e5 for the safer and silent continuation.

However, b4 after Nb3 seems playable except of drawing the queen on c7 preventing the move Na5 picking up the fianchetto bishop. Makes sense until a combination strikes at the weak pawn at d7.

1.) Nb3, b4
2.) f6, Qe6
3.) fxg7, Bxg7
4.) Na4, Qxh3
5.) gxh3, Bxe4
6.) Nb6, Rd8
7.) Nc5, f5

The position sits prettily well for white as he has the initiative and play, however, black has more pawns to conserve until the endgame. The fate depends on white's hand on how he can deliver the complete dominance to finish the game as black tries to hold it until the end phase in which he has the endgame advantages.

After Nb3, taking the e4 pawn with the bishop is a blunder as white can recapture the piece after Nd2 attacking both the queen and the bishop. There are several choices to continue the play except e5, which seems silent and unsound, but somewhat black, is willing to do so.

Above all, the e5 response after Rhf1 by black is not that good enough as it weakened the d7 square and opened an access road for the rook and queen after the move f6 by white to infiltrate the king's position. At this moment, black is really in behind of development, its pieces are stuck and not joining the play while white's are active and its rooks are dominating the center files. This is the result of too many unnecessary moves of black letting white to gain tempo in which Wei Yi converted to development.

Game 26
The Sicilian Brilliancy

16.) Kb1, Rc8
17.) f6, Nxf6
18.) Rxf6, gxf6

Move 18: gxf6

Wei Yi sacrificed his rook for his dreamed position on the board; the king at the center, exposed to attacks. In this set up, a rook for a knight seems a fair trade for the Chinese prodigy.

19.) Bb6, Qc6
20.) Na5, Qe6
21.) Nxb7, Rb8

White is threatening the one-move mating attack at the d7 pawn while black is defending it accordingly, seeking a safe trade to breath at his gripped position.

22.) Nd5, Rxb7
23.) Qc3, Qc6
24.) Nxf6+, Ke7

At this position, black is almost hopeless to hold longer, there are mating attacks from every sides and the bishop and the rook at the corner can't help but to watch the suffocation of their king. Trading queens after Nd5 instead of capturing the b7 knight seems the answer to open up and escape the gripping, but still there are no ways to run.

1.) Nd5, Qxh3
2.) Nc7+, Ke7
3.) Bc5+, d6
4.) Rxd6, f5
5.) Nd5+, Ke8
6.) Nf6+, Ke7
7.) Rxa6# (1-0)
The mating attack is unstoppable and black can't do anything but to accept the forcing checks.

25.) Bd8+, Ke6
26.) Qh3# (1-0)

Move 26: Qxh3#

This is one of the staggering ends of the tournament. Wei Yi delivered a very beautiful and classical piece sacrifices that lead to a mating pattern black can't resist. This is one of the finest matches of Wei Yi, showing that wrong continuations and inaccurate responses if exploited, will win the game in the most dominating possible. Tempo is important, black is in haste of attacking white even if his own position is not really safe from any form of counter attacks. Despite of his undeveloped position, she forces to have the initiative but forget to make the defense ready for white's counter plays.

Game 27
The Crushing Hikaru

**Wesley So – Hikaru Nakamura
Sinquefield Cup (2015)**

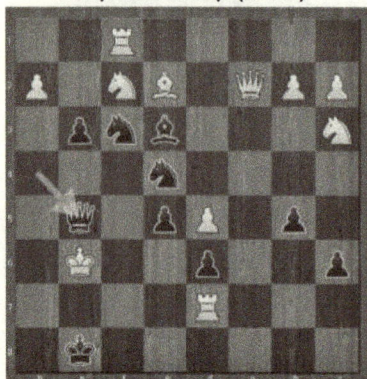

Move 39: Qg5#

One of the finest and famous amongst chess players in the modern era, Hikaru Nakamura, being one of the top guys who can stand against Carlsen on top level match crushes Wesley So in the most satisfying mate ever, where he dragged down the white king in his premises and beaten by several checks leading to mate. In this game, Nakamura is in his strongest form, the machine-like sacrifices are so deep that even Wesley So can't stop the aftermath of losing his materials.

    1.) d4, Nf6
    2.) c4, g6
    3.) Nc3, Bg7

Nakamura had prepared his King's Indian Style against white. The early castling followed by the break on the f file is the critical moment in this continuation.

    4.) e4, d6
    5.) Nf3, 0-0
    6.) Be2, e5

Black is provoking white to capture the e5 pawn, as it seems to be defenseless, but black can easily regain after the following continuation:

    1.) Be2, e5
    2.) dxe5, dxe5
    3.) Nxe5, Qxd1
    4.) Bxd1, Nxe4
    5.) Nxe4, Bxe5

Black regained the pawn and as if nothing happened, the position is even and so the materials.

    7.) 0-0, Nc6
    8.) d5, Ne7
    9.) Ne1, Nd7

Black didn't try to enter such variation and go for the typical continuation of development. Realizing this position, both sides are already prepared to push their f-pawn for domination, seeking squares and grabbing spaces to occupy.

    10.) f3, f5
    11.) Be3, f4
    12.) Bf2, g5

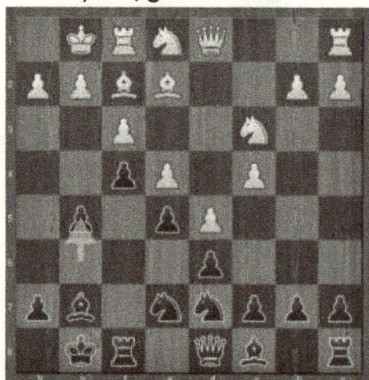

Move 12: g5

Playing f3 seems silent and defensive, and after Be3, white just let black gain some tempo to play f4, gripping the kingside to slow down further development but Wesley just wants to conserve his position as his pawns are a little bit over-extended and black will going to explode his pieces once the white's center pawns broke their chains. At 10th move, moving f4

83

Game 27
The Crushing Hikaru

immediately stops the problem as shown in the following variation:

1.) Ne1, Nd7
2.) f4, f5
3.) Nf3, Nc5
4.) exf5, e4
5.) Nd4, Nxf5
6.) Nxf5, Bxf5
7.) Be3, Nd3
8.) Qd2, Qe7

White is slowly breaking up the queenside while black tries to part the defenses of the white's kingside. However, this is a very close position and both sides have winning advantages in hand.

13.) Nd3, Ng6
14.) c5, Nf6
15.) Rc1, Rf7

Move 15: Rf7

Both players are not ready to light the fire, but slowly creeping forward, grabbing squares and maneuvering pieces in preparation to attack. This is a queenside against the kingside domination.

16.) Kh1, h5
17.) cxd6, cxd6
18.) Nb5, a6

In this position, as both sides are initiating an attack, black is somehow has the better chances of winning as he is attacking the kingside. White will be forced to defend to protect his king losing tempi and initiatives which is not the scenario in the queenside battle.

19.) Na3, b5
20.) Rc6, g4
21.) Qc2, Qf8

Move 21: Qf8

White is the first to open up and break the c-file. Does this enough as black is soon to get the domination on the kingside and his pawns are along the way? Few exchanges and the game would be swindled in favor of black.

22.) Rc1, Bd7
23.) Rc7, Bh6
24.) Be1, h4

White can't now shift to defend the king from pawn storm attacks; he might not gain the initiative and tempo and lose his position whatsoever. In this matter, attacking is the best response; black might stop and slow down his plans if white dominated fully affecting black king's safety, but as we can see, the king is well placed and defended on the corner. This makes white's plan nonsense and will be useless, as after few moves, white's position will cripple and gripped.

84

Game 27
The Crushing Hikaru

25.) fxg4, f3
26.) gxf3, Nxe4
27.) Rd1, Rxf3

Move 27: Rxf3

Black now in this moment starts crushing the white's kingside. There are several choices white may respond after f3, but all of them are leading to a losing position:
1.) f3, Rd1
2.) fxe2, Qxe2
3.) Bxg4, Rxf7
4.) Qxf7, Qf2
5.) Bxd1, Kg1

Black has all the initiative in position and in materials. Clearly white is in the verge of losing.

However, if white accepted the knight sac, an incredible mating attack is just waiting to uncover.
1.) f3, gxf3
2.) Nxe4, fxe4
3.) Rf1+, Kg2
4.) Be3, Bxf1
5.) h3+, Kxh3
6.) Qf3+, Bg3
7.) Bxg4# (1-0)

However, there are numerous responses and variations to continue this position, but we are just uncovering lines capable to see by human eyes.

If white didn't take the h3 pawn, still a mating combination can take down the position.
1.) Be3, Bxf1
2.) h3+, Kg3
3.) Qxf1, Rc8+
4.) Kh7, Qf2
5.) Bf4+, Nxf4
6.) exf4+, Kf3
7.) Qd3+, Qe3
8.) Qxe3#

The mating continuations are very difficult to find but black had established a control on the kingside, making every response from white is still can't hold the game even more.

Hikaru is throwing all of his pieces, sacrificing on every move just to open up white's kingside. His confidence to deliver a winning position really pushes him to play insanely aggressive. On the other hand, Wesley must be very careful as his king is slowly breaking down from black's dominations.
28.) Rxd7, Rf1+
29.) Kg2, Be3
30.) Bg3, hxg3

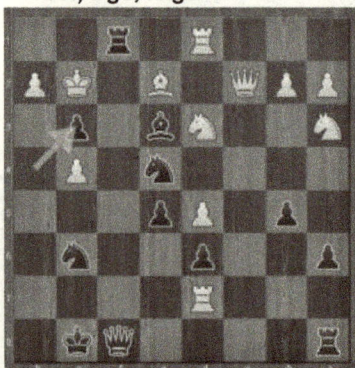
Move 30: hxg3

White didn't capture the rook, instead sacrificed his bishop to prevent prior mating set ups.

85

Game 27
The Crushing Hikaru

Let us show the following continuations if Bxf1 took place:

1.) Kg2, Be3
2.) Bxd1, h3+
3.) Kxh3, Ng5+
4.) Kg2, Qf3#

A same situation from prior mating attacks. Black was forced to move his bishop to open the 8th rank for his rook and prevent the threat of Rg1+-Ng5+ mating the king, but instead of sacrificing it, moving the bishop to f2 is also possible to block some white's pieces and simplify.

1.) Kg2, Be3
2.) Bf2, Rxf2+
3.) Nxf2, Qxf2+
4.) Kh1, Bf4
5.) Bf1, Qe3
6.) Rd2, Qxd2
7.) Qxd2, Nxd2
8.) Rxd6, Nxf1
9.) Rxg6+, Kf7
10.) Rc6, Nxh2

After several trades, black is ahead in position and material advantages in which itself is winning position.

Another normal response is Bb4, not distracting black's plan and may continue to lose the king in a mating net:

1.) Kg2, Be3
2.) Bb4, h3+
3.) Kxh3, Qh6+
4.) Kg2, Nf4+
5.) Kxf1, Ng3+
6.) Ke1, Ng2#

This combination is very difficult to realize with the human eye, but with Hikaru, anything can be possible.

Above all, Bg3 is the best response, sacrificing it to prevent white's mating plans at least for some time.

31.) Rxf1, Nh4+
32.) Kh3, Qh6
33.) g5, Nxg5+

The white king can't go to h1, as g2+ is a mate. Playing g5 is a must giving the king his only escape after Ng5+. Wesley must see everything is this position, all of the mating attacks are hanging around, and finding the escape square is difficult to recognize.

34.) Kg4, Nhf3
35.) Nf2, Qh4+
36.) Kf5, Rf8+

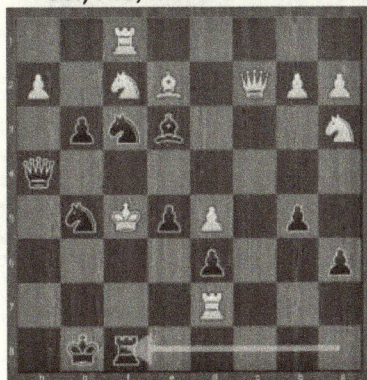
Move 36: Rf8+

Black couldn't capture the g3 pawn to escape; a classical mating attack is waiting at the end.

1.) g5, Nxg5+
2.) Kxg3, Nf5+
3.) Kg2, Qh3+
4.) Kh1, Ng3#

The rook can't capture the f5 knight after Nf5+, as the mate in one by Qh3+ is waiting; instead moving away the king is the better idea to hold longer.

To prevent these continuations, black is forced to move his king toward the center. This is the Hikaru's dream, driving the king somewhere then ambush thereafter.

Game 27
The Crushing Hikaru

37.) Kg6, Rf6+
38.) Kxf6, Ne4+
39.) Kg6, Qg5#

Move 39: Qg5#

Totally a shameful ending for white, black again sacrificed a full rook for the mating attack to happen. Hikaru just completely crushed white's defenses, destroying anything in its path, to garner an unstoppable combination ending white's hope to continue the game. Since 26th move, black blows out series of sacrifices that ruined white's position, its domination in the queenside doesn't matter and affects enough to the safety of the black king. Because of this, black is really comfortable in his repertoire, garnered an inevitable crushing combinations with ease.

Generalizing the game to think where white gone wrong, as its response are logical too and defensive at the same time lead us to believe that the 25th move, f3, made the position passive and gripped by the black structures. The spaces black had occupied in the kingside slow down the development of white pieces while black's position improves drastically until the end. This made black achieved a very comfortable and dominative position.

Hikaru Nakamura is an American chess prodigy, Twitch livestreamer, content creator and a five-time United States champion.

Game 28
The Impossible Checkmate

Wilhelm Steinitz – Curt Bardeleben
Hastings (1895)

Move 24: Rg7+

One of the classical players of history, Steinitz, nothing can escape in his positional understanding of the pieces. In this match, he converted the slightest disadvantages of black's position into a winning endgame which black can't hold no more.

1.) e4, e5
2.) Nf3, Nc6
3.) Bc4, Bc5

Entering one of the aggressive openings to learn, Guioco Piano hides many tricks and traps suitable for classical style players. Both are fighting for the center control which is the key to lead the initiatives and control the game.

4.) c3, Nf6
5.) d4, exd4
6.) cxd4, Bb4+

One of the typical continuations in the Piano line, Steinitz is eager to place his two pawns to outpost the center for the middle game control.

7.) Nc3, d5
8.) exd5, Nxd5
9.) 0-0, Be6

As we can clearly see, at 7th move, d5 seems not the best response to punish white's position. A more logical response is Nxe4 as the knight is pinned and can't recapture. But somehow, black avoided the possible continuation if Nxe4 took place:

1.) Nc3, Nxe4
2.) 0-0, Nxc3
3.) bxc3, d5
4.) cxb4, dxc4
5.) Re1+, Ne7

Black is up a pawn, but was stuck in an uncomfortable position; taking the e4 pawn in exchange of white's development is not a great choice in this position. Steinitz must play d5 first instead of taking the c3 pawn with the bishop, preventing this continuation.

1.) Nc3, Nxe4
2.) 0-0, Nxc3
3.) bxc3, Bxc3
4.) Ba6, d5
5.) Bb5, Bxa1
6.) Re1+, Be6
7.) Qc2, Qd7
8.) Ne5, Qd8
9.) Nxc6, bxc6
10.) Qxc6, Qd7
11.) Qxd7#

First, the pawn is poisoned and next is the rook, white just sacrificed his whole a1 rook to gain extra tempo of improving its position and exploiting the black king at the center. Black has the choice to give away his queen to prevent the mating attack that also leads to a playable losing position, a very poisonous indeed.

Moving the bishop to e6 instead of taking down the c3 pawn at 9th move became clear to be more logical than the latter as the positions are still the same, where the rook will be offered as a sacrifice to steal some tempo and exposing the black king to attacks. Above all, black is still doing well.

Game 28
The Impossible Checkmate

10.) Bg5, Be7
11.) Bxd5, Bxd5
12.) Nxd5, Qxd5

Move 12: Qxd5

Retreating the bishop to e7 somewhat loses a tempo for black, instead Qd7 is a better response. Steinitz seems already realized the position after some trades. With some possible positional advantages, white seizes the chance to exploit the black king at the center.

13.) Bxe7, Nxe7
14.) Re1, f6
15.) Qe2, Qd7

The game is now approaching to endgame, and positional repertoires are in need to win the game. In this moment, black is forced not to castle to save his knight from the capture. The momentum and initiative is now already on white's hand.

16.) Rac1, c6
17.) d5, cxd5
18.) Nd4, Kf7

The black rooks are still undeveloped which is the weakness in position, White just want to exploit it, sacrificed a pawn, paving ways for the knight to participate the gripping. Above all, Steinitz saw even further, after several moves, the mating combination arises from nowhere.

19.) Ne6, Rhc8
20.) Qg4, g6
21.) Ng5+, Ke8

This is where the madness start, white continues to do forcing moves against black, its dominance and mobility shows the importance of piece development. Black loses several tempos in the opening which in turn after some trades, leaving its position defenseless against white's infiltrations.

22.) Rxe7+, Kf8
23.) Rf7+, Kg8
24.) Rg7+, Kh8
25.) Rxh7+ (1-0)

Move 25: Rxh7+

A shocking rook sacrifice has forced the game to end. At 22nd move, black is forced not to take the rook with the queen saving the king from the mate shown in this variation:

1.) Rxe7+, Qxe7
2.) Rxc8+, Rxc8
3.) Qxc8+, Qd8
4.) Qxd8+, Kxd8

White has the piece, and this position can easily be winning. However, if king took the rook, there are still mating combinations after several moves in which black realized not to play.

89

Game 28
The Impossible Checkmate

Taking the rook with the king seems a logical response. But the continuation shows this is also leading to a losing position:

    1.) Rxe7+, Kxe7
    2.) Re1+, Kd6
    3.) Qb4+, Rc5
    4.) Qf4+, Kc6
    5.) Re6+, Kb5
    6.) a4+, Ka5
    7.) b4+, Kxa4
    8.) bxc5+, d4

White is up a knight, and the black king is gripped in the corner, still can't hold and forced to defend continuous attacks.

However, if the king after Re1+ goes to d8 instead of d6, loses faster than the latter shown in this line:

    1.) Rxe7+, Kxe7
    2.) Re1+, Kd8
    3.) Ne6+, Ke7
    4.) Nc5+, Kd6
    5.) Qxd7+, Kxc5
    6.) Rc1+, Kb6
    7.) Rxc8, Rxc8
    8.) Qxc8, a5

Black will most probably resign than playing this position against white having the whole queen in hand.

Above all, black chose to play Kf8 letting white to take the queen, but leaving its c1 rook hanging and after black's Rxc1+, the white king will be mate. With that in mind, black is confident in his position, but Steinitz has all the resources to attack counter intuitively, he didn't take the queen, instead, moves the rook defenselessly and attacks the king regaining the tempo for his own mating chances shown at the following variations. This is one of the best endgame swindle in our game collections so far.

Black is forbidden to taste the rook in any way whatsoever, as the continuations, will all lead to the same set up and a losing position. At 24th move, after black's Kg8, white continues to play brilliantly, playing Rg7+, which in turn a wrong move if black dares to take.

    1.) Rg7+, Qxg7
    2.) Rxc8+, Rxc8
    3.) Qxc8+, Qf8
    4.) Qxf8+, Kxf8

White is then a piece up and winning the game with ease with a whole knight in his hand.

All of the continuations will fall to the same set up if black dares to take the poisoned rook. Moreover, at 25th move, if black continues to play Kg8 after Rxh7+, still a long maneuver will end the game in favor of white as shown in this position:

    1.) Rxh7+, Kg8
    2.) Rg7+, Kf8
    3.) Nh7+, Kxg7
    4.) Qxd7+, Kh6
    5.) Rxc8, Rxc8
    6.) Qxc8, Kxh7

Black still lose the game, however, if the king doesn't take the rook and move Ke8 instead, a deadly mate is going to happen as shown:

    1.) Rxh7+, Kg8
    2.) Rg7+, Kf8
    3.) Nh7+, Ke8
    4.) Qxd7+, Kf8
    5.) Qf7#, mate

Black can't escape the mating threat and the losing position since the rook sacrifice at 22nd move, whereas white has plenty of choices to play the winning line. Each white's pieces are placed correctly to deliver a terrible mating attack which in turn, black had no way to defend.

Game 28
The Impossible Checkmate

If the black king goes back to h8 instead on f8 after Rxg7+, it will face the worst fate than before; white will maneuver the queen to garner the best domination possible:

1.) Rxh7+, Kg8,
2.) Rg7, Kh8
3.) Qh4+, Kxg7
4.) Qh7+, Kf8
5.) Qh8+, Ke7
6.) Qg7+, Ke8
7.) Qg8+, Ke7
8.) Qf7+, Kd8
9.) Qf8+, Qe8
10.) Nf7+, Kd7
11.) Qd6#

White delivers a mate in front of the black queen's face saying that even its two rooks can't defend the unstoppable threat.

There are more plenty of ways black can respond to the game's last 3 moves until its finish at move 25. And all of them lead to mate or an inferior losing position. Steinitz is superior in his repertoire, his positional mastery skills in the endgame, makes his opponents lose hope to bounce back. His pieces are well coordinated and his timing really sets the board on fire. With just few pieces in his hand, he can drag the game in complications and drowned the opponent's chances to fight back. Hardly see is his realization after the trades. Simplifying the position to hold and conserve his advantages and control at the center, until after several continuations, black is left with all its will, defending. Moreover, black didn't respond better in the opening phase, made his position, inferior from defending white's attacks with his undeveloped rooks, that Steinitz had been exploited successfully.

Wilhelm Steinitz is an Austrian and later American chess master, and the first official World Chess Champion, from 1886 to 1894. He was also a highly influential writer and chess theoretician.

Game 29
The Simplicity of Tal

Mikhail Tal – Bent Larsen
Montreal (1979)

Move 18: Bc6+

Take a look at this another masterpiece from the famous "Magician of Riga", Mikhail Tal, where he showed too much brilliancy winning the game with ease in just 22 moves of utmost attacking lines.

1.) e4, c5
2.) Nf3, Nc6
3.) d4, cxd4

This is the typical Sicilian continuation. Tal in his repertoires is good in playing this opening as it requires the combination of keen visualization and mind stamina needed to understand the complications ahead in time.

4.) Nxd4, Nf6
5.) Nc3, d6
6.) Bg5, e6

As usual, black will be slightly behind in development and must learn to make first its defenses as the opening calls to. While white, on the other hand, clearly has the space and activity on the board. Black must just wait for the counter attacking chances to seize in the upcoming middle game.

7.) Qd2, Be7
8.) 0-0-0, a6
9.) f4, Qc7

Both sides are still in their middle game preparations, activating their pieces and honing their positional defenses. White has the initiative on the kingside whereas black has on the queenside. He who first to infiltrate gains the tempo and the full momentum of the game.

10.) Be2, Nxd4
11.) Qxd4, b5
12.) e5, dxe5

Move 12: dxe5

Black exchanged the knight, letting the black queen recapture and outpost the d4 square with tempo in which seems to be a helping move on white's domination. Also, Tal forced black to capture the e5 pawn, opening the a8 to h1 diagonal and at the same time controlling the d-file with the strong queen-rook combination.

13.) fxe5, Nd5
14.) Bxe7, Nxc3
15.) Bf3, Nxd1

The game is now starting the middle phase and black seems to be behind in development. The move, e5 is so immense that it opens up several choices for white to attack, forces black to defend and slow down its preferred development. After a few moves, white already infiltrated black's position.

Game 29
The Simplicity of Tal

Black is forced to take the c3 knight, instead of recapturing the e7 bishop with the knight to prevent the mating attack as shown:

1.) Bxe7, Nxe7
2.) Nxb5, axb5
3.) Bxb5+, Bd7
4.) Qxd7+, Qxd7
5.) Rxd7+, Kf8
6.) a4, f6

White has the winning position; the three passed pawns are unstoppable from promotion, while the h-rook was stuck and the black king is gripped.

However, if black had just moved the king to f8, after white's Bxb5+, an inevitable mate is already in time.

1.) Bxb5+, Kf8
2.) Qd8+, Qxd8
3.) Rxd8#

The king faced the worst fate possible. The pieces can't help to block the check, and it's a shameful way to lose the game.

However, if black retake with the queen, Tal would have love to play his dominating position:

1.) Bxe7, Qxe7
2.) Nxd5, exd5
3.) Qxd5, Bb7
4.) Bxb5+, axb5
5.) Qxb5+, Kf8
6.) Rd7, Qg5+
7.) Kb1, Bxg2
8.) Rf1, Bxf1
9.) Qd5, Qe7
10.) Qxa1+, Qe1
11.) Rd1, Ke7

A quite playable continuation, but still black is losing the endgame, the passed pawn are enough to take down black's hope to win, also playing without the queen is just provoking black to resign.

Tal saw that his bishops are so strong, even stronger than his rooks. To continue the attack, he played Bf3, saving the bishop while attacking the black rook, sacrificing his d1 rook for the sake of combinations.

16.) Bd6, Qc4
17.) Qb6, Nf2
18.) Bc6+, Bd7

Move 18: Bd7

Tal threw one of his strongest moves in this game, Bd6 placing his bishop permanently to hinder black's will to castle kingside. On the other hand, Nf2 is provoking white to capture the knight, but stopping the initiative and leaving the white a material down in the incoming endgame. Tal is not really interested on the giveaways; even not tasting the rook instead, or even saving his own at h1, to continue the attack; Tal played Bc6+ for the sake of positional domination.

19.) Bxd7+, Kxd7
20.) Qb7+, Kd8
21.) Qxa8+, Qc8
22.) Qa7 (1-0)

All of the moves are forced and unstoppable. The move Qa7 is threatening mate in one and capturing the f2 knight which black can't stop both.

Game 29
The Simplicity of Tal

There are several choices black can hold longer but all will lead to the same losing set-ups.

1.) Qxa8+, Kd7
2.) Qa7+, Kc6
3.) Qxf2

Black is a piece down while white has a dominating center outpost by his bishop.

Summarizing the game in all, Tal has really dominated the position since move 12th, e5, which in turn opens several lines for white to coordinate his pieces and infiltrate. After that move, almost all of the responses seems forced and logical leading to a winning advantages in favor of white. But as we can see, where did the tragedy started? Black started to lose tempo and its defenses since the capture on the poisoned rook on d1, as it lets white to play the strong move Bd6, attacking the queen with tempo, and after Bc6+, a series of forcing moves is inevitable in white's favor.

Instead, black should have played a difficult to see, Ne2+ on the 15th move to continue the even position as shown:

1.) Bf3, Ne2+
2.) Bxe2, Qxe7
3.) Bf3, Bb7
4.) Bxb7, Qxb7
5.) Qd6, Rc8
6.) Rd2, Qc6
7.) Rhd1, Qxd6
8.) Rxd6, Ra8
9.) Rb6, h5

And the game continues evenly in position and in material. Black didn't saw this line and blinded by the hanging rook on d1, not realizing that after a series of continuations, his position would be fatal than before.

Known as "The Magician from Riga", Tal was the archetype of the attacking player, developing an extremely powerful and imaginative style of play.

Game 30
The Pinoy Pride

Wesley So – Mark Paragua
4th Pichay Cup International Open (2008)

Move 24: Qxf6

Wesley So, the player with a great accuracy and one of Carlsen's greatest rival beside Giri. Here, he is playing against the finest player from the Philippines, Mark Paragua where he showed multiple marks of sacrifices and combinations that destroyed black until the very endgame.

    1.) e4, e6
    2.) d4, d5
    3.) Nc3, Bb4

This is the French Winawer variation, one of the most complicated lines in this opening. In this continuation, white will be attacking the black's kingside, while black is sneaking the queenside to return the favor. Correct and accurate continuations are really important in this insane line of the French.

    4.) e5, c5
    5.) Qg4, Ne7
    6.) dxc5, Bxc3+

Wesley after taking the c5 pawn has now the tripled pawn structure which is a typical formation in the French Winawer. While both sides are grabbing spaces for their development, black at move 5,

provoked white to enter a crazy line in which white didn't try to enter, but a very interesting continuation to see.

    1.) Qg4, Ne7
    2.) Qxg7, Rg8
    3.) Qxh7, cxd4
    4.) a3, Qa5
    5.) axb4, Qxa1
    6.) Nce2, Nc6
    7.) Nf3, d3
    8.) Qxd3, Nxb4
    9.) Qd1, Bd7
    10.) h4, Rc8

Both king are in the middle and may become exposed anytime once the pawns are driven out. White has the disadvantages in position and material but his h4 pawn are the key in saving the game. White's pieces are there to defend the position, it seems black has more way to go to crack white's defenses. It's an interesting line to play but a difficult time to decide which side has the edge in winning the game.

    7.) bxc3, Qc7
    8.) Nf3, Qxc5
    9.) Bd2, 0-0

Move 09: 0-0

The black's g and h pawn are defenseless for a long time but Wesley seems already in preparation of not to capture it. He just wants to preserve

95

Game 30
The Pinoy Pride

the set up and let white castling in the kingside. White defended the e5 pawn as it is the only outpost in the center hindering black's mobility for some extent.

10.) Bd3, f5
11.) exf6, Rxf6
12.) Qh5, g6

Move 12: g6

At almost 10th move, white had achieved an attacking position towards the black's kingside. The bishop pair is dangerously eyeing the king while black's pieces are still not developing for the defense. Castling on the kingside seems a risky decision to take, making the king in an awkward situation afterwards. The doubled pawns together with the bishops are solidly defending the white king clearly shown at the board or should we say, white has the initiative.

13.) Qg5, Nd7
14.) 0-0, Nc6
15.) c4, d4

Wesley moved c4, wanting to rip out the diagonals to break open and directly attack the king. But black didn't want that to happen and played d4 instead. However, it will give more domination for white if black had taken

the pawn as the following continuation is going to happen:
1.) c4, dxc4
2.) Qxc5, Nxc5
3.) Bxc4, b6
White has the bishop pair and a developed position while black has an awkward king in the corner and the rook is not perfectly placed at f6 which itself an uncomfortable game to play.

16.) Rfe1, b6
17.) Qg3, Ba6
18.) Ng5, Qe7

Move 18: Qe7

White is threatening to play Ne4 forking the queen and the rook forcing the queen to move at e7 while defending the weak e6 pawn. Wesley is controlling the important squares for domination and it seems that black is trying hard to develop its defenses behind in time.

19.) Be4, Rc8
20.) Bd5, Nd8
21.) Nxe6, Nxe6

White is throwing a series of forcing moves against black, trading up to free the g5 knight and pinning the rook after Bg5. Clearly, white has the domination and control in the position; the bishops and rook are paralyzing black's pieces in many ways possible.

96

Game 30
The Pinoy Pride

22.) Bg5, Nc5
23.) Qa3, Qf7
24.) Bxf6, Qxf6

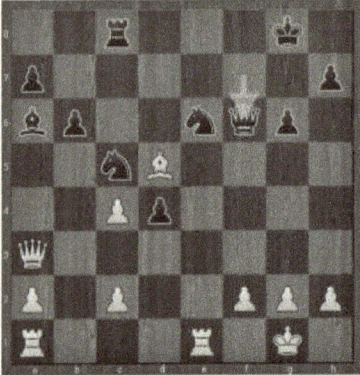
Move 24: Qxf6

Wesley sacrificed his knight for a pawn just to pin the rook after Bg5. We can see that black's pieces are paralyzed and gripped; the bishop on a6 is not on its good square, and kind of not participating, so is the rooks and the knights. While white's bishop pair and the rook are pinning down from different directions gripping black's access to move. It seems that any response of black will lead to a losing position as white is continuing the series of forcing moves making black striving from good counter chances.

25.) Qxa6, Nxa6
26.) Rxe6, Qd8
27.) Rd6+, Kg7

Wesley forced to enter the endgame and just threw out a sneaking queen sacrifice that eventually can still be regained after several trades. After that combination, both sides have equal pieces and an even position, but an endgame white want to play. His doubled pawns on the c-file which makes white a pawn up can slightly change the course of the match and can use to win the game.

28.) Rxd8, Rxd8
29.) Rd1, Nb4
30.) Rxd4, Nxa2

Paragua had breath himself out of that uncomfortable position in the middle game after the seemingly even trades. Wesley goes to catch the d4 pawn in exchange of his a2 giving black a chance to make a passed pawn and threatens a possible promotion. At this moment, black had managed to even the advantages and regained some initiative.

31.) f4, Nc3
32.) Kf2, b5
33.) Ke3, bxc4

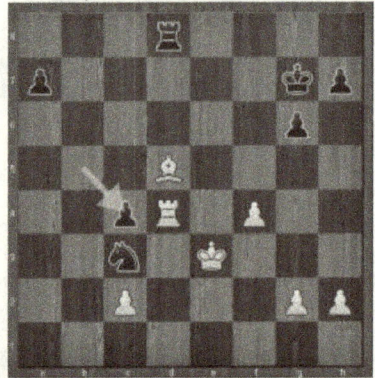
Move 33: bxc4

Both players are playing their endgame now; Wesley had moved his king to participate while Paragua exploited white's doubled pawn structure, had device a trap to even in material, it would be a draw if the bishop took the c4 pawn, a variation shown in the following:

1.) Ke3, bxc4
2.) Bxc4, Nd1+
3.) Kd3, Nf2+
4.) Kc3, Nd1+

This is a draw due to threefold repetition; the king couldn't leave the rook at d4, and forced to face the repetitive checks knight has in hand.

97

Game 30
The Pinoy Pride

34.) Bf3, Re8+
35.) Kf2, a5
36.) Rxc4, Nb5

Move 36: Nb5

At some extent, white regained the pawn. Black continues saving his isolated a-pawn instead of protecting the c4 square entering this line:

1.) Kf2, Rc8
2.) Rd7+, Kf6
3.) Rxa7, Rd8
4.) Rxh7, Rd2+
5.) Ke3, Rxc2

A more complicated endgame to see where black has to protect his only promoting pawn and his only key to win the game. Advancing it is not that easy as white's three connected pawns are ready to march up toward the king, saving the a-pawn would be a better choice to play.

37.) Bc6, Rb8
38.) Ra4, Rb6
39.) Bf3, Ra6

Wesley is using his might to stop the promotion and get a blockage against the black's a-pawn. He had free up his c-pawn preparing to lead towards the last square. Now, white has regained his advantages and now ready to kill black's hope in winning the game.

40.) Be2, Nc3
41.) Bxa6, Nxa4
42.) Ke3, Nb2

Wesley had pressed black to trade and play a knight against bishop endgame. In theory, bishop is better than the knight in an open position because it can attack farther and moreover, can diminish pawn chains easily. Knight, on the other hand, is just boasting for forks but can easily be trapped by the bishop.

43.) Kd4, a4
44.) Bc4, h5
45.) g3, Kf6

Move 45: Kf6

The white king had first to control the situation, helped by the bishop to stop the a-pawn from advancing. In this position, both sides must be careful in their responses as just one mistake can completely destroy the possibilities of winning. We are now in the endgame, and there's no hope of bouncing back.

46.) Kc3, a3
47.) Bd3, g5
48.) fxg5+, Kxg5

White seems slowly killing the position and just waiting for black to realize that the hope of promoting his a-pawn is over and can't do anything to change that.

Game 30
The Pinoy Pride

49.) Kb3, Nxd3
50.) cxd3, Kg4
51.) Kxa3, Kh3

Move 51: Kh3

A clear winning position for white, after the trade, the d-pawn starts to advance towards the promotion square, which the black king can't run into as he is leaving the stronger g and h pawn chains. It is now a losing position for black, but Paragua is willing to press more for hopes.

52.) d4, Kxh2
53.) d5, Kxg3
54.) d6, h4

Black decided to take down the pawn chains as Wesley is surely winning the queen a few moves after. Clearly white is winning here.

55.) d7, h3
56.) d8=Q, Kg2
57.) Qg5+, Kh1
58.) Qf4 (1-0)

Now we are studying this endgame in pieces, move by move, and we can see some important variations.
If at 56th move, black hasted to move h2, it is a mistake due to following reasons:

1.) d8=Q, h2
2.) Qd5, Kf2
3.) Qh1, Kg3
4.) Kb2, Kh3

5.) Kc3, Kg3
6.) Kd4, Kh3
The pawn is eventually stopped and the white king is slowly creeping in to garner a mating attack.

If the king moved to f2, it is losing after some continuations:
1.) d8=Q, Kf2
2.) Qh4+, Kg2
3.) Qg4+, Kh2
4.) Kc3, Kh1
5.) Qxh3+, Kg1
It is still a losing line for black. The pawn is eliminated and the king would soon be mated.

Above all, Paragua choses to place his king to g2, securing the support on the promoting pawn. But after Qg5+, Kh1, hoping for some stalemating chances, the game would continue as the following:
1.) Qg5, Kh1
2.) Qf4, Kg2
3.) Qg4+, Kh2
4.) Kb3, Kh1
5.) Qf3+, Kh2
6.) Qf2+, Kh1
7.) Kc2, h2
8.) Qf1# (1-0)
After several maneuvers, the queen had place itself in its dream square, f2, creating a zugzwang that forces black to move its only move, h2, and a one move from mate.

It is a great game for Wesley indeed; He dominated the middle phase and forced black to enter the endgame in position favor of himself and in time, slowly killing black's hope to win. The queen sacrifice is just too difficult to see and despite of the even position after the trades, black is left with a difficult endgame to play.

Game 31
The Tal Tales

Mikhal Tal – Vasily Smyslov
Bled-Zagreb-Belgrade Candidates (1959)

Move 19: Qxf7

One of the most attacking players with the most unexpected move, Tal always shocks most of the observers in his era as he continue searching for rare lines forcing his opponents make inaccurate responses.

1.) e4, c6
2.) d3, d5
3.) Nd2, e5

This is the Caro-Kann defense, closed variation, a defensive opening which in turn, transformed into a very complicated middle game.

4.) Ngf3, Nd7
5.) d4, dxe4
6.) Nxe4, exd4

A little mishap for black arises from these opening continuations, as we can see the two knights are on the center controlling squares while black's pieces are still not moved in anyway. Black lost a tempo from the 5th move, dxe4 letting the knight to come on the center, and develop. Smyslov may try this line instead:

1.) Ngf3, Bd6
2.) d4, exd4
3.) exd5, cxd5
4.) Nxd5, Nc6
5.) N2f3, Nf6

6.) Bd3, 0-0
7.) 0-0, Bg4

Black has the isolated d-pawn but its development is immense that it can defend the pawn in any way whatsoever. But this is still in the opening phases which there are several choices for the responses.

7.) Qxd4, Ngf6
8.) Bg5, Be7
9.) 0-0-0, 0-0

Move 9: 0-0

White now is starting to dominate and complicate the situation. However, it seems that Ne6+ by white is quite logical at move 9 instead of going to castle queenside. But Tal saw that black can hold such attack as shown in this variation:

1.) Bg5, Be7
2.) Ne6+, Bxe6
3.) Qxe6, Ne4
4.) Bxd1, Nxe6
5.) Bc7, Ne4
6.) Nd4, 0-0
7.) f6, Nef6
8.) 0-0-0, Nd5

Black had escaped the attack as Ne4 saves the major problem. After the trades, both sides have an even position in which Tal didn't like to enter.

Game 31
The Tal Tales

10.) Nd6, Qa5
11.) Bc4, b5
12.) Bd2, Qa6

Move 12: Qa6

The d-file is already pressing down by the white queen as it is supported firmly by the rook after the castle. Black has to come out and defend the gripping, advancing its queenside pawns to create threats toward the king but the white's bishop pair is already active and strong in its domination.

13.) Nf5, Bd8
14.) Qh4, bxc4
15.) Qg5, Nh5

This moment is the turning point of the match. A very difficult to see Qh4,
Tal is giving away his bishop for free! This is a totally computer move in time in which algorithms doesn't exist yet. Smyslov accepted the challenge and took the bishop, after several moves, black will be left with hopeless and doubtful mind in the end.

However, at 13th move, black may capture the knight already and not saving the e7 bishop in which is still okay for his position afterwards as shown in the following lines:
1.) Nf5, bxc4
2.) Nxe7+, Kh8

3.) Bc3, a6
4.) Nb6, Rhe1

White is in domination but black can still handle the situation. The open b-file can easily be taken by the black rook to infiltrate and attack the king sometime in the future which gives black a chance to counter play.

At some point, black made an inaccurate response, moving its knight to h5 reacting on the Qg5 threat. He might just play g6 instead, facing the following continuation:
1.) Qg5, g6
2.) Nh3+, Kh8
3.) Bc3, Qxa2
4.) Rxd7, Qa1+
5.) Ke2, Qa5
6.) Nxf7+, Kg8
7.) Nh3+, Kh8
8.) Bxa5, Ne4+
9.) Kc1, Bxg5+
10.) Nxg5, Bxd7
11.) Nxe4, Kg7

This is a very complicated line for black but is playable enough to win at some ways. But instead of entering such line, Smyslov could force to draw as follows:
1.) Qg5, g6
2.) Nh3+, Kg7
3.) Nf5+, Kg8
4.) Nh3+, Kg7

It is a draw due to threefold repetition. Preventing the latter complicated positions and also avoiding the drawn variations, Smyslov pressed for more, trying the second option of preventing the mate after Qxg7+, moving the knight to h5 is somewhat better.

16.) Nh6+, Kh8
17.) Qxh5, Qxa2
18.) Bc3, Nf6

Game 31
The Tal Tales

There are several options in response of Tal's Bc3; black could play Bf6 blocking the white bishop's diagonal and forcing it to trade. The continuation is shown in the following lines:

    1.) Bc3, Bf6
    2.) Ng5, Bxg5
    3.) Qxg5, f6
    4.) Qf5, Rb8

The mating threat neutralizes and the position is now almost even for both sides. The knight on g5 must be taken by the bishop to prevent the following mating attack:

    1.) Bc3, Bf6
    2.) Ng5, Bxc3
    3.) Nxf7+, Kg8
    4.) Qxh7#

The knight really did a good job on holding the mating pattern.

Another way is to play f6, to solidly close and block white's access on the mating attack.

    1.) Bc3, f6
    2.) Rhe1, Bc2
    3.) Nf7+, Kg8
    4.) Nd6, Qa1+
    5.) Kd2, Qxd1+
    6.) Kxd1, Bxe6

An interesting line to consider for black, the material is theoretically even but the position and the initiatives are immensely difficult to evaluate.

Above all, Smyslov just want to drive away the queen in its path. Stopping its plan and neutralize the threats toward him but Tal has many resources in hand. He created a more complicated play after few moves.

    19.) Qxf7, Qa1+
    20.) Kd2, Rxf7
    21.) Nxf7+, Kg8

Tal had just thrown a staggering queen sacrifice for a mating pattern but black has to escape using his resources in time however, if at 20th move, the queen had just took the rook on d1 instead of letting it be captured freely, was not a right choice to make.

    1.) Qxf7, Qa1+
    2.) Kd2, Qxd1+
    3.) Kxd1, Rxf7
    4.) Nxf7+, Kg8
    5.) Nxd8, Ne4+

Black is left with a piece down towards the endgame, with an isolated passed a-pawn after Nxc3, but a doubled pawn in the c-file and a pawn down in the kingside.

    22.) Rxa1, Kxf7
    23.) Ne5+, Ke6
    24.) Nxc6, Ne4+

Move 24: Ne4+

After the combination, white chose to steal a pawn and attack the a7 square twice but providing a way to bishop pair access the open diagonals, instead playing Rhe1 would be better controlling the center file and preventing the nasty Ne4+ taking down the bishop and creating some double pawn structure.

Game 31
The Tal Tales

25.) Ke3, Bb6+
26.) Bd4 (1-0)

Move 26: Bd4

"You must take your opponent into a deep forest where 2+2=5, and the path leading out is only wide enough for one." - Mikhail Tal

In this position, black can still hold the game but choses to resign maybe due to the following continuation:

1.) Bd4, Nc5
2.) Bxc5, Bxc5+
3.) Nd4+, Kf7
4.) c3, Bd7

Black is down a pawn, but has the bishop pair, while white has the rooks and the connected pawn islands which seem to have the edge but a long way ahead before a completely losing position.

At some chance, playing against Tal in a disadvantageous endgame would be a no hope after all. Smyslov didn't dare to try continuing the game and although he can exploit his bishop pair for some complications, he resigned immediately as the materials were not enough to end the game in winning chances. Above all, black could make it to draw but tried to make a slightly weak response leading white to deliver some tricky and deadly mating attacks, he escaped the fate but left with a weaker position afterwards.

The position he didn't want to press more.

Game 32
The Norway Pride

Magnus Carlsen – Hans Krogh Harestad
XXV Politiken Cup (2003)

Move 35: Nh5+

The true form of the World Champ, in its domination and accuracy, destroyed his opponent in this game. Carlsen sacrificed his knight and queen to deliver a clean and smooth mating combination, the game in which didn't go that far.

1.) e4, e5
2.) Nf3, Nc6
3.) Bb5, a6

White enters the Ruy Lopez line, a silent and very positional approach giving both sides the freedom to maneuver the minor pieces and control the center with pawns.

4.) Ba4, Nf6
5.) 0-0, b5
6.) Bb3, Be7

Both players are continuing the typical line and improving their positions for the middle game. However, if black tried to taste the e4 pawn, another interesting line is shown as follows:

1.) Ba4, Nf6
2.) 0-0, Nxe4
3.) Re1, Nc5
4.) Bxc6, dxe6
5.) Nxe5, Ne6

The center line is cleared and there are so much open spaces for mobility.

7.) Re1, d6
8.) c3, 0-0
9.) h3, Na5

Both players are silently developing their positions instead of grabbing the initiatives immediately, playing conservatively to garner a solid defense for their premises in the future.

10.) Bc2, c5
11.) d4, Qc7
12.) Nbd2, Nc6

Move 12: Nc6

Still, there were no threats in the board and white doesn't want to take either c5 or the e5 pawn avoiding the opening of the d-file which is good for the black's f-rook to enter. The spaces and mobility was shared even for both sides and there were no captures going on still.

13.) d5, Nd8
14.) a4, Ra7
15.) Nf1, g6

Magnus closed the pawn chains and made the knight awkward at d8. At this point, placing the knight on c6 at black's 12th move is not a good response, as white slightly gained tempo and spaces as well as the initiatives in the game after d5. The pawn is blocking almost all of the squares of the black's bishop pair.

104

Game 32
The Norway Pride

16.) Bh6, Re8
17.) Ng3, Nd7
18.) Nh2, f6

Both players are playing conservatively until at this point, wanting to break open the f-file for the control. But black made the move, g6 letting the bishop to outpost the h6 square and outpost the black's kingside. Still, there are no trades made on the board.

19.) Be3, Nb6
20.) axb5, axb5
21.) Bd3, Bd7

Move 21: Bd7

It is difficult to see the unseen motifs of the move f6, seems defending something but the real reason behind is trapping the bishop after the move g5, immediately responded by Magnus as he retreats it to e3 square. White decided to rip out the a-file as the first trade was made on the 20th move in the middle game.

22.) Qd2, Nf7
23.) Rxa7, Qxa7
24.) Qe2, Qa6

Still, there are no concrete advantages in the position from either side. Both players are playing defensively and the trades are just to simplify the positions in the board.

The minor pieces are just sitting there and waiting to free up once the pawn chains are ripped out.

25.) Ng4, Kg7
26.) Bc1, Na4
27.) Bc2, Ra8

Move 27: Ra8

Slowly but surely, both sides are creeping through their plans of sneaking. While black is aiming to dominate the a-file, white is planning to break the kingside structures. Both of their defenses are solid and concrete needing so many resources to infiltrate. As we remember, this situation happened before on game 27 of this book on the match between Wesley So and Hikaru Nakamura at the Sinquefield Cup, year 2015, that may gave us insights on how can we handle this very situation where both sides are preparing an immense attack against each other on both wings. Realizing that situation, we can say that white has the initiative and advantages, as he is attacking the king directly forcing black to defend and withdraw his attacks on the a-file afterwards depending on the weight of the white's threat. After several moves, the same aftermath will happen in favor of white.

Game 32
The Norway Pride

28.) Qe3, c4
29.) Rf1, Nc5
30.) Nh6, Ng5

Move 30: Ng5

White is starting to infiltrate the loophole on the h6 square. As black had no clear plans on the a-file, white is threatening to break open its f-file to continue infiltrate the kingside. At this moment, black should stop its attack and defend immediately.

31.) f4, exf4
32.) Qxf4, Bxh3
33.) Qh4, Bd7

Amidst the attack, black had found a counter play sacrificing his bishop to take the pawn and if white recaptures, the fork is heading the way to win the initiative and eventually win the game afterwards:

1.) Qxf4, Bxh3
2.) gxh3, Nxh3+
3.) Kh1, Nxf4
4.) Bxf4, Kf8

The queen is traded in exchange for the bishop and knight but still white's four minor pieces are actively wandering the board and it's a long way to go before black can fully dominate. As being the World Champ, this trap can be avoided easily; he moved the queen busting the trap, and saved the knight.

34.) e5, dxe5
35.) Nh5+, gxh5
36.) Qxg5+, fxg5

This is the critical moment of the game. Black didn't notice that at this very position, the mating combination is already realized before Magnus eyes. Taking the h5 knight at 35th move is considered a blunder for black, to prevent the trap, moving the king to h8 is a safer response instead.

1.) Nh5+, Kh8
2.) Bxg5, fxg5
3.) Qg3, Nd3

The mating combination is busted and the threats are neutralized. However, black dares to taste the knight and open up his position from white's attacks.

37.) Rf7+, Kxh6
38.) Rxh7# (1-0)

Move 38: Rxh7#

The mating attack is inevitable since the queen captured the g5 knight even if not accepting the queen sacrifice or not, despite of the existing pieces on the board black have in hand. This is a very tricky combination and a great visualization from the World Champ who clearly sees the opportunity of mating amidst the defending pieces on the board.

Game 33
Almost Immortal

Garry Kasparov – Lajos Portisch
Niksic (1983)

Move 35: Qb3+

After studying the game of the present World Champ, now, we will be heading to another chess legend, Kasparov, played an almost immortal game against Portisch where he sacrificed several pieces to gain positional advantages leading to a mating attack.

1.) d4, Nf6
2.) c4, e6
3.) Nf3, b6

Both sides entered the queen's Indian game, after a few moves, black is trying to play defensively blocking some chances from white to garner a combination, but white's aim is unstoppable, the unseen sacrifice forced black to defend continuously until its end.

4.) Nc3, Bb7
5.) a3, d5
6.) cxd5, Nxd5

Black choses a conservative approach to develop his pieces while white is not yet ready to castle his king as the bishop is not yet already been freed. But it's too early to decide which side has the winning advantages.

7.) e3, Nxc3
8.) bxc3, Be7
9.) Bb5+, c6

Black now seems wanting to simplify the board preventing Kasparov to have a dynamic position in the middle game. He just moves and defends some chances of tactics, the question is until when.

10.) Bd3, c5
11.) 0-0, Nc6
12.) Bb2, Rc8

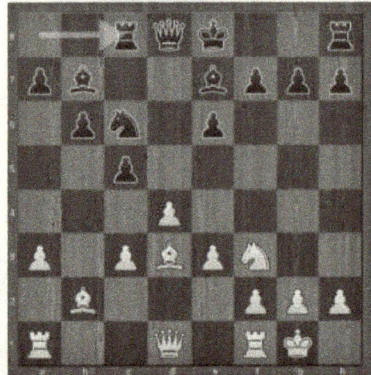

Move 12: Rc8

The position now is equal in its sense; both sides had their best squares and spaces for maneuvering except on the black bishop at b2 but in general way, its quiet difficult to say who has the winning chances of the game.

13.) Qe2, 0-0
14.) Rad1, Qc7
15.) c4, cxd4

Both defenses are too concrete and pure; there are no threats on the board just clumps of pieces waiting for their time to be ignited.

16.) exd4, Na5
17.) d5, exd5
18.) cxd5, Bxd5

Kasparov decided now to set up the fire, obeying his will to open up the board for the dynamics of his pieces.

107

Game 33
Almost Immortal

In this position, Garry smells an action to take, his two bishops are preying the kingside and ready to take over the places on the board. However, at 17th move, if knight would take the c5 pawn instead, black would face his downfall continuously thereafter as shown in the following lines:

    1.) d5, Nxc5
    2.) Qe4, g6
    3.) Bxc5, Qxc5
    4.) Qe5, f6
    5.) Qxe6, Rf7
    6.) Rc1, Qa6
    7.) d6, b5

And white continues his domination. A one wrong response in a complicated position is enough to lose the game immediately.

    19.) Bxh7+, Kxh7
    20.) Rxd5, Kg8
    21.) Bxg7, Kxg7

Move 21: Kxg7

This is the most instructive play in this match. The first bishop sacrifice makes sense but the second one is just aiming to open up the kingside for future attacks. The question is can Kasparov exploit those open spaces with its leftover resources as black still has many pieces ready to defend? With his positional mastery, only him

and the computer knows why. It seems that black let the h7 pawn falls since the recapture on d5. Instead of retaking, continuing the closed line is a better response to avoid Kasparov play his repertoires in the open field. The best response is the silent a6, preventing white the chance to continue his attacks.

    1.) cxd5, a6
    2.) Rfe1, Rfe8
    3.) Qe4, g6
    4.) Qe5, f6
    5.) Qg5, Bc5

White is just wandering his plan but can't fully execute to destroy king's defenses, or if white just take the a6 pawn:

    1.) cxd5, a6
    2.) Bxa6, Bxa6
    3.) Qxa6, Rfd8

Black let a pawn sacrifice that neutralizes white's initiative and gives black a tempo to prepare his development.

    22.) Ne5, Rfd8
    23.) Qg4+, Kf8
    24.) Qf5, f6

Move 24: f6

In that given position, white just want to exploit black's king open spaces with his only pieces left on the board.

Game 33
Almost Immortal

Now, black has the material advantages but is not well coordinated to defend white's attacks. Kasparov must seize every opportunity to take down the king before his opponent has the time to defend it well.

    25.) Nd7+, Rxd7
    26.) Rxd7, Qc5
    27.) Qh7, Rc7

Move 27: Rc7

Black is forced to exchange his rook for a knight. Just moving the king will lead to a losing position as shown in the following continuation:

    1.) Nd7+, Kg7
    2.) Re1, Rxd7
    3.) Rxd7, Qc5

Taking the knight is forced to simplify the position, if the king would go somewhere, a more tragic result may end as follows:

    1.) Nd7+, Kf8
    2.) Qg6+ (1-0)

The king is mated, if the king goes to g8, another mating pattern is inevitable:

    1.) Nd7+, Kg8
    2.) Qg6+, Kh8
    3.) Rh5# (1-0)

Another mating attack is shown if the king tried escaping on the f7 square:

    1.) Nd7+, Kf7
    2.) Qh7+, Ke6

    3.) Re1+, Kxd5
    4.) Qe4+, Kd6
    5.) Rd1# (1-0)

The entire escaping move can't escape the mating attack and so, black is forced to trade.

After the trade, the material now is even for both sides, but still, the black king is under attack though it feels a little bit comfortable after the exchange. Black wants to trade more to neutralize white's attack against the king.

    28.) Qh8+, Kf7
    29.) Rd3, Nc4
    30.) Rfd1, Ne5

Move 30: Ne5

Kasparov still has the aces in his hand and didn't want to simplify. He exploits black's awkward knight and its dislocated bishop to infiltrate the weak squares surrounding the black king. As black re-maneuvered its knight to participate the game, white is setting his mating pattern against the black king. As we can see, black spent two tempos to put his knight in the play, the cost of the awkward move, Na5.

    31.) Qh7+, Ke6
    32.) Qg8+, Kf5
    33.) g4+, Kf4

109

Game 33
Almost Immortal

Kasparov saw the unseen mating pattern in the position. Black didn't notice that its pieces can't stop the series of mating attacks white has to deliver. However, there are plenty of ways to slow down but all will lead to mate.

> 1.) Qh7+, Kf8
> 2.) Rd8+, Bxd8
> 3.) Rxd8# (1-0)

The only pieces remaining for white end the game. If the king went to e8, the same aftermath will happen:

> 1.) Qh7+, Ke8
> 2.) Qg8+, Bf8
> 3.) Qe6+, Qe7
> 4.) Rd8# (1-0)

A beautiful mating attack that black prevented, instead, he moves the king to e6 to survive longer.

However, at 32nd move, if black tried to block the check by its knight, another pattern is inevitable:

> 1.) Qg8+, Nf7
> 2.) Re1+, Kf5
> 3.) Rf3# (1-0)

This is another mating threat that must be prevented, so black was forced to move again his king and face the rooks.

> 35.) Rd4+, Kf3
> 36.) Qb3+ (1-0)

There are no remaining choices possible to escape the threats except from sacrificing pieces which in the end can't help the situation from winning. Black chose the longest possible mating attack and after Ke2, Qe3+, the dish was served. The king is mated, hunt down in a series of checks and its fellow pieces can't stop or even slow down the mating process. Kasparov being the beast (in chess) had destroyed black in the meanest possible way.

Garry Kimovich Kasparov is a Russian chess grandmaster, former World Chess Champion, writer, political activist, and commentator. Kasparov was ranked world no. 1 for 255 months overall for his career.

Game 34
File Control

Peter Svidler – Conny Hoist
Copenhagen op (1991)

Move 21: Qg6

Peter Svidler is one of the strongest players since before the computer era until up to date. This Russian always showing his concrete structural defenses that is difficult to grip and crack under pressure. His defenses are widely known to beat several modern day masters including the World Champion and until at this point in time, continuously crushing at several chess tournaments.

1.) e4, c5
2.) Nf3, d6
3.) Nc3, Nf6

Black tried to enter the Sicilian line, letting white to be aggressive at some part in the middle game while black is defending and waiting to find some chances of counter attack.

4.) d4, cxd4
5.) Nxd4, a6
6.) f4, e6

The move e6 makes sense, despite of blocking the bishop's diagonal, it prevented the white's next move f5, dominating the kingside spaces to control the gripping thereafter. On the other hand, as black is expecting, Svidler starts to open up his spaces for the kingside domination.

7.) Bd3, Qc7
8.) 0-0, Nc6
9.) Nf3, Be7

Black's Qc7 seems not a good response for the continuation of this line but white can't exploit it fully due to structural defenses of black in hand. However, Svidler avoided the trade of his knight, keeping it in its pace to participate on the plan. Still, both sides are playing the typical continuation of the Najdorf, a line that usually explodes in the middle game depending on the player's initiative.

10.) Kh1, 0-0
11.) Qe1, Nd7
12.) Qg3, Nc5

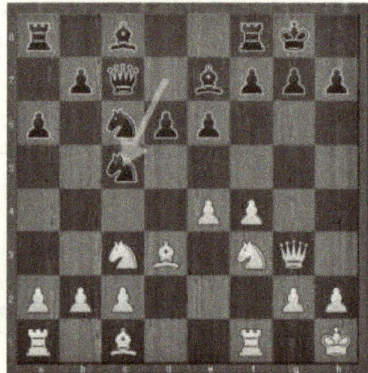

Move 12: Nc5

We can see here in the position that both of the white's bishops are hiding preying the kingside pawns, with the help of the queen, it can cause threats and damages if black didn't pay attention. Moving the knight to d7 is logical at some extent, providing the bishop its control squares essential for the defense of the dark squares surrounding the king, but moving it again attacking d3 lost a tempo, Nb4 serves the same purpose instead.

13.) f5, Kh8
14.) fxe6, fxe6
15.) Bg5, b5

111

Game 34
File Control

White didn't bother to exchange his bishop instead; played f5 opening up the access to play Bh6, black must react defensively in this situation, to prevent the incoming threat, moving the king is the best response as taking the f5 pawn seems simplifying the board but leading the game to lose afterwards.

1.) f5, exf5
2.) Bh6, Bf6
3.) Nd5, Qd8
4.) exf5, Kh8

Black has to drawback here, as white clearly controls the game with several choices to dominate.

However, retaking the e6 pawn with a bishop is more logical than opening up the f-file; it connects the rook and develops the bishop to participate the game.

1.) fxe6, Bxe6
2.) Be3, Nxd3
3.) cxd3, Qd7

The position gets even and all the incoming threats are neutralized but instead of entering this line, black made a mistake of retaking e6 by the f-pawn.

16.) e5, dxe5
17.) Bxh7, Kxh7
18.) Bxe7, Rxf3

This is the most critical moment of the game, where black has to response correctly to survive the following strike. There are several choices to choose from the 16th move of the game, here are the following:

1.) e5, Nxe5
2.) Nxe5, dxe5
3.) Bxe7, Qxe7
4.) Qh5, Rxf1+
5.) Rxf1, g5
6.) Qh5, Nxd3

7.) Rf7, Rxf7
8.) Qxf7, Bb7
9.) Qxb7, Rf8

Black is losing this position, white continuously forced black to defend and sacrificing several pieces to avoid the mate. However, if knight took the d3 bishop first, again, white can gain a little bit of positional advantages.

1.) e5, Nxd3
2.) Bxe7, Qxe7
3.) exd6, Qe8
4.) cxd3, Bd7

White has up a pawn and an active knight formation in the center which gives a little bit of initiative but this is a better move after e5, eliminating the bishop on preying the h7 square is essential to prevent sacrificial mating pattern as this is the main reason why white chose to open up. After all, black chose the least preferred line, retaking the e5 pawn creating its own doubled pawns in the center.

Going to the 17th move of the game, Svidler saw a forcing line, sacrificing his bishop to open up the kingside and execute his plan. Black is forced to retake or else he will completely be dominated after Bg6.

However, at 18th move, black choses to sacrifice his rook considering these several possible mating combinations:

1.) Bxe7, Qxe7
2.) Ng5+, Kg8
3.) Qh4, Rxf1+
4.) Rxf1+, g6
5.) Rf8+, Qxf8
6.) Qh7# (1-0)

And the king will be still in mate if black responded Kxf8,

1.) Rf8+, Kxf8
2.) Qh8# (1-0)

Sacrificing the rook is a must.

Game 34
File Control

If black recaptured with his knight, white can fork the a8 rook afterwards.

1.) Bxe7, Nxe7
2.) Ng5, Kg8
3.) Rxf1+, Kxf1
4.) Qf3+, Nf5
5.) Qxa8, Ke7

And white advances in material and in king's safety as the black king is now in the middle of the board longing for defenses for the incoming white's attacks.

To prevent these losing continuations, black chose to sacrifice his rook and take the f3 knight which is one of the most important pieces in the mating pattern.

19.) Rxf3, Qxe7
20.) Raf1, Kg8
21.) Qg6 (1-0)

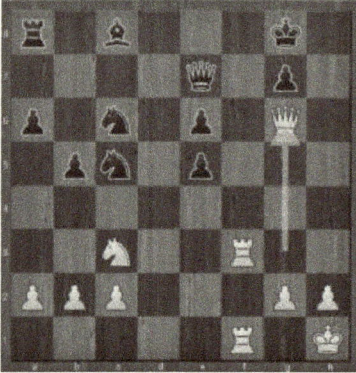

Move 21: Qg6

Black made the last horrible mistake here, played Kg8 and at an instant, lose the game as white can win in any way possible with his resources and controls in the f-file. The line may continue as shown:

1.) Qg6, Nd8
2.) Rh3, Nf7
3.) Qh7+, Kf8
4.) Qh7# (1-0)

Conny's day is surely ruined.

To prolong the situation, black may have played Nd8, guarding the f7 square from white's Rf7 threat continuing the match as follow:

1.) Raf1, Nd8
2.) Qg4, Kg8
3.) Qh5, bb7
4.) Rh3, Bxg2+
5.) Kxg2, Qb7+
6.) Kg1, Nf7
7.) Rxf7, Rf8
8.) Rxb7, Nxb7

And the mating attack continues, and eventually afterwards, white wins the match.

Generalizing the game, we can see that there are several inaccuracies black had made and exploited by white. Its development seems logical in the opening but not preparing for the middle game defense against white's attacks. Black responded poorly on the infiltrations and as the situations became worst, all pieces left don't have enough time to stop the mating combination. Black's pieces are wandering the queenside while king safety had been easily unnoticed. At the end, the Russian who has the most dominative moves won the game.

Game 35
Aronian's Immortal

Levon Aronian – Andrei Volotikin
European Club Cup (2008)

Move 23: e6+

Aronian is a tough player to beat in chess, once ranked world's no. 2 in the FIDE Rating and a great contender to Carlsen in his prime. He is a combination of defensive and dynamic style of play, his accurate moves always crushing several GM's and until now, winning and dominating several chess tournaments.

1.) d4, d5
2.) c4, c6
3.) Nc3, Nf6

Both players entered playing the Slav, said to be a slow and boring opening which in turn became Aronian's immortal game after several continuations. However, taking the c4 pawn will give not that much compensation considering these variations:

1.) c4, dxc4
2.) e3, c5
3.) Bxc4, Nf6
4.) Nf3, e6
5.) 0-0, a6

Black's center pawn was eliminated with tempo by developing the bishop giving white a slight advantage in developments.

4.) e3, g6
5.) Nf3, Bg7
6.) h3, 0-0

Both sides are concreting their defensive structures for king safety, slowly developing and preparing for middle game dominations.

7.) Bd3, Be6
8.) Ng5, Bf5
9.) Bxf5, gxf5

Move 09: gxf5

Black's Be6 threatening to capture the c4 pawn is not really a good move in this continuation due to white's Ng5 striking the bishop and if recaptured giving black a doubled pawns at the center which is not a strong defense. Playing c5 instead is better as shown in this line:

1.) Bd3, c5
2.) 0-0, e6
3.) cxd5, exd5
4.) Re1, Be6

A typical continuation of piece development and a right time to play Be6.

To not lose the tempo, black's bishop was moved to f5, willing to be exchanged to open the g-file against the white's kingside. Aronian took the chance and exploited the weakness in the position.

114

Game 35
Aronian's Immortal

10.) Qb3, Qb6
11.) Qc2, e6
12.) g4, h6

As white strikes the b7 pawn, black immediately want to trade queens as his position is slightly inferior but as expected, white avoided and starts infiltrating the black's weakness.

13.) Nf3, fxg4
14.) hxg4, Nxg4
15.) e4, dxc4

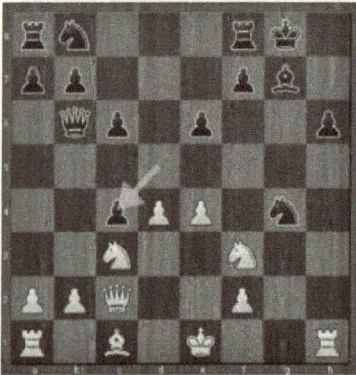

Move 15: dxc4

Taking the c4 pawn is somewhat not helping black for the defense as its pawn will be doubled and will be slightly stuck. After several moves, white is ready to destroy the black's kingside structures. Instead, at 15th move, f5 by black is better slowing down the attack.

1.) e5 ,f5
2.) c5, Qa6
3.) exf5, exf5
4.) Bf5, Qc5
5.) 0-0-0, Na6

Both players shared an even count of initiatives. There are several chances to infiltrate and a difficult time to decide which has the winning edge.

16.) e5, Nd7
17.) Be3, f5
18.) 0-0-0, c5

Black had played f5 closing the pawn chains but a little bit too late as white's rooks are coming to control the g and h-files and black needs to get rid of its doubled pawns for faster counter attacking chances.

19.) d5, f4
20.) Ng5, hxg5
21.) Qh7+, Kf7

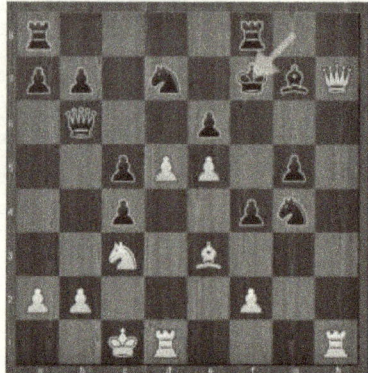

Move 21: Kf7

White is slowly controlling the center after d5 leaving the c-pawns doubled for a long time. At the same time, Black made a losing response, opening up the queen's access at the h7 square, Aronian found a brilliant knight sacrifice attacking the e6 pawn and threatening a mate in one forcing black to accept the poisoned piece and face the combination. However, Rf5 seems better but a little bit complicated as shown in the following variation:

1.) Ng5, Rf5
2.) Na4, Qb5
3.) dxe6, Rxg5
4.) exd7, Nxe5
5.) d8=Q, Rxd8
6.) Rxd8+, Bf8
7.) Bxf4, Ne3+
8.) Kb1, Nxf4

A complicated line but stronger than accepting the knight sacrifice.

Game 35
Aronian's Immortal

22.) Ne4, exd5
23.) e6+, Kxe6
24.) Qxg7, Ngf6

Move 24: Ngf6

Black faced the domination since the move f4, its king is then became the center of attacks from white's sneaking chances. Playing e6+ is not really in need as taking the g5 pawn after exd5 ruins king safety immediately. At 24th move, there are several choices black had to play, the white's bishop is hanging but its king seems in danger from the queen. At this critical moment, Volotikin must be very careful in executing his defenses. However, if black took the bishop, he will face the situation worse than before.

1.) Qxg7, fxe3
2.) Nxg5+, Kd6
3.) Rxd4+, Kc7
4.) Rxd7+, Kc6
5.) Rd6+, Kxd6
6.) Rd1+, Kc6
7.) Qd7# (1-0)

Aronian could execute an almost immortal mating pattern literally crushing black with no mercy. However, taking the hanging knight is not suggested as after dxe4, Qxd7+, the king safety made worse.

The king now is literally wandering the center of the board as playing Ngf6 is a defensive response making the knights intact and at some chances covering the king of the incoming threats from white.

25.) Bxc5, Nxc5
26.) Nxc5+, Qxc5
27.) Rde1+, Kf5

Move 27: Kf5

This position covers so many choices for white to continue, and all of them will lead to a crush black's defenses. The most obvious one if Nxg5+, crushing the king as shown:

1.) Nxg5+, Kd6
2.) Ne4+, Kc6
3.) Bxc5, Nxc5
4.) Nxf6, Kb5
5.) Nxd5, Qc6
6.) Rh6, Qc8

The series of attacks is unavoidable and enough for black to resign the game immediately preventing the losing continuation. If the king chose to escape on f5, the same aftermath will happen as shown in the following lines:

1.) Nxf5+, Kf5
2.) Rxd5+, Nxd5
3.) Qxd7, Kxg5
4.) Qxd5+, Rf5
5.) Qg2+, Kf5

Game 35
Aronian's Immortal

6.) Rh6+, Ke4
7.) Rxb5, axb5

The forcing moves are just easy to find as the black king is defenseless from white's resources. At 27th move, if black choses to escape at d6 square, it is still loses the hope of winning the game.

1.) Rde1+, Kd6
2.) Qe7+, Kc6
3.) Re6+, Kb5
4.) a4+, Kb4
5.) Qxb7+, Kxa4
6.) Ra6+, Qa5
7.) Kc2, Qxa6
8.) Ra1# (1-0)

A shameful mating trick destroyed Volotikin.

Instead of escaping to d6 square, the last resort is blocking the check by Ne4. The losing position awaited and white's attacks continue to prevail.

1.) Rde1+, Ne4
2.) Rh6+, Kf5
3.) Qd7+, Ke5
4.) Qe6+, Kd4
5.) Rd1+, Nd2
6.) Rxd2# (1-0)

There are plenty of mating patterns arises since black's Ngf3, and all of them are just waiting to unlock depending on the responses of Volotikin. Taking the g5 pawn by knight at 25th move wins immediately but Aronian has his own version of choices to end the game and execute the chances differently.

28.) Rh5, Nxh5
29.) Re5+, Kg4
30.) Qxg5+, Kf3

Aronian brilliantly sacrificed his whole rook driving the king away from his pieces. A very risky move as at this point in time, white loses his rook and

knight already. The execution now must be perfect and must leave black no counter attacking chances or else the game will be swindled. However, let's take a look if black didn't accept the poisoned piece and responded Ne4 instead; a more logical approach to safely continue the game as we hope to.

1.) Rh5, Ne4
2.) Qd7+, Ke5
3.) Rxg5+, Ke4
4.) Rd1+, Nd2
5.) Rxd2+, Ke4
6.) Qe6+, Kf3
7.) Qe2# (1-0)

The king hunt continues and the mating threats are unstoppable.

31.) Qxh5+, Kxf2
32.) Qe2+ (1-0)

White finally delivered the last blow of its mating threats and the game may continue as follows:

1.) Qe2+, Kg3
2.) Rg5+, Kh4
3.) Qg4# (1-0)

And the game ended in a brutal mating trick. If black didn't take the pawn hoping to complicate something and slow down the mating pattern, the line may be as shown:

1.) Qxh5+, Kg2
2.) Qg4+, Kf1
3.) Qe2+, Kg2
4.) Rg5+, Kh3
5.) Qa5# (1-0)

The game followed the same aftermath as before.

This miniature created by Aronian is too rare to repeat itself in history. The positional and material sacrifices are brilliantly executed to garner the most dominative play possible, deserving to be called an immortal game.

Game 36
Digging the Ruy Lopez

Garry Kasparov – Anatoly Karpov
World Championship Rematch (1986)

Move 24: e5

It's the 18th day of April 2021, where the world is still longing to survive the pandemic of the covid-19 virus. Everyone is trying to adapt the challenges of starvation. In the middle of the night, going back to chess board, let us look at the battle of the two greatest chess players in their prime, the one who is aggressive attacker like a beast against the conservative gripping like the boa constrictor. Both are totally opposite styles that when clashed, creating a dynamic middle game set ups and a staggering finish.

1.) e4, e5
2.) Nf3, Nc6
3.) Bb5, a6

Kasparov chose the dynamic Ruy Lopez. This opening is known for its silent hidden traps commonly exploded in the middle phase of the game, the Kasparov preferred line.

4.) Ba4, Nf6
5.) 0-0, Be7
6.) Re1, b5

Karpov didn't seize the chance to grab the e4 pawn as after several continuations, the game would approach an open position that he thinks white would be more comfortable.

1.) 0-0, Nxe4
2.) Re1, Nc5
3.) Bxc6, dxc6
4.) Nxe5, Ne6
5.) Qa5, Qf6
6.) d4, Bd6
7.) Nc3, Bxe5

White seizes the opportunity to attack early on the game while black is then forced to defend.

7.) Bb3, d6
8.) c3, 0-0
9.) h3, Bb7

Both of the players are improving their position, silently claiming the domination on the center of the board. As white approaches to break the center, black is managing to counter on the left wing.

10.) d4, Re8
11.) Nbd2, Bf8
12.) a4, h6

Move 12: h6

The two players are conserving their play, reserved for the near future, seems ready to fight fully and give everything in the middle game. The initiative is still shallow to see, as there are still no exchanges on the board.

Game 36
Digging the Ruy Lopez

13.) Bc2, exd4
14.) cxd4, Nb4
15.) Bb1, c5

Black is counter attacking the queenside but white can still handle the situation. To conserve the bishops, Kasparov placed it at the first rank disconnecting its rooks but eyeing black's kingside for further infiltration.

16.) d5, Nd7
17.) Ra3, c4
18.) Nd4, Qf6

Move 18: Qf6

Black made an outpost knight at the b4 square controlling white's mobility. The b7 bishop is trapped after d5 silently shutting down from defending the kingside. And now, black must react, freeing its queen for kingside protection. An intelligent move, Ra3 is a good idea in this line, as the rooks now can't be connected; activating it at the 3rd rank will cause more threats in the future. After Nd4, white is threatening to capture the b5 pawn; Karpov let it as his position will became weak after several continuations as shown:

1.) Nd4, Qb6
2.) Nf5, Ne5
3.) Rg3, Kh8
4.) Nf3, Bc1
5.) Be3, Qd8

6.) Nxh6, gxh6
7.) Nxe5, dxe5
8.) Qh5, Qf6
9.) Bg5, Qg6
10.) Qh4, Kh2
11.) Bf6, Ra2

With the aid of computer, it is the most accurate way of defending the white's play. Black is up in material but has a long way to go to neutralize white's aggressive lines against the king. However, just taking the a4 pawn immediately is not a suggested response to save the b5 pawn.

1.) Nd5, bxa4
2.) Nxc4, Rc8
3.) Ne3, Ne5

The pieces are dynamically set up but the a4 pawn will also soon fall in favor for white.

19.) N2f3, Nc5
20.) axb5, axb5
21.) Nxb5, Rxa3

Move 21: Rxa3

Now, white is up a pawn but the positions are too messy to secure a win. The major pieces are still wandering the board and black slightly gained some positional advantages for a pawn which balances the situation.

119

Game 36
Digging the Ruy Lopez

22.) Nxa3, Ba6
23.) Re3, Rb8
24.) e5, dxe5

Move 24: dxe5

White sees that the d3 square is dominated by black and if placed by knight, attacks the rook and force the bishop to trade. Evaluating the position, e3 is the safest square for the rook preventing such situation and if maneuvered to c3, another pawn will fall, to counter such plan, black made the silent move Rb8, saving the c4 pawn at the end.

1.) Re3, Rb8
2.) Rc3, Nbd3
3.) Bxd3, cxd3
4.) Be3, Nxe4

Black regained a pawn and made a stronghold structure at white's premises, a variation which Kasparov didn't permit. Instead breaks up the e-file to open the bishops' diagonal for further attacks.

25.) Nxe5, Nbd3
26.) Ng4, Qb6
27.) Rg3, g6

Karpov made an inaccurate response which weakens his structure, a move g6, instead of Ne4 at 27th move. Realizing this, we could see interesting lines that is hidden below the board.

1.) Rg3, Ne4
2.) Nxc4, Bxc4
3.) Bxd3, Nxg3
4.) Bxc4, Ne4

An interesting imbalance in the position, white has two isolated passed pawns with a strong pair of bishop while black is up a piece but doesn't have the dominative position in hand, still, a great chance for both of the players to tackle the game.

28.) Bxh6, Qxb2
29.) Qf3, Nd7
30.) Bxf8, Kxf8

Move 30: Kxf8

Black let white to weaken the kingside structure in exchange of the b-pawn: both are in race to destroy each of their position. Kasparov let his pawn fall confident to destroy black's kingside before the isolated c4 pawn promotes: quiet a risky move against black raging pieces. White is a pawn up but pieces are scattered on the board, possibilities are endless and predicting which side has the upper hand is difficult to tell.

31.) Kh2, Rb3
32.) Bxd3, cxd3
33.) Qf4, Qxa3

Game 36
Digging the Ruy Lopez

This was the most intriguing parts of the game where black has taken the initiative, grabbed a piece and fully dominated the queenside squares. Can black continue the domination or can Kasparov himself has the ace cards waiting for chances to counter attack?

34.) Nh6, Qe7
35.) Rxg6, Qe5
36.) Rg8+, Ke7

Move 36: Ke7

Karpov didn't fully know that white's pieces are all set to garner a strong attack against his king, just waiting for the perfect chance to tackle the position. The king is forced to escape toward the middle squares. At 36th move, one response is Kd8, preventing the king to be exposed but also facing the same fate as the latter. After several moves, we can realize that the knight is poisoned, captured in exchange for tempo in favor of white's attack.

1.) Rxg6, Kd8
2.) Rg8+, Nf8
3.) Nf5, Qd7
4.) Rxf8+, Kxf8
5.) Qh6+, Ke8
6.) Qh8# (1-0)

Nh6 followed by Rxg6 lit the fire and burned the hope to win against black.

37.) d6+, Ke6
38.) Re8+, Kd5
39.) Rxe5+, Nxe5

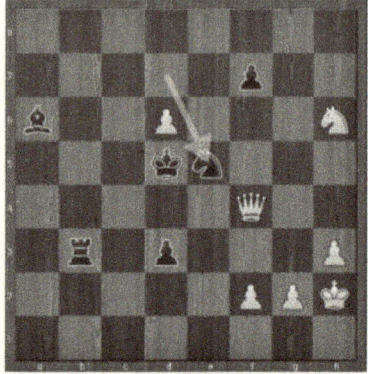

Move 39: Nxe5

This is one of the most staggering parts of this match, where the black king roams on the middle of the board while the other is sitting prettily on the side. Both the king and the queen are scared to taste the pawn to prevent these fatal continuations.

1.) d6+, Kxd6
2.) Nxf7+, Kd5
3.) Nxe5, Nxe5

The knight delivers the fork and wins the game in a dominative style. If the queen took the pawn, another fork with a mate reveals.

1.) d6+, Qxd6
2.) Nf5+, Ke6
3.) Qxd6+, Kxf5
4.) g4+, Ke4
5.) Re8+, Ne5
6.) Qxe5, Kf3
7.) Qe3# (1-0)

White's attack is unstoppable. The continuous threats drove the king in a mating net, an irreversible fate.

40.) d7, Rb8
41.) Nxf7 (1-0)

Everything fell down on Kasparov's hands and black can't do anything to stop this, a game worthy to remember.

Game 37
An Irreversible Fate

Boris Spassky – Robert James Fischer
World Championship Match (1972)

Move 27: Bxa4

Robert Fischer, everybody knew him and he is the toughest in his prime. This is one of the best games he played against the Russians. A mystic move, creating a dangerous mating attack left the audience shocked with a story to tell.

1.) d4, Nf6
2.) c4, e6
3.) Nc3, Bb4

Spassky played the Nimzo-Indian Defense, avoiding lines from Fischer's repertoire, the king's pawn openings. Black's kingside pieces now are free and anytime, ready to castle.

4.) Nf3, c5
5.) e3, Nc6
6.) Bd3, Bxc3+

Still, players are following the typical continuation of the opening. Black captured the knight, creating a doubled pawn and a stronger defense at the center.

7.) bxc3, d6
8.) e4, e5
9.) d5, Ne7

After several moves, white garnered wider spaces for its pieces, black is slightly cramped and we can say that Spassky is in better set ups.

10.) Nh4, h6
11.) f4, Ng6
12.) Nxg6, fxg6

Move 12: fxg6

Spassky has the bishop pair and a spacious advantage but can he really exploit such chances to dominate the position? At this moment, no pawns were captured and are still firming both players' structural defenses. Pawn formation plays a great role in leading the middle game; these tiny minions can tell which side has better chances in the endgame.

13.) fxe5, dxe5
14.) Be3, b6
15.) 0-0, 0-0

Spassky being a Russian, is slowly killing Fischer's defenses, now he has the d-pawn to consider, an isolated passed pawn eyeing the promotion square and limiting black's mobility. White had created a very strong structure on the center of the board, together with the bishop pair, smells a winning positional advantage waiting in the endgame.

16.) a4, a5
17.) Rb1, Bd7
18.) Rb2, Rb8

Both sides are slowly creeping through with their plans to infiltrate. Maneuvering their pieces in

Game 37
An Irreversible Fate

preparation for the approaching endgame with their pawn structures; the only hope to exploit and win the match.

 19.) Rbf2, Qe7
 20.) Bc2, g5
 21.) Bd2, Qe8

Move 21: Qe8

At Fischer's perspective, we can realize what he is thinking at this position; as white having the bishop pair is an advantage in the incoming endgame, those pieces can't maximize their potential and mobility as the board is crowded with pawns blocking the diagonals. Fischer's pawns are all set to black squares gripping the black bishop at some extent as white's white squared bishop is slightly cramped due to its white squared pawns and at some reasons, black's bishop can defend. Spassky's doubled rook and the isolated d-pawn are the threats at this moment, although white seems to be more dominating, its e4 pawn is the weakness in the structure.

 22.) Be1, Qg6
 23.) Qd3, Nh5
 24.) Rxf8+, Rxf8

White simplifies the position, playing defensively while black prefers finding some winning chances.

 25.) Rxf8+, Kxf8
 26.) Bd1, Nf4
 27.) Qc2, Bxa4

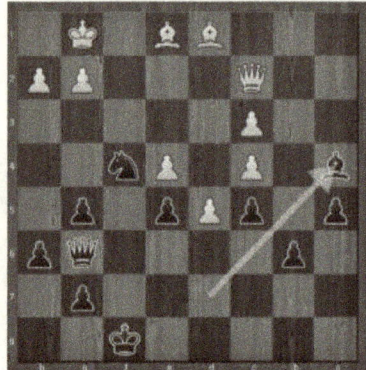

Move 27: Bxa4

Before Bxa4, the game would end to a dead draw. The position and the pieces are not so active and can't infiltrate for more. But Spassky, having a wide variety of choices, made an inaccurate move, a blunder that hinder everything in his path, on the spot, gives Fischer the edge to surely win the match. However, white may play silently as the following continuations:

 1.) Bd1, Nf4
 2.) Qf3, g4
 3.) Qe3, Qf6
 4.) Bd2, Kg8
 5.) Qf2, Nh5

And the game continues. Draw is along the way after several moves. Moreover, the game would continue in favor of black.

 1.) Qc2, Bxa4
 2.) Qc1, Bxd1
 3.) Qxd1, Qxe4
 4.) Qd2, Qxc4
 5.) d6, Qd3

Black can manage to dominate easily after the downfall of the e4 pawn and white can't stop or slow down the infiltration.

Game 38
Sealing the Checkmate

Tigran Petrosian – Ludek Pachman
Bled (1961)

Move 18: Rd8

This is one of the classical favorites of a defensive playing style. Petrosian choses king safety above all else, accompanied by solid attacking tricks. His forcing moves always shock the face of his opponent. This queen sacrifice, Qxf6+ made black no squares to hide from its fate.

1.) Nf3, c5
2.) g3, Nc6
3.) Bg2, g6

A defensive opening, the Reti, concreting first the king structure in preparation for a balanced middle game set-up. Good maneuvering of the pieces will tell which side has the winning hand.

4.) 0-0, Bg7
5.) d3, e6
6.) e4, Nge7

Both players are moving out of the book, but still sensible of their responses. Playing their defensive repertoires, each has the mind to grasp and applying the theories of the middle game set ups.

7.) Re1, 0-0
8.) e5, d6
9.) exd6, Qxd6

Still, the position is equal and there are no clear plans to rip out the other side. We are in the halfway of the match, after several moves, the winning game will be in favor of white.

10.) Nbd2, Qc7
11.) Nb3, Nd4
12.) Bf4, Qb6

Move 12: Qb6

This seems the losing part of the game story; the queen was moved twice preventing Nc4 and the Bf4 threat giving white tempos which in turn slow down black's development. Black may try e5 after Re1 at 7th move, making spaces and concreting the structures and avoiding such uncomfortable line.

13.) Ne5, Nxb3
14.) Nc4, Qb5
15.) axb3, a5

Black is moving inaccurately at this continuation. The queen is then moved in an awkward square and the knight made an outpost at c4 which made white's structures stronger. Pachman must see this safe variation:

1.) Ne5, Bxe5
2.) Bxe5, f6
3.) Bxd4, cxd4
4.) Rc1, Bd7

The knight must capture first to prevent the latter. The position is then equal and the tempos are regained.

Game 38
Sealing the Checkmate

16.) Bd6, Bf6
17.) Qf3, Kg7
18.) Re4, Rd8

19.) Qxf6+, Kxf6
20.) Be5+, Kg5
21.) Bg7 (1-0)

Move 18: Rd8

Move 21: Bg7

After axb3, white is threatening to play Ra5, black is forced to play a5 to block the rook's path, and after Bd6, black inaccurate moves lead to its losing path. However, at 16th move, the suggested response is Re8, just defending the knight and solidifying the position. The draw is possible continuing the line as follows:

1.) Bd6, Re8
2.) Bc7, Rf8
3.) Bd6, Re8
4.) Be5, Bxe5

White may choose to end the game in a draw by threefold repetition, or may continue the game as he wants. However, black may sacrifice his a-pawn to prevent the draw as this line shows:

1.) Bd6, Re8
2.) Bc7, Qd7
3.) Bxa5, Ra6

This is still a good line, than playing Bf6 at the first time.

After several moves, black can't escape the fate from white's mating threat Petrosian had prepared, a queen sacrifice is yet to be served.

This is literally the best tactical blow in the game. White had driven the king towards the mating net with an awesome queen sacrifice. The continuations are forced so as the mating attack and the game would end as shown:

1.) Nf5, h4+
2.) Nxh4, gxh4+
3.) Kh5, Bf3#

Black king is brutally mated and if the king escaped to f5, it will be followed by Ne3+ and still a mate.

As early as 17th move, the same mating pattern can be applied, as shown on the following lines:

1.) Qf3, Kg7
2.) Qxf6+, Kxf6
3.) Be5+, Kg5
4.) Bg7, Rg8
5.) f4+ or h4+, Kg4
6.) Ne3+, Kh5
7.) Bf3# (1-0)

If the king went to f5:

1.) f4+ or h4+, Kf5
2.) Ne3# (1-0)

Those beautiful ways to end the game are so fulfilling to watch.

Game 39
The Breakdown

Anatoly Karpov – Garry Kasparov
World Championship Match (1984/85)

Move 32: d2

The best by test! Both players showed their strengths against each other longest in chess history, the time when the Russians dominate the sport. In the end, as the saying goes, there could be no two lions in the same hill, the better will stand out.

1.) Nf3, Nf6
2.) c4, e6
3.) d4, d5

The queen's pawn game, the typical defensive opening with plans slowly creeping through the other side. Kasparov hasted the plan and dominated early on the match.

4.) Nc3, c6
5.) Bg5, Nbd7
6.) e3, Qa5

As Karpov moved e3, Kasparov seized the chance to tackle the queenside as white's black bishop can't now defend the upcoming pin, slightly making the position a little bit of an awkward. But still not enough to win the game with that initiative, Karpov has several choices to defend and too early to decide who has the winning card.

7.) cxd5, Nxd5
8.) Qd2, N7b6
9.) Nxd5, Qxd2+

The position gets more complicated, and Karpov choses to simplify preventing the dynamic middle game set up, the forte of Kasparov's style. A safer approach to battle black's repertoire.

10.) Nxd2, exd5
11.) Bd3, a5
12.) a4, Bb4

Move 12: Bb4

White continued the pin and outpost the b4 square. Still, the position is equal and the pawn structure will tell the fate of the game.

13.) Ke2, Bg4+
14.) f3, Bh5
15.) h4, 0-0

The white king is in the center of the board, still a good move as the pawn structure is still closed. Both players are raging to battle their minor pieces at the incoming middle game. Still, deciding which has the winning hand is not in the right time.

16.) g4, Bg6
17.) b3, Bxd3+
18.) Kxd3, Rfe8

Karpov wants to simplify the board to get to the endgame faster as it is his advantage to battle black as his king can now roam the center squares. Can this idea work as the rooks are still actively engaging the play?

126

Game 39
The Breakdown

19.) Rac1, c5
20.) Bf4, Rac8
21.) dxc5, Nd7

Move 21: Nd7

Black wants to complicate the position even more. Preventing the idea of exchanging the pieces, Kasparov did everything to slow down the upcoming endgame.

22.) c6, bxc6
23.) Rhd1, Nc5+
24.) Kc2, f6

Slowly but surely, black tries to hold the middle game phase and exploit white's king in the center. Karpov made an inaccurate decision at 22nd move, a better response is Bd6, solidifying the structure of the center as shown in this continuation:

1.) dxc5, Nd7
2.) Bd6, Bxc5
3.) Bxc5, Nxc5+
4.) Ke2, b6
5.) h4, d4
6.) e4, Rcd8

And the black king is safe. The trades are in favor and the position gets simpler than before.

However, the white king couldn't get into the e2 square after Nc5+ to avoid this deadly knight trick shown in the following variation:

1.) Nc5+, Ke2
2.) Ne6, Bg3
3.) Nd4+, Kf2
4.) Bxd2, Rxd2
5.) Nxb3, Rcc2
6.) Nxd2, Rxd2

And from this, black clearly wins the upcoming endgame. The knight is unstoppable even if following this line:

1.) Bxd2, exd4
2.) Be3+, Kg2
3.) Bxc1, Rxc1

Due to this line, the king is forced to enter the c2 square. Moreover, if white entered the Bd6 line after black's Nd7, the white king could go to e2 safely as the bishop on f4 is now eliminated on the trades so as the move, Bg3. And the king can now escape the fork and pin.

Above all the suggested lines, Karpov played c6 and let black to centralize his b-pawn and join the attack after the bxc6. This gave Kasparov a more solid and stronger approach to battle the exposed king.

25.) Nf1, Ne6
26.) Bg3, Red8
27.) Bf2, c5

Move 27: c5

Game 39
The Breakdown

Black now is approaching his pawns as the frontline. White's minor pieces are slightly passive and its king is exposed. In this way, Kasparov must do anything to exploit his advantages.

    28.) Nd2, c4
    29.) bxc4, Nc5
    30.) e4, d4

Move 30: d4

Black wants to complicate more, and didn't want to simplify the position as he weaken the white's pawn structure and just waiting for his attack to ripen up, Karpov can't do anything but to defend.

    31.) Nb1, d3+
    32.) Kb2, d2

At this time, Karpov was in a breakdown; his Nb1 move was not that stronger and let black to haste the winning line. Seeing the upcoming continuation, Karpov resigned immediately. However, the better move to continue the play is Ra1 defending the weak pawn before the downfall.

    1.) e4, d4
    2.) Ra1, Rb8
    3.) Ra2, d3+
    4.) Kc1, Ne6
White can still breathe more and play an even position.

The game may end in the following line if Karpov chose to continue:

    1.) Kb2, d2
    2.) Rc2, Nd3+
    3.) Kb3, Nxf2
    4.) Rdxd2, Bxd2
    5.) Rxd2, Rxd2
    6.) Nxd2, Nd3
Karpov is down a full rook left with a losing position. The continuation he didn't dare to play.

Generalizing the play, Kasparov has the greater edge in pushing his advantages into a bigger plan. White played several inaccurate responses seized by Kasparov. The king safety played a big role in this match in addition to the stronger pawn structure in which black easily utilized. It seems that Bd6 instead of c6 at 22nd move can make the game longer and stronger for white. A move which Karpov didn't saw and considered thus made his position weaker and stronger for his opponent. Kasparov didn't immediately seize the chances. He holds the opportunities in his hand, waited for the right time to ripen up and as the weakness accumulates, starts the blow and let his attack crushed the position. A style like the boa constrictor, but at this time, he lose the match against his greatest nemeses in his prime, Kasparov accepted the resignation and smiled.

Game 40
The Heart Stop

Garry Kasparov - Anatoly Karpov
World Championship Match (1985)

Move 22: Rcd8

Kasparov showed his real ability in this match of 1985. His fatal queen sacrifice fully destroyed the defenses of black as well as the hope to counter play. White seized the opportunity in the position exploiting the weakness and left Karpov in a losing middle game.

    1.) d4, Nf6
    2.) c4, e6
    3.) Nc3, Bb4

Entering the Nimzo-Indian line, black is preparing to castle kingside very early on the game while white goes for the center control with his pawn structure.

    4.) Nf3, 0-0
    5.) Bg5, c5
    6.) e3, cxd4

Kasparov chose not to defend but to return the pin at g5. White keeps his pawn formation in the center while black decided to put his king into safe.

    7.) exd4, h6
    8.) Bh4, d5
    9.) Rc1, dxc4

Although white is keeping his king in the center, the position is still safe and black's pieces are not been fully developed to garner an attack.

    10.) Bxc4, Nc6
    11.) 0-0, Be7
    12.) Re1, b6

Both players continue their logical continuations of the position. As white castled his king and the b4 bishop left with no purpose to pin, Karpov retreat his bishop to e7 to defend. The position is still balanced and too early to say who has the winning hand.

    13.) a3, Bb7
    14.) Bg3, Rc8
    15.) Ba2, Bd6

Move 15: Bd6

The position seems perfectly well for both sides. Their pieces are well organized and intact as well as their pan structures which is a great asset on the endgame. Both GM's are playing conservatively, slowly creeping their plans to exploit once the blow was enough to rip out.

    16.) d5, Nxd5
    17.) Nxd5, Bxg3
    18.) hxg3, exd5

At 15th move set up, Kasparov decided to open up. Seems everything is okay after the exchanges except for his doubled pawn on g-file but at some reasons, it creates a more defensive structure on his king. The conservative position, turned out to be open for dynamic plays.

Game 40
The Heart Stop

19.) Bxd5, Qf6
20.) Qa4, Rfd8
21.) Rcd1, Rd7

22.) Qg4, Rcd8
23.) Qxd7, Rxd7
24.) Re8+, Kh7
25.) Be4+ (1-0)

Move 21: Rd7

At this moment, the Kasparov spirit begins. After Qa4, Kasparov seized the chances to infiltrate. The black knight is attack thrice as black can't take the free pawn on b2 removing its defense on the c6 knight. The b7 bishop is kind of stuck in the corner, defenseless as the a7 pawn once the knight is moved or eliminated. Now, the initiative is on white's hand, but still not enough to cramp black's position. After Rfd8, white may try to trade with the knight to garner the a7 pawn but achieved nothing afterwards as shown in the following:

1.) Qa4, Rfd8
2.) Bxc6, Rxc6
3.) Qxa2, Rxc1
4.) Rxc1, Qxb2
5.) Re1, Bd5

The board simplifies, the initiative is gone from white, and becomes equal for both sides. Another variation is a trick to capture the white queen.

1.) Bxc6, Rxc6
2.) Rxc6, Qxc6
3.) Qxa7, Ra8
4.) Qxa8, Bxa8

And the queen is traded for a rook.

Move 25: Be4+

Little that Karpov know is the plan of white to exploit his position. Rcd8 immediately loses the game for black as white can sacrifice his queen to dominate the back rank and totally grip Karpov's pieces. Instead of Rcd8, black's better response after Qg4 is Rc7 keeping the play and preventing such combination. Everything now is totally forced and a decisive winning line for Kasparov as the game may continue as the following:

1.) Be4+, g6
2.) Rxd7, Ba6
3.) Bd5, Kg7
4.) Re6, Qf5
5.) Nh5, Qb1+
6.) Kh2, Bc1
7.) Rxf7+, Kxf7
8.) Re1+, Kf6
9.) Rxb2, Ne5

The sacrifice is compensated and white has the winning line. The black queen can't escape the capture as losing the game. Black played conservatively but that little inaccuracy can destroy the game as well as its defensive position.

130

Game 41
The Rapport Card

Levon Aronian – Richard Rapport
European Club Cup (2016)

Move 41: Qd3+

He is the ever dynamic and one of my favorites, Rapport always showing the crowd his preparation and wit in the middle phase of every game. Here, he grip and shattered the defensive play of Aronian. The king hunt is so dramatic to watch and the impressive maneuver end the game in favor of black.

1.) d4, d5
2.) c4, Nc6
3.) Nc3, Nf6

Both sides played the queen's pawn game, declining the free pawn, entering the queen's gambit declined and a typical continuation is seen in the position.

4.) cxd5, Nxd5
5.) Nf3, e5
6.) dxe5, Bb4

Rapport early goes to an attack sacrificing his e5 pawn to pin the white king with tempo. A good and aggressive continuation, a more defensive approach is Be6 solidifying the structure as white's doubled pawn can be defenseless in the future.

7.) Bd2, Nxc3
8.) bxc3, Ba5
9.) e3, 0-0

Black took the opportunity to weaken white's pawn structure. After Nxc3, white is forced to trade with his pawn rather than his bishop keeping that in the game as the pawns will be shattered anyway. If white recaptures with the bishop the position will be weaker as the following:

1.) Nxc3, Bxc3
2.) Bxc3, bxc3
3.) Qe7, g3

As the e5 pawn will soon fall, white is left with a weaker queenside position as the black bishop was eliminated and can't support the holes in the pawn structure. However, if white decided to defend the e5 pawn, he will let black continue with a more massive development.

1.) Bxc3, bxc3
2.) Qe7, Qa5
3.) 0-0, Re8
4.) e4, Qc5
5.) Rc1, Nxe5
6.) Nxe5, Rxe5
7.) Be2, Bd7

The pawns are all even in number but the development and initiatives are on black's hand.

Moreover, e3 seems not a best choice to solidify white's position. As it shut black's bishop mobility. However, e4 or g3 are the better moves to free up the white bishop in preparation for the kingside castling.

10.) Qa4, Bb6
11.) Qf4, Qe7
12.) h4, f6

Aronian chose not to play in a defensive way and attack early black's kingside. As white's queen is suddenly exposed to attacks and the king is still in the center of the board, it's a quiet risky response against black's solid and threatening plans.

Game 41
The Rapport Card

13.) exf6, Rxf6
14.) Qc4+, Kh8
15.) Bd3, Bf5

Move 15: Bf5

White let black to develop the tempo more after the trades as the queen is forced to escape the threat but that tempo is then regained after Qc4+. Evaluating the position, the white king is still in the center but is not literally exposed to infiltrations as both the bishops and the defensive pawn structure are guarding the position. The white queen is exposed and slightly in an awkward square but there are still safe squares to escape.

16.) Bxf5, Rxf5
17.) Ng5, Ne5
18.) Qe4, Qd7

Black is keeping the complications on the board and some of the pieces were eliminated. After the exchange, the position became clearer now for both sides as the threats are neutralized. The only weakness now for white is his stuck bishop on d7 and his isolated c-pawn.

19.) 0-0, Re8
20.) Qc2, h6
21.) Ne4, Rh5

As the rooks are now positioned to attack, the white queen is forced to retreat.

The black rooks now are active and ready to tackle the chances. Rapport is threatening to attack white's kingside after the castle.

22.) Ng3, Rxh4
23.) Rad1, Rf8
24.) Bc1, Qg4

Move 24: Qg4

To hold the position, Aronian choses to give up his h4 pawn and positioned his knight to protect the structure. If white defended the pawn with g3, white's structure will weaken as the f3 square is then become exposed to exploitation as shown in the following continuation.

1.) Ne4, Rh5
2.) g3, Qh6
3.) f3, Nc4
4.) Rae1, Rxe4
5.) Qxe4, Qxg3+
6.) Kh1, Rxh4+
7.) Qxh4, Qxh4+
8.) Kg2, Nxd2

All of the pieces are perfectly organized to garner an aggressive attack at the white king and Aronian can't do anything to stop this. Moreover, there is another continuation that will also lead to the same fate as the latter.

1.) g3, Qh6
2.) f4, Ng4

132

Game 41
The Rapport Card

3.) Bc1, Rxe4
4.) Qg2, Rxe3
5.) Bxe3, Bxe3+
6.) Rf2, Bxf2+
7.) Kf1, Ne3+
8.) Kxf2, Qxg2+
9.) Kxe3, Rd5

Still a losing position for white, that g3 move can surely ruin everything and end the game immediately.

At this moment, black pieces are heading for a combination while the undeveloped pieces of white are just defending the incoming threats.

    25.) Rd5, Qg5
    26.) Qe2, c6
    27.) Rd4, Rh1+

Move 27: Rh1+

Black seized the chances to exploit the undefended d5 rook and heading for Nf6+, gxf6, Qxd5 trick. To respond at this, Aronian sets a somewhat complicated continuation. After Qe2, black could not make the plan as this will lead to the following line.

    1.) Qe2, Nf6+
    2.) Qxf6, Rxf6
    3.) Rxg5, Rxf2
    4.) Kxf2, hxg5
    5.) Nf5, Ra4
Then black is down a piece.

As Levon want to even the structure of the game, he provoked black to capture his rook at d4 to garner a stronghold position after the trade and regain the initiatives. As after Bxd4, exd4, the position would be in favor of white as shown at the following:

    1.) Rd4, Bxd4
    2.) exd4, Nf3+
    3.) gxf3, Qf6
    4.) f4, b5
The game evenly ended and the threats are neutralized. Should we say that the rook was poisoned at this time?

Instead of grabbing the material, Rapport has another card in mind, sacrificing also the rook to garner the beautiful mating attacks. Aronian must be very careful in his responses as his pieces are not well prepared to organize the defense. His bishop is still stuck in the back rank and clogged from defending the threats. Guess what's white's next move here?

    28.) Kxh1, Bxd4
    29.) f3, Bb6
    30.) Ne4, Qh5+

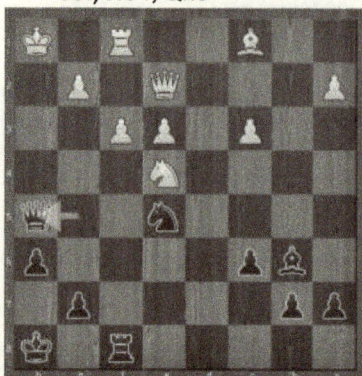

Move 30: Qh5+

White had found the safest move to continue the play, f3 giving up his whole rook and blocking knight's g4

133

Game 41
The Rapport Card

access to the mating attack. However, if Aronian retake the bishop with exd4, black can have a strong initiative to win the game.

1.) Kxh1, Bxd4
2.) exd4, Qh4+
3.) Kg1, Ng4
4.) Re1, Qh2+
5.) Kf1, Qxg3
6.) Be3, Rf6
7.) c4, Qh4
8.) Qc2, Qh1+
9.) Ke2, Qxg2
10.) Kd1, Nxe3+

Unlike this time, the rook is in the right time to capture. Black can keep the grip and slowly kill white's defenses. Aronian didn't choose to play this variation as the position is losing to continue.

Moreover, after f3, if black seized the chance to grab the knight instead of saving the bishop, the position will sit prettily well in favor of white as shown in the following continuation:

1.) f3, Qxg3
2.) cxd4, Qh4+
3.) Kg1, Ng6
4.) f4, Rd8

The position is now cleared for complicated plans and infiltrations and approaching now for an even endgame. Aronian safely escaped the chances of mating and neutralized the threats in his premises.

31.) Kg1, Bc7
32.) Kf2, Qh2
33.) Ke1, Rd8

Rapport now starts to hunt down the king's mobility but still not enough to tackle white's defenses. There are still many defenders on board and the pawns are still quite difficult to isolate. After the escape, the game now has even chances for both sides but black hold the positional advantages.

34.) Bd2, Nd3+
35.) Kd1, Qe5
36.) g4, Qb5

Move 36: Qb5

This is the third time Aronian had moved his bishop on the same square, d2. His position is so weak and the pieces are not in their best square to defend. The knight on d3 is the monster in white's premises, blocking, forking, and pinning any piece in the future while the f1 rook guards no one so as the white queen, and its minor pieces are in the awkward squares which must be exploited immediately.

37.) Qg2, Nb2+
38.) Kc2, Nc4
39.) Bc1, Rd5

The queen must be moved away from the Qa4+ threat, a beautiful mating set up gift for black. There are plenty of choices to choose from after Nb2+ and white preferred the safest one. If the king goes to e1 hoping to perpetual checks, the game would continue as the following:

1.) Qg2, Nb2+
2.) Ke1, Nd3+
3.) Kd1, Bb6
4.) g5, Bxe3

Game 41
The Rapport Card

5.) gxh6, g5
6.) f4, Qa4+
7.) Ke2, Bxd2
8.) Nxd2, Nxd2
9.) Nxf4+, Rxf4
10.) Qxf4, Nb3

White can push some plans but it will not be worth it in the end as black may tear up the files and exploited its advantages in hand. If the king choses to go on c1, he will face a worse situation than before.

1.) Qg2, Nb2+
2.) Kc1, Nc4
3.) Re1, Qb2+
4.) Kd1, Bg3
5.) a4, Nxd2
6.) Nxd2, Qb1+
7.) Ke2+, Qxe1#

The queen can't take the bishop at the first place due to the following combinations:

1.) Re1, Qb2+
2.) Kd1, Bg3
3.) Qxg3, Rxd2+
4.) Nxd2, Qxd2#

The king is just too exposed on the mating attacks and white pieces can't defend the threat at the possible time.

40.) g5, Na5
41.) Bd2, Qd3+ (1-0)

Rapport kept and executed the grip properly like the boa constrictor. At this position, the Nc4 threat are waiting and black can't stop the king hunt again. Moreover, the game would continue as below:

1.) Bd2, Qd3+
2.) Kd1, Nc4
3.) Rf2, Rb5
4.) Ke1, Rb1+
5.) Bc1, Rxc1#

White is forced to grant the mating attack than to suffer the losing position lately in the endgame.

It is important to see another variation of this continuation:

1.) Bd2, Qd3+
2.) Kd1, Nc4
3.) Ke1, Nxd2
4.) Qxd2, Bg3+
5.) Rf2, Bxf2+
6.) Qxe4, fxe4
7.) Rxd2+, Kf3

White is still playing the losing endgame here suffering the fate of his weak position.

White's position immediately falls as the bishop is then placed on d2 for the fourth time, clearly a full domination of black's play. Moreover, instead of playing Bd2, Nd2 is still playable but the fate is the same as shown in the following lines:

1.) g5, Na5
2.) Nd2, Qd3+
3.) Kd1, Nc4
4.) Re1, Bg3
5.) Re2, Rxg5

The grip is awesome; the forces of black's pieces are too strong and white can't keep playing this line as it will then lose at the end of the game.

Through all of the variations cited, white's losing move is exposing its queen on the center, black exploited the chances to gain tempo and position and after the 20th move Qc2, Rapport has seen and hold fully the advantages of attacking the kingside.
At 9th move, g3 is better instead of e3 freeing the f1 bishop at the same time not blocking the other. The clogged bishop of white weakened its position and as Rapport complicates the situation more, white couldn't bear and hold the attacks and eventually ended the game in resignation. A dominative play of Rapport card!

Game 42
Creeping the Pawn

Alexander Beliavsky – Pentala Harikrishna
FIDE World Championship Knockout Tournament (2001/02)

Move 38: Bd8

Sometimes, a small inaccuracy can ruin the play and end the game immediately. This happened on Harikrishna. White let his queen be trapped but after a couple of moves, we can realize that the queen is poisoned and the game ended in favor of white.

1.) d4, d5
2.) c4, c6
3.) Nf3, Nf6

Both sides entered the Queen's gambit declined, Slav variation. Slow, maneuvering lines can be seen. Several pieces together with the pawn structures will clash at the center. The initiatives are shared evenly for both colors.

4.) Nc3, e6
5.) e3, Nbd7
6.) Qc2, Bd6

Following the typical lines, both players are carefully setting their defenses and strengthening for the middle game structures, slowly but surely developing the pieces and maximizing their full mobility to garner domination in the near future.

7.) Bd3, 0-0
8.) 0-0, dxc4
9.) Bxc4, b5

Still the positions sits prettily even, both kings run in their safe square and still there are no threats in the board as all the weak points are well defended.

10.) Be2, Bb7
11.) Rd1, Qc7
12.) Bd2, a6

Move 12: a6

As black gained a tempo after dxc4-b5, he used this to solidify his queenside and paving the way for the fianchetto. Black's bishops are eyeing the kingside together with the queen while white keeps the minor pieces in the center not threatening anything.

Black now has a slight edge in the position but there are still several chances for white to regain.

13.) b4, a5
14.) a3, axb4
15.) axb4, Nd5

Harikrishna didn't chose to take the b4 pawn even it is playable, maybe it is outside his opening preparations:

1.) b4, Bxb4
2.) Bxb5, axb5
3.) Bxb4, Rfc8

The edges are even, nothing gained after the sacrifice.

Game 42
Creeping the Pawn

16.) Nxd5, exd5
17.) Qf5, Nf6
18.) Qc2, Qe7

Move 18: Qe7

Due to the concrete pawn structure in a closed position, both sides can't execute both of their bishop pair unless they break the pawn chains.

All were well defended, the queen side is slightly locked and the kings were undisturbed.

19.) Qb2, Nd7
20.) Rxa8, Rxa8
21.) Ra1, Rxa1+

The most possible rook trade will take place on the a-file as it is the only open file on the board. Now, the rooks were eliminated and possibly the only pieces would be left in the endgame were the minors. The game now is approaching the end phase.

22.) Qxa1, Nb6
23.) Ne5, Qc7
24.) h3, Nc4

As the board is still crowded with pawns, bishops will be just waiting to open up while the knights will do the maneuver. He who chose the better outpost can greatly affect the course of the endgame. There are no bigger threats on the board and a drawn game is more likely to happen.

25.) Bc3, Qb6
26.) Bg4, Nxe5
27.) dxe5, Be7

Pawn structure is important to secure a win in an endgame. Black made a slight inaccuracy of taking the knight, as it paved path to the c3 bishop to extend its mobility towards the kingside. Due to that, white now has even the position, regain the initiatives and has the better position.

28.) Bd7, Qd8
29.) e6, f6
30.) Qa7, Qa8

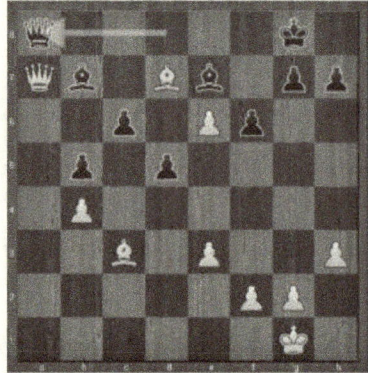

Move 30: Qa8

White starts to dominate his bishop pair as it is now free to roam the kingside. Black is forced to move f6 instead of taking the e6 pawn to prevent the following continuation:

1.) e6, fxe6
2.) Bxe6+, Kf8
3.) Bxg7+, Ke8
4.) Qe5, Qd6
5.) Qf5, Kd8
6.) Bd4, c5
7.) Bxc5, Qc6

White immediately dominates the board with his very active bishop pair. Preventing this line, black decided to block the c3 bishop's diagonal but letting white to have a stronghold in black's premises.

137

Game 42
Creeping the Pawn

31.) Qb6, Bd6
32.) f4, h6
33.) Bd4, Be7

Move 33: Be7

Black now is suffering the outcomes of his inaccuracy. The b7 bishop was locked in his own pawns and can't help to solidify his defense. White's plan now is to eliminate the e7 bishop in his diagonal to pave path for the e6 pawn towards the promotion. Black can't take the free b4 pawn preventing the following situation:

1.) Bd4, Bxb4
2.) Bc5, Ba5
3.) Qxa5, Qxa5
4.) e7, Qa8

The white queen is then trapped but the promoting e6 pawn is unstoppable.

34.) Kh2, Kh8
35.) Bc5, Bd8
36.) e7, Bxb6

Beliavsky placed his king into safety before executing his plan as black can't do anything and can't take the c5 bishop realizing the following position afterwards:

1.) Bc5, Bxc5
2.) Qxc5, Bc8
3.) Qd6, Bxd7
4.) exd7, Qd8

5.) Qxc6, Kf7

White is dominating the board and black can't do anything but to defend.

37.) Bxb6, c5
38.) Bd8 (1-0)

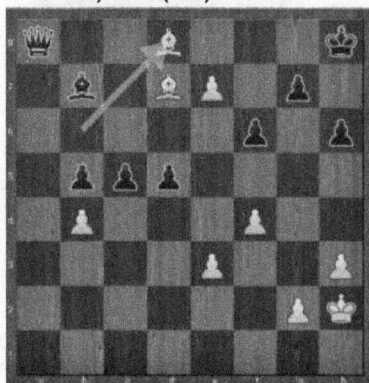

Move 38: Bd8

As the only threat of the promoting pawn eliminated, white can easily dominates the situation and regain the queen afterwards. His bishop pair are so immensely active and even the black queen can't hold and defend the threats. White exploited black's tiny inaccuracy of taking the knight on e5 as it opens a strong diagonal eyeing the kingside, followed by the move, e6, a right timing plan forcing Harikrishna to remove one of the threats of the promoting pawn. Black's bishop pair didn't achieved a great mobility in the middle game, blocked in his own structures, and was easily dominated by white. A solid gripping ended the game in a convincing winning style.

Game 43
Feeding the Dragon

Alexey Shirov – Veselin Topalov
FIDE World Championship Knockout
Tournament (2001/02)

Move 16: a3

We will study now the simple way to tackle the Sicilian Dragon opening. No too much complications, no sacrifices and combinations, just a shear endgame repertoire ended the game in favor of white. In this match, Shirov defeated the Sicilian Dragon user in a simple and solid manner.

1.) e4, c5
2.) Nf3, Nc6
3.) d4, cxd4

Shirov is facing the ever dangerous Sicilian line from the hands of Topalov. Both players are famous in their respective repertoires, their style and achievements are evident in the history of their career.

4.) Nxd4, g6
5.) Nc3, Bg7
6.) Be3, Nf6

Following the typical opening lines, Shirov didn't dare to see another interesting continuation in this opening. As black opened up the g6 square, white may try the following variations:

1.) Nxd4, g6
2.) Nxc6, bxc6
3.) Qd4, Nf6

4.) e5, Nd5
5.) e6, Nf6
6.) exf7+, Kxf7
7.) Bc4+, d5

White instantly has the edge as the black king can't castle anymore. But still there are several pieces on the board that can defend the incoming threats. However, black may try another response, a safer response against white.

1.) e5, Nd5
2.) e6, f6
3.) exd7+, Bxd7
4.) Bc4, Be6
5.) 0-0, Bg7

Black now has a weak kingside but his bishop pair is active and can strengthen the defenses afterwards. A playable variation Shirov didn't dare to try, instead he goes for the typical Sicilian lines.

7.) Bc4, 0-0
8.) Bb3, d6
9.) f3, Bd7

Move 9: Bd7

The solid line, both are prepared following the typical continuations of the game. Here, we may see that black has the initiative just waiting on the queenside while white must risk his kingside to attack.

139

Game 43
Feeding the Dragon

10.) Qd2, Rc8
11.) 0-0-0, Nxd4
12.) Bxd4, b5

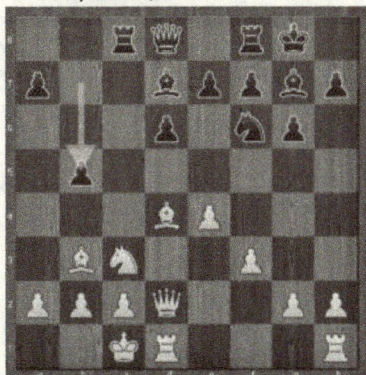

Move 12: b5

Topalov starts now to tickle the queenside structure, taking down the d4 knight first before forwarding the b5 pawn immediately. Shirov can easily choose where to castle his king but he wants his rook pile be placed against the black's kingside and let himself to face the pawn storm, although taking the free a7 pawn looks obvious, Shirov didn't dare to taste as it will give way to open file for the rook to participate the game, a primitive humanly response to evaluate the position. White didn't want to play defensive here, instead he want a dynamic and aggressive match in the middle game.

13.) Nd5, Nxd5
14.) exd5, Bxd4
15.) Qxd4, a5

A trade to simplify the game, as black is attacking the white side; Shirov must defend against the pawn storm to continue to game; the outcome of his decision after castling on the queenside. White king now is in danger as black is holding the initiatives and threatening to open up his defenses. White now must defend

and if he neutralizes the situation, only then he can forward his pawns too and return the attack.

16.) a3, b4
17.) a4, Qe8
18.) h4, Bxa4

Move 18: Bxa4

Topalov now starts his pawns to storm white's structure as he can't take the b4 pawn preventing the opening of the files towards his king. White's plan now is to close the position by using the black pawns as a blockage for the rook to participate the attack while sneaking some tempo to counter attack on the black's kingside. There are other lines playable and still a good response to continue the game:

1.) a3, b4
2.) axb4, Rb8
3.) Rhe8, Rxb4
4.) Qc3, Bb5
5.) Rd4, Rxd4
6.) Qxd4, a4
7.) Ba2, Qc7

White neutralizes the danger but didn't regain the initiatives in this variation and it was not a closed position after all as b and c files are open for a rook pile to attack the king afterwards. Shirov choses the slowest line for black to infiltrate his premises.

140

Game 43
Feeding the Dragon

19.) Kb1, Bxb3
20.) cxb3, a4
21.) h5, f6

Move 21: f6

At the right moment in time, white has reached the kingside and threatening black's defenses. Topalov can't keep his resources to continue the threat and now, white has even the initiative forcing black to play f6, to prevent a very neat mating combination.

> 1.) cxb3, a4
> 2.) h5, axb3
> 3.) hxg6, fxg6
> 4.) Rxh7, Kxh7
> 5.) Rh1+, Kg8
> 6.) Qh8+, Kf7
> 7.) Rh7# (1-0)

The mating combination was simple, but if black didn't expect the rook sacrifice, he can still escape the mating combination but will also lead to a losing position:

> 1.) h5, axb3
> 2.) hxg6, fxg6
> 3.) Rxh7, Rf6
> 4.) Rdh1, Rc1+
> 5.) Kxc1, Qc8+
> 6.) Kb1, Qf5+
> 7.) Ka1, g5
> 8.) Rh8+, Kg7
> 9.) Rah7+, Qxh7
> 10.) Rxh7+, Kxh7

A rook against the queen in an endgame set up can't win unless white blunders the play. Above all, Topalov forced to play f6 blocking the white queen's diagonal and at the same time, letting his own queen to defend.

22.) hxg6, Qxg6
23.) Qd3, axb3
24.) Rh4, Qxd3+

Move 24: Qxd3+

This is where the endgame starts, as black didn't have any choice but to trade off the queens, white has the more active rook now after the trades. He placed the queen to d3 to gain tempo and attack the b3 pawn after the exchange. In this response, white has the more dominative rook pair in the endgame. But it's a long way to go deciding which has the better chance in winning the game.

25.) Rxd3, Rb8
26.) Rxb3, Rb5
27.) Rd4, Rfb8

We are entering now the end phases of the game with black a pawn up and his king in a safer square but white rooks has the more control in the center of the board. The initiative again is even for both sides and its difficult now to decide which has the better card.

141

Game 43
Feeding the Dragon

28.) Kc2, Kf7
29.) g4, f5
30.) gxf5, Kf6

Move 30: Kf6

Black made a tiny bit of inaccuracy here, sacrificing his f5 pawn to weaken white's pawn structure. This is not a must response; instead there is healthier way to continue the game without giving up the advantages in hand. After several moves, the f5 pawn will be a trap for the black king; a poisoned pawn that ended the match.

1.) Kc2, Kf7
2.) g4, Rc5+
3.) Kd3, h5
4.) gxh5, Rh8
5.) Rbxb4, Rxh5
6.) f4, Rcxd5
7.) Rxc5, Rxc5+

The pawn was kept and intact essential to win the game easily afterwards.

31.) Re3, b3+
32.) Kd3, R8b7
33.) Re6+, Kxf5

This is a simple rook maneuver to corner the king. As black rook pair can't help their king's situation, white can now exploit and execute on how to

mate the king in the center of the board. If only then that the king didn't taste the poisoned pawn, the game would be like the following:

1.) Kd3, R8b7
2.) Re6+, Kf7
3.) Ke3, Rb4
4.) Rde4, h5
5.) Rh6, Rxe4+
6.) fxe4, Rc7
7.) Rxh7+, Kg8
8.) Rxh5, Rc2
9.) Rh6, Rxb2
10.) f6, Kf7
11.) fxe7, Kxe7

And a long theoretical game roams the board. The pawns were even but black can still have the chances in his b-passed pawn.

34.) Rh6, Rb4
35.) Re4, R4b5
36.) Ke3, Kg5
37.) Reh4 (1-0)

Move 37: Reh4

Black must take the e4 rook at 35th move and must not retreat to b5 square. Kg5 doesn't make sense as it let white to trap the king. Now, white is threatening a one-move mating tactic, Rhe5+, and black can't do anything to stop this; A brilliancy indeed!

142

Game 44
Too Strong to Beat

Wei Yi – Ding Liren
Chinese Team Championship (2015)

Move 64: Kc4

Ding Liren is one of the elite masters in the field of this sport. His brilliancy to positional understanding is so immense and beating the younger players of this generation. On the other side, Wei Yi, a young prodigy, famous in his classical repertoires and dynamic style didn't bring the bacon in the end. Black is so well prepared, sneaking chances to even the initiatives. In the end, white ended in a helpless position and lose the match.

1.) e4, c6
2.) d4, d5
3.) Nc3, dxe4

The Caro-Kann Defense, an opening that dynamically sets the pieces for the incoming middle game. We can sense now the threats waiting aboard as both of the players want to play in an aggressive approach.

4.) Nxe4, Bf5
5.) Ng3, Bg6
6.) h4, h6

Both are eagerly developing their pieces and positions following the typical continuations of the opening.

The winning bar now is even for both players as we are still in the opening phase of the match.

7.) Nf3, e6
8.) h5, Bh7
9.) Bd3, Bxd3

As the h7 bishop can't escape the attack, trading it off is a better choice to make. At this point, the two knights are already active but black was left underdeveloped. Although white now gained tempo after Qxd4 and in a developed position, black is still strong in its defense, and there are no clear weakness white can exploit immediately.

10.) Qxd3, Nf6
11.) Bd2, Be7
12.) 0-0-0, 0-0

Move 12: 0-0

Both had taken their king into safety. White is a one move left for full development while black is still has several pieces waiting at the back rank. At this position, white clearly has the positional advantages.

13.) Ne4, Nxe4
14.) Qxe4, Qd5
15.) Qg4, Kh8

Black again traded his developed knight at 13th move, he must play Nbd7 instead. Yi has the open spaces to roam for his plan while Liren seems wanting to simplify the board as he is comfortable playing closed position against this classical young GM.

Game 44
Too Strong to Beat

16.) Kb1, Nd7
17.) Qh3, Rad8
18.) g4, e5

Move 18: e5

Black can't hide the fact that he is behind in development and must keep defending. White is threatening to play g5 and shatter king's defenses as white is really comfortable with his set up black must hold the position and defend carefully.

19.) g5, e4
20.) Nh4, Bxg5
21.) c4, Qxc4

Wei Yi in his classical form had fully mastered his art of sacrificing the materials for better complications in his favor. He can't take the e5 pawn to prevent a mating combination as shown in the following:

1.) g4, e5
2.) dxe5, Nxe5
3.) Nxe5, Qxe5
4.) Qf3, f5

And black neutralizes the attack as he can't take the h6 pawn threatening the queen due to Bxh6, Qxd1+, Rxd1, Rxd1#.

Liren pushes his pawn to drive the knight away and eliminate the defender but Yi is prepared on the situation, moving c4 to prevent the

queen from retaking and forcing black to take with the h-pawn. At this instance, black have no choice to open his kingside and defend with his doubled pawn structure. Is it a worth it pawn sacrifice? But now, black is in a real danger.

22.) Bxg5, hxg5
23.) Ng6+, Kg8
24.) Ne7+, Kh8

Move 24: Kh8

The real deal here is whether Wei Yi let the perpetual check and draws the game, or continues the match with a winning position. At 23rd move, black can't move his king to h7 preventing white's Qf5 placing the king in a more uncomfortable square as shown in the following:

1.) Bxg5, hxg5
2.) Ng6+, Kh7
3.) Qf5, Kg8
4.) Ne7+, Kh8
5.) Qxg5, Qe6

There is no need to put the king to h7 as it will then move to g8 afterwards.

25.) Ng6+, Kg8
26.) Nxf8, Nxf8
27.) h6, g6

Wei Yi decided to grabbed the chances and continue the game against the elite.

Game 44
Too Strong to Beat

28.) Qa3, Qe6
29.) Qxa7, Qe7
30.) Rhe1, g4

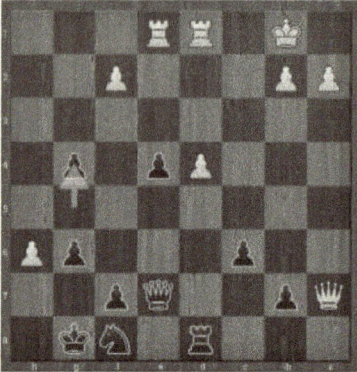
Move 30: g4

After the exchange at 26th move, white's threat neutralizes and Wei Yi runs out of resources to continue the attack. Black was left with a clump of pawns at the kingside and a very defensive structure afterwards. As white holds the rook pair, black's defensive structure can keep the game and the initiatives even.

31.) a4, Kh7
32.) a5, Rd7
33.) Qc5, f5

White didn't made his plan happen as he can't crush black's kingside structure while black now is silently building his advantages into reality. Slowly but surely, black is aiming to swarm his pawns toward the promotion while holding the situation. Wei Yi must take an action before the plans of Liren ripen up.

34.) a6, Qxc5
35.) dxc5, bxa6
36.) Rd6, Rc7

The game approaches the end phase and the winning bar slowly lighting up in favor of black. However, Liren can immediately take the d6 rook instead

of defending the c6 pawn and the game instantly ended for a win.

1.) dxc5, bxa6
2.) Rd6, Rxd6
3.) cxd6, Kxh6
4.) Rc1, Kg5
5.) Rxc6, e3
6.) fxe3, g3
7.) Rc1, Kg4
8.) Rg1, Kf3
9.) Kc2, Kf2

Black now had the real pawn storm and Yi can't really slow down the swarm or even advance his own.

37.) Rf6, Nd7
38.) Rf7+, Kxh6
39.) Rd1, Kg5

Move 39: Kg5

Black let white to trade their pieces pushing to simplify the board and make Yi face the difficulty of defending the approaching promotion, or should I say promotions. White can't accept the provoking exchanges as the lone rook can't complicate more at the end against the pawn storm. A slowly well-organized movement of black is just too hard to stop.

40.) Kc2, e3
41.) fxe3, g3
42.) Rg7, g2

145

Game 44
Too Strong to Beat

Carefully, Liren must hold his pawn formation intact before the c6 pawn falls and grabbed the chances to advance toward the last rank. Every move now will decide the end. Just one inaccuracy will make the hope slipped in their hands.

    43.) Rg1, Kf6
    44.) Rg8, Kf7
    45.) Rh8, Kg7

Move 45: Kg7

White may try to immediately place his rook at h7 instead of placing it first to g8 to not lose control the 7th rank. The position may get better as the following shown:

*   1.) Rg1, Kf6*
*   2.) Rh7, Rb7*
*   3.) Rxg2, Nxc5*
*   4.) Rxb7, Nxb7*

The position gets better for white and a little comfortable to continue as the pawns were not that intact approaching the last rank.

    46.) Rh2, Rb7
    47.) Rhxg2, Ne5
    48.) Ra1, a5

White must keep his rook pair and don't want to push the board into the endgame; seems Yi want to complicate things up. But Liren can't let him do his plans, and even set up a trap for the a1 rook. It looks that the a5 pawn is free but dangerous to taste after the following continuation:

*   1.) Ra2, a5*
*   2.) Rxa5, Nc4*
*   3.) Kc3, Nxa5*

And that simple fork immediately wins the game in favor of black. If after Nc4, white's response is Ra2, another winning continuation is on hand.

*   1.) Ra2, a5*
*   2.) Rxa5, Nc4*
*   3.) Ra2, Nxe3+*
*   4.) Nxg2, Kd2*

And white has the same fate as the latter.

    49.) Ra3, Nc4
    50.) Rb3, Rxb3
    51.) Kxb3, Nxe3

Move 51: Nxe3

Wei Yi had just made a horrible blunder, moving his rook to a3 and letting black to fork it with Nc4 attacking twice the b2 pawn and at the same time, threatening to capture the hanging e3 pawn. At this moment, Yi is forced to trade his rook, moving it to b2 to protect the pawn but as after the trades, black now has expanded his gain. Another pawn fell and he is now ready to easily forward his little armies up until the last square.

Game 44
Too Strong to Beat

White now is in serious trouble. He doesn't have enough time to advance his pawns and must defend the two connected passed pawns of black, as the knight is helping them, he may now face serious difficulty on how he will defend the swarm.

    52.) Rf2, g5
    53.) Re2, f4
    54.) Kc3, g4

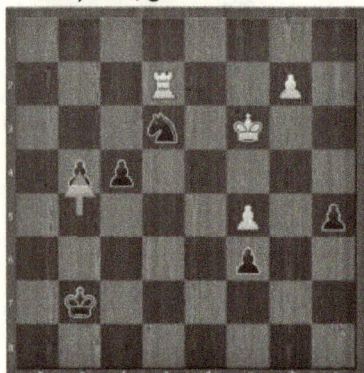

Move 54: g4

It was a big shame for the white rook, as it can't defend the advancing of the g and f pawns towards the promotion. At this position, black has the greater edge to win the game but still this is not the right time to resign the game as white.

    55.) Kd3, Kg6
    56.) Re1, Kf5
    57.) Ra1, g3

As the white king is helping to stop or to slow down the march, Wei Yi seizes the chance to attack the a-pawn hoping to pave way for his own to advance too afterwards, once the threats are neutralized.

    58.) Ke2, Ng4
    59.) Rxa5, Nh2
    60.) Ra8, f3+

The pawns now are both two moves before queening. It was a literally losing position now for the young GM,

but still hoping to find little chances to sneak, he push the game and continue the play.

    61.) Ke3, f2
    62.) Rf8+, Ke5
    63.) Ke2, Kd4
    64.) Rf5, Kc4 (0-1)

Move 64: Kc4

As white want to push the game for more, he loses his tempo and stuck in the zugzwang position. The rook is locked defending the c5 pawn and guarding the f-pawn from promotion. The king however, is defending the f1 square too preventing the promotion to happen. The only available response is to move the b-pawn in which can easily be taken by the black king. Soon the b and c pawn will fall next is the rook after f1=Q by white, leaving a winning position for black with his pawn or pawns readily advancing to the last rank. A great game from Ding Liren showing no mercy to his opponent in anyway whatsoever, he slowly suffocates white's chances to continue the game and in the end, Yi lost in the center of the desert craving for air.

147

Game 45
Out of the Book

Mikhail Tal – Andrei Sokolov
Brussels World Cup (1988)

Move 14: Nxf7

As black is comfortable developing his position, Tal is busy doing his magic. The difficult to see Nxf7 shattered the preparation of Sokolov, sacrificing the knight for a pawn leading to unfamiliar variations he hadn't met before. In the end, black was left with a losing endgame set ups and white wins the game.

1.) d4, Nf6
2.) c4, e6
3.) g3, d5

The Catalan Opening, Tal was ready to improve his position, wanting to place his bishop in the fianchetto and put his king into safety before sneaking into domination. Nowadays, this is an interesting line Anish Giri plays, beating some of the best elite modern GM's of the present era of chess.

4.) Bg2, dxc4
5.) Nf3, c5
6.) 0-0, Nc6

Following the typical continuations of the game, Tal had sacrificed his pawn for a tempo of developing his position. His king is already safe, and as black took the c4 pawn, it opens the long diagonal for the g2 bishop. After several moves, both will fight for the center control.

7.) Ne5, Bd7
8.) Na3, cxd4
9.) Naxc4, Bc5

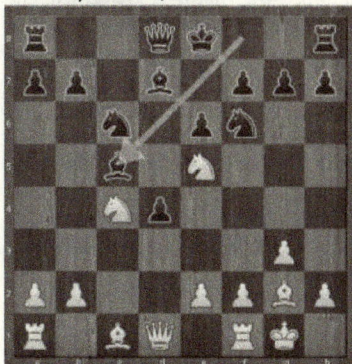

Move 9: Bc5

All of the minor pieces are supporting the center craving for domination. Black is a pawn up but white clearly has the safer position. We can see that the d7 bishop was stuck but it was difficult to tell on how it can be exploited.

10.) Qb3, 0-0
11.) Bf4, Qc8
12.) Rfd1, Rd8

Both sides continue developing their position. White's pieces seems more active than those of black as they are holding more spaces and eyeing important squares on the opponent's premises. But that is not enough to say that black will certainly lose the game afterwards or maybe there are something hidden in the bush waiting to be unlock in the right possible time.

13.) Rac1, Nd5
14.) Nxf7, Kxf7
15.) Ne5+, Nxe5

As black didn't expected, white decided to sacrifice the pawn out of pure understanding of the position.

Game 45
Out of the Book

Giving up the knight for a pawn, Tal achieved a stronger build up against black. White seized the chances of black's clogged minor pieces and immediately went to attack the king with his mating threats. Sokolov is forced to take the e5 knight as after Ne5+, it opens a file for the rook to attack the bishop. The c6 knight must take for the bishop to be defended.

If Sokolov saw what will be his fate after the Kxf7 and played a defensive Rf8 instead, he could prevent the mating threats but will face the same losing position:

> 1.) Nxf7, Rf8
> 2.) Ncd6, Bxd6
> 3.) Nxd6, Qd8
> 4.) Bxd5, exd5
> 5.) Qxd5+, Kh8
> 6.) Nxb7, Qe8
> 7.) Nd6, Qg6

White had established a good control on the board and a solid pawn structure. Black is down two pawns which itself hopeless to win against Tal. But an interesting line will exist if black can manage to give up his queen saving his position.

> 1.) Ncd6, Bxd6
> 2.) Nxd6, Nxf4
> 3.) Nxc8, Nxe2+
> 4.) Kh1, Nxc1
> 5.) Rxc1, Rxc8
> 6.) f5, Rb8

It was a long game to go but still black is suddenly in a better position than the latter.

> 16.) Bxe5, b6
> 17.) Qf3+, Kg8
> 18.) Qg4, g6

Everything now seems forcing for black. Its two minor pieces are pinned by the bishop and rook and its queen is in a very awkward square. White is down a piece and it must action immediately before the threats were neutralized as still, black king is not in a complete danger after the exchange or is it? On the other hand, white can regain his lost piece anytime threatening to move b4 and harvest the fruit of his pin. The complications suddenly arise after black took the poisoned knight. And after several more moves, black will be lost in the midst of the forest, walking alone in a vulnerable position.

> 19.) Be4, Be8
> 20.) b4, Nxb4
> 21.) Bxa8, Qxa8

Tal starts now to reap his labor, playing b4 forcing black to give up his rook as the bishop can't take to protect the queen. Every move now is awkward for black while very comfortable for white; the results of his staggering knight sacrifice. But however, Nc3 instead of Nxb4 seems to be a playable response as it blocks the c1 rook's file toward the black queen at the same time it attacks the other. But after some evaluations, it will lead to a horrific losing position afterwards as shown:

> 1.) b4, Nc3
> 2.) bxc5, Nxd1
> 3.) Qf4, Qd7
> 4.) Qf6, d3
> 5.) Qh8+, Kf7
> 6.) Qg7# (1-0)

Black's pieces are just too far to defend the king. The mating combinations was unstoppable as white didn't need to seize materials and went immediately for the mating attack.

> 22.) Qxe6+, Bf7
> 23.) Qf6, Kf8
> 24.) Qh8+, Ke7

Game 45
Out of the Book

Tal starts now the hunt, driving the king in a more exposed square. As he had regained now his lost material and shattered the king's position, the winning bar is mostly in favor for white. Seeing this position, the fate of the game is on white's hand.

    25.) Bf6+, Kd7
    26.) Bxd8, Nc6
    27.) Bf6, Qxh8

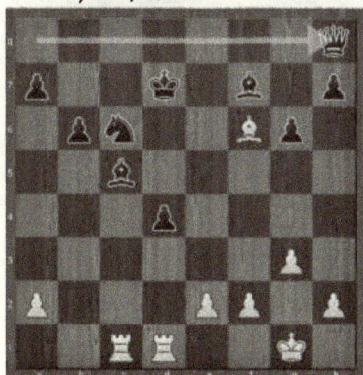

Move 27: Qxh8

At 26th move, black is doubtful if he retakes the bishop with his queen as the incoming trades will result to the following endgame:

    1.) Bf6+, Kd7
    2.) Bxd8, Qxd8
    3.) Rxd4+, Bxd4
    4.) Qxd4+, Nd5
    5.) e4, Qg5
    6.) Rd1, Kd6
    7.) exd5, Bxd5

The position gave a theoretical endgame in which white has the upper hand. As black is down a material, he must keep and hold the position or make more complications preventing to simplify the game but first taking the queen is essential to limit the threats from white.

    28.) Bxh8, Bxa2
    29.) e3, a5
    30.) Bxd4, Nxd4

White is taking advantage of the pin and as black has several active minor pieces; Tal must simplify first to dominate.

    31.) exd4, Bd6
    32.) d5, a4
    33.) Rc6, Bc5

Move 33: Bc5

Tal must eliminate one of the bishops to slow down and weaken the approaching pawn swarm. One little tempo wasted here can swindle the position and the winning bar. As white holds better materials, black holds a more dangerous position.

    34.) Rc1, Bd4
    35.) R6c4, Bxc4
    36.) Rxc4, b5

White must sacrifice his rook for a bishop to weaken the structure. If black took the free d5 pawn at 34th move, it will be a winning endgame for white as shown:

    1.) Rc1, Bxd5
    2.) R6xc5, bxc5
    3.) Rxc5, Bb3

A more simplified set up will let the rook dominates more.

Giving the full piece to connect the pawns seems not logical but stronger as the obvious Bc5 instead of b5 gives a weaker position afterwards.

150

Game 45
Out of the Book

As shown in the following variation:
1.) Rxc5, Bc5
2.) Rxa4, Kd6
3.) Ra7, Kxd5
4.) Rxh7, b5
5.) Kf1, b4
6.) Ke2, b3
7.) Kd3, b2
8.) Kc2, Bxf2
9.) Rg7, Ke6
10.) Rxg6+, Kf7

Slowly but surely, white is holding the position and keeping his advantages in the position and in materials. Black decided to put aside his only piece just to connect his passed pawns making it stronger against the white rook.

37.) Rxd4, a3
38.) Rd1, b4
39.) Ra1, Kd6

Move 39: Kd6

As the pawns are the soul of the game, black suddenly had tweaked the magic wand and made white defend the promotion. White's king is far from stopping the march while the black king can freely take the d5 pawn and on the way to support the swarm. Tal is suddenly losing here; the brilliant b5 raises the winning bar in favor of black but was it still enough to win the match?

40.) Kf1, Kxd5
41.) Ke2 (1-0)

Move 41: Ke2

The invincible winning trick, Tal had escaped the brink of a certain defeat.
As the position shown, white is winning after several continuations:
1.) Kf1, Kxd5
2.) Ke2, Kd4
3.) Kd2, Kc4
4.) Rc1+, Kb3
5.) Rb1+, Kc4
6.) Kc2, a2
7.) Re1, b3+
8.) Kb2, g5

And white can hold the pawns then gradually eliminate them after.

Tal had the most intuitive understanding of the fate of the position. The complication he makes always left his opponent in the midst of doubt raises the possibility to make inaccurate moves in unfamiliar continuations and eventually loses the game in the end, a very classical miniature from the 'Magician of Riga'.

Game 46
The Complicated Winawer

Mikhail Tal – Mikhail Botvinnik
World Championship Rematch (1961)

Move 16: Rh8

We have come to study the complicated game of the two intuitive players in the history of this sport. Tal is always shocking the crowd with his dynamic and artistic combinative style, and Botvinnik, a positional theoretician, playing with complete accuracy and precision on board. Both are playing the French, showed one of the most interesting games in the world stage.

1.) e4, e6
2.) d4, d5
3.) Nc3, Bb4

The early moves showed the Winawer variation of the French game; one of the most aggressive and risky approach of the opening. Both sides are sacrificing their king's safety and literally giving up several pawns and the chance to castle. In the middle game, every piece will face the threats of each other and as the complication accumulates, the chaos will be out of control.

4.) e5, c5
5.) a3, Bxc3+
6.) bxc3, Qc7

Now, white has the doubled pawn structure and has a weaker pawn formation against black. But, we are still in the opening phase of the game and both sides are following the theoretical continuations of the Winawer.

7.) Qg4, f5
8.) Qg3, Ne7
9.) Qxg7, Rg8

Move 9: Rg8

Black goes for force rather than the material giving up his pawns for the g and h file rook control. Although this is a typical pawn sacrifice in this opening, seeing this in the modern times is quietly rare. It seems that the black king is in danger but history says that it is completely safe sitting in the center. Afterwards, black could now counter on the queenside.

10.) Qxh7, cxd4
11.) Kd1, Bd7
12.) Qh5+, Kd8

We are in the 12th move of the match and still in a deep theory. As both players didn't bother to keep their king in the center, white has the edge in the queenside while black has to pressure the c3 pawn to sneak towards the white king. Both positions are awkward in a logical sense. There are no clear threats but there are varieties to choose where to attack.

Game 46
The Complicated Winawer

13.) Nf3, Qxc3
14.) Ra2, Nbc6
15.) Rb2, Kc7

Move 15: Kc7

Instead of taking the pawn Tal used the tempo to develop his knight, as black is concreting a strong pawn structure in the center and a very safe king in the c7 square. However, the d4 pawn will soon fall if white took it in the first place, the same fate with his winning bar:

1.) Qh5+, Kd8
2.) cxd4, Qc3
3.) Rb1, Qxd4+
4.) Bd2, Qxf2
5.) Nf3, Nbc6

And black has weakened the defenses and got full advantages realizing that the pawn was poisoned afterwards.

16.) Rb5, Rh8
17.) Qxh8, Rxh8
18.) Bb2, Qxf3+

White is already preparing itself to trap the queen after Rb5 threatening Bb2. But however, a different story will come out if after Rh8 Tal didn't give up the white queen for an h8 rook. The black queen will have the chance to escape the net if white played Qg5 after Rh8 instead of taking

it. A very different line from the latter as shown in the following variations:

1.) Rb2, Kc7
2.) Rb5, Rh8
3.) Qg5, Qa1
4.) Qd2, Rag8

Black had found the only square outside the threats pinning the bishop and still keeping the king awkward. The black rooks are defending the right wing; at this position white is still defending from black's initiatives. Hence, to keep the white's tempo, at the right time, Tal sacrificed his queen and traps the opponent's queen thereafter.

19.) gxf3, Ng6
20.) h4, Ngxe5
21.) h5, Nf7

Move 21: Nf7

As white captured the rook Botvinnik took the knight and starts the material imbalances. Tal made a trick in the position, at 20th move; it seems that he is giving up his only passed pawn but there is a deeper meaning behind h4 as we can see in this variation:

1.) gxf3, Ng6
2.) h4, Rxh4
3.) Rxh4, Nxh4
4.) f4, Ng6

Game 46
The Complicated Winawer

5.) Bc1, Ncxe5
6.) fxe5, Bxb5
7.) Bxb5, Nxe5
8.) Bf4, Kb6
9.) Be8, Ng4

This will be a very interesting line both in favor for both sides. White will have the active bishop pair while black is holding the strong center pawns. An endgame Botvinnik didn't chose to play.

22.) f4, Nd6
23.) Rb3, Ne4
24.) Ke1, Rh6

Move 24: Rh6

White has the rook pair but black is more dominating; its center pawn formation together with his knight pair is a future threat to endgame. The pawns of white are isolated posing weakness in the position and its bishops are not in their active squares, its only edge is the passed pawn in the h-file which can easily be blocked by the rook. We can say now that the initiatives and the controls are on black's hand.

25.) Be2, Be8
26.) Rd3, Nf6
27.) Bxd4, Nxd4

As white tackled the d4 pawn, black counter on the h-pawn, and the game

continues as both players are slowly minimizing the threats on the board.

Black must maintain his posture to bring the endgame in favor of him against Tal, and Tal must simplify things more to lighten the complications in the center in order to maximize his rook pair and dominate.

28.) Rxd4, Bxh5
29.) Rd3, Rh7
30.) Rdh3, Bg6

Move 30: Bg6

Black must not let white to simplify the board and better to maintain his closed center pawn formation. The capture on the h-pawn slightly made the game even for both sides, slowly approaching, as the pieces were traded now, the endgame in white's favor. At 28th move, black may try a different variation to play instead:

1.) Rxd4, Kd6
2.) Rb4, Bc6
3.) Ra2, Ne4
4.) Rb3, Ke7
5.) Rbh3, Be8

Still white can't dominate as there are no weak points in the defenses; the board is still crowded with solid pawn structure, and black's minor pieces

154

Game 46
The Complicated Winawer

are actively defending; a better continuation than the latter.

31.) Rxh7+, Nxh7
32.) Rh6, Nf8
33.) Rh8, Nd7

We are in the endgame story now; Tal is doing the obvious move, attacking the minor pieces as they can't defend each other simultaneously. It will be a rook against a knight endgame or is it going to be that far?

34.) Rg8, Bf7
35.) Rg7, Be8
36.) Re7, Kd8

Move 36: Kd8

The rook is tickling the bank rank and finally got a winning line. Now, Tal is heading to capture the e6 pawn which greatly weakened black's pawn structure; the outcome of the falling of the poisoned h-pawn.

37.) Rxe6, Bf7
38.) Rh6, Ke7
39.) Bd3, Be6

As the e6 pawn falls, the now isolated d5 and f5 pawn are exposed to attacks. As the board clears, white surely is winning now; the rook is very active doing his full domination at the back rank and we can see now the endgame is near to happen.

40.) Rh5, Nf6
41.) Rg5 (1-0)

Nf6 here is the last inaccuracy which made black finally loses his left hope to continue the game. The better version to just defend the f5 pawn is Kf6 as shown in the following lines:

1.) Bd3, Be6
2.) Rh5, Kf6
3.) Rh6+, Kf7
4.) Kd2, Nf8
5.) Ke3, Kg7
6.) Rh1, Ng6
7.) Rh5, Kf6
8.) Rh7, Ne7
9.) Be2, Bf7

Still black can hold the position and keep his defenses intact instead of Nf6 as it is losing after the trades as shown in the following below:

1.) Bd3, Be6
2.) Rh5, Nf6
3.) Rg5, Ne4
4.) Bxe4, fxe4
5.) Kd2, Kf6
6.) Ke3, Bf7
7.) Kd4, a6
8.) c4, dxc4
9.) Kxe4, b6

Tal can easily win this theoretical endgame as the bishop can't defend all of its pawns and the white king is holding the center squares. It will be a long time to go but it's still a winning endgame for white.

All in all, Tal played beautifully in this match. His combination of risk, theory, and classical complications lead black to respond in slight inaccuracy that had been exploited and converted to winning position afterwards. It was then a must study classical match of the French winawer.

Game 47
Simply Instructional

Mikhail Tal – Jonathan Speelman
Reykjavik World Cup (1988)

Move 22: Nxf7

It was several days ago that I turned to be a 25 year old continuing my passion in the game. It's so happen that Tal's games are my favorite. His favorite square that is always a subject for sacrifices is the f7. Through this, his plan always prevail making his opponent defending and striving to survive on his mating nets until the end.

1.) e4, d6
2.) d4, g6
3.) Nf3, Bg7

White immediately grabbed the center squares while black prioritized his king's safety. Playing defensively, Speelman didn't tackle the chance to face white's repertoires in the center and decided to solidify his position afterwards.

4.) Be2, Nf6
5.) Nc3, 0-0
6.) 0-0, c5

Now the game slowly emerges as the Pirc; a conservative and solid choice to battle white's mastery of the e4 variations. Thinking of the fact that one of the ways to face the classical players' aggressive styles is playing a solid and defensive opening.

7.) d5, Na6
8.) Re1, Nc7
9.) Bf4, b5

Move 9: b5

Black now has the edge in the queenside and threatening to play b4, driving away the c3 knight to capture the e4 pawn. There are still no exchanges on the board, the minor pieces are in their best squares; the position sits prettily well for both colors.

10.) Nxb5, Nxe4
11.) Nxc7, Qxc7
12.) Bc4, Nf6

White took the chance to weaken black's attack on the left wing in exchange of his center e4 pawn. Due to this, Tal neutralized the threats on the queenside then opening up his rook file to put pressure on the e7 pawn, at 12th move, white slightly is in a better position.

13.) h3, Re8
14.) Rb1, a5
15.) Qd2, Qb6

Slowly and silently, both players are preparing the middle game set up. Strengthening their weak points and solidifying their defenses more. Evaluating the positions, all of the pieces are actively participating, and defending together but black has the

Game 47
Simply Instructional

isolated a-pawn in result of the b5 move which itself posing positional imbalances. But as we are still in the middle game stage, that pawn is difficult to exploit.

    16.) Re3, Ba6
    17.) Bxa6, Qxa6
    18.) Rbe1, Kf8

Move 18: Kf8

White continues to put pressure on the weak square at e7, the d5 pawn is perfectly placed and the bishop on f5 is keeping its threat on d6 square if ever the e7 pawn advances, and now the rooks are being piled up; the time that black is in trouble as his pieces are not yet active so far and must defend the pressure.

    19.) Ng5, Qb7
    20.) c4, Qb4
    21.) Qe2, h6

Black wants to simplify the position and neutralize the threats but did a wrong response, h6, letting Tal to think deeply and shift his plan. Now his favorite square, f7 is a subject for infiltrations. All of the following moves after this are forcing now for black and very dominative for white. Instead of h6, Nxd5 seems a tricky sacrifice but not winning as shown below:

    1.) c4, Qb4
    2.) Qe2, Nxd5

    3.) cxd5, Qxf5
    4.) Ne6+, fxe6
    5.) Rf3, Qxf3
    6.) Qxf3+, Kg8
    7.) dxe6, Bxb2

Still the position is not in favor for black as white can shatter the kingside afterwards easily by its pawn swarm.

    22.) Nxf7, Kxf7
    23.) Rb3, Qa4
    24.) Qe6+, Kf8

Move 24: Kf8

Now Tal decided to sacrifice his knight for his mating plans. White is down a piece but threatening to dominate the mating attack as after Rb7 the pressures are simply unstoppable. The black queen can't really help to defend after it was driven away and all of the black's pieces are not in their best places to hold the pressures even more. We can trace back where the losing part starts for black and this is on the 20th move, Qb4, a silent and not seemingly a blunder but gave white a tempo to add stress on the e7 pawn forcing black to defend with its resources. As early as possible, a4 must be played to save the game from approaching combinations.

    1.) Ng5, Qb7
    2.) c4, a4

Game 47
Simply Instructional

3.) R3e2, Rab8
4.) Qc2, Qd7
5.) Nf3, Ng8

Tal could not steal tempi from its Rb3 as the a4 pawn guarded the b3 square and the black queen will be prevented from being stuck at the corner. But now it's too late for black to decide as white is now dominating the back rank premises.

25.) Rb7, Qxc4
26.) Bxd6, Ng8
27.) Re3, Bf6

Move 27: Bf6

We are now seeing the full gripping at the corner with the black king as the lone victim. Black can't recapture the d6 bishop due to the threat of Qf7#. All of the pieces are actively participating to suffer black's position. As Tal is dominating, Speelman was left with a weak and exposed set up dangerous for his king's safety. After several moves, the bomb is ready to explode and clear the board.

28.) Rf3, Kg7
29.) Bxe7, Rxe7
30.) Rxe7+, Nxe7

The exchanges wiped out all of the defending pieces and left black with a lone king with its pieces away from the rescue. The trades are so carefully managed by black to prevent these mating continuations.

1.) Rf3, Kg7
2.) Bxe7, Nxe7
3.) Qxf6+, Kg8
4.) Qe6+, Kh8
5.) Rf7, Qc1+
6.) Kh2, Qg5
7.) d6, Ra6
8.) Rbxe7, Rxe7
9.) Rf8+, Kg7
10.) Qg8# (1-0)

A mating threat is just unstoppable to watch and doesn't make any difference than the latter variations. The worst fate could happen if the bishop retakes as after Rf7+, the black king is then mated afterwards:

1.) Rf3, Kg7
2.) Bxe7, Bxe7
3.) Rf7+, Kh8
4.) Qxg6, Qc1+
5.) Kh2, Qf5+
6.) Rxf5, Rad8

Black is forced to sacrifice his queen to continue the game, preventing the unstoppable Qg7# but more or less, he will lose the match as early as possible.

31.) Qxf6+, Kg8
32.) Qf7+, Kh8
33.) Qxe7, Qxd5
34.) Rf7 (1-0)

Black now couldn't stop the net after Rh7+, Kg8, Qg7# or even if the queen moved to d4 at 34th move continuing the game, white can still manage by moving Rh7+, Kg8, Qf7#.

This is a great game by Tal showing us a very neat and tactical combination to beat the Pirc. Started by his knight sacrifice, the match continued forcing black to defend his attacks until the very end of the royal game. Indeed truly the "Magician from Riga".

Game 48
Reviving the Risk

Robert J. Fischer – Larry Melvyn Evans
US Championship (1963/64)

Move 16: h5

Is there anyone of you used to play and master the King's Gambit? It's one of the craziest opening repertoires on the board. This opening is rarely used in professional matches due to its very risky and aggressive manner of playing. But here, Fischer played it so well and crushed his opponent easily in the end.

1.) e4, e5
2.) f4, exf4
3.) Bc4, Qh4+

White eagerly wanted to test black's wit on how to tackle his king, as it is forced to move very early on removing its right to castle. This idea is quite illogical for the king's safety. Although it is not the strongest opening in town, white's fate will depend on how black manages to grip white's kingside but he can't do that easily if white is well prepared. The king will be forced to move instead of blocking the checks preventing the early king hunt as shown below:

1.) Bc4, Qh4+
2.) g3, fxg3
3.) Bxf7, Kd8
4.) Kf1, gxh2
5.) Nf3, Qh3+

6.) Ke2, Qg2+
7.) Kd3, Nc6

And the game would be so easy to win for black. The white king is just driven out instantly and yes it can regain its position but Evans can't do it in front of Fischer, and everybody knows why.

4.) Kf1, d6
5.) Nc3, Be6
6.) Qe2, c6

Move 6: c6

As white is inviting the chaos to happen, letting black to create the complications more, Evans tried to be conservative and hold his position. He can't fight Fischer in a theoretical middle game and preventing the typical move to play is his idea to level his gain against the classical Bobby. Black is up a pawn but the position sits prettily even for both sides. The only thing that differ the two colors is the white king on f1.

7.) Nf3, Qe7
8.) d4, Bxc4
9.) Qxc4, g5

Then black starts his pawn march. As the rook on h1 is kind of blocked, the white king couldn't run to a safer square once his pawns are all exchanged. At this position, black is

159

Game 48
Reviving the Risk

better but there are still more moves to go to solidify his advantages.

10.) e5, d5
11.) Qd3, Na6
12.) Ne2, Nb4

Move 12: Nb4

From several moves cited above, black has the right to attack but doesn't last long, as after e5, forcing to block the pawn chains preventing to expose the black king, Evans was left with an awkward position as continuing to attack the Fischer's king will make his premises open for infiltrations. The e5 and d4 pawns are against the black bishop's diagonal which itself deals a good grip for Evan's position. Now, both sides had even positional initiatives with a complicated set up. However, if white took the e5 pawn at 10th move, the game would continue as below:

1.) e5, dxe5
2.) Nxe5, f6
3.) Nf3, Nd7
4.) Bxf4, Nb6
5.) Qd3, 0-0-0
6.) Re1, Qd7

This is an almost even position, white had regained the initiatives and both colors are prepared for a dynamic middle game. Avoiding this, white played d5 and preserved the position.

13.) Qd1, 0-0-0
14.) c3, Na6
15.) h4, g4

Move 15: g4

Now things are getting more complicated. White allowed black to storm his own king safety, as pawns are coming towards his premises so are the rooks afterwards. But he can attack the queenside too by playing b4-a4-b5 maneuver, seems a little late but defending his kingside is more important now. After several continuations, let us see how the play transformed in favor of white or is the risk worthy to be played?

16.) Nh2, h5
17.) Nxf4, Qxh4
18.) Kg1, Nh6

As the white king is slowly surviving the attack, black is securing his positional advantages. Fischer must defend carefully to hold his premises and must find a way to escape the awkward square. However, white can still defend the king with his pieces.

19.) Nf1, Qe7
20.) Nxh5, Rg8
21.) Nfg3, Rg6

Although black pawns are over-extended and defenseless on exchanges, black rooks can now participate fully on the partially open

Game 48
Reviving the Risk

files. Black king is sitting prettily in the corner and the other in danger although the minor pieces are more active and can hold and defend well. KGA is such a risky opening to play.

22.) Nf4, Rg5
23.) Be3, Nc7
24.) Qd2, Rg8

Move 24: Rg8

As all of the minor pieces of white are holding and defending the place, black provoked to allow an exchange of its minor pieces for his rook to lessen the defenses, in which Fischer didn't allowed. However, let us see the how the situation will be if white seized Nxd5 at 23rd move, a very tempting to play.

1.) Nf4, Rg5
2.) Nxd5, Rxd5
3.) Bxg5, Qxg5
4.) Qe2, Nc7
5.) Rf1, Bg7

Black will be slightly better in this position, as his minor pieces are slowly creeping toward the white king.

25.) Nfe2, f6
26.) exf6, Qxf6
27.) Bxh6, Bd6

Unnoticeably, white is silently eyeing the isolated h6 knight which was captured defenselessly. Now, Fischer

has the upper hand, winning the position immediately. Fischer's active and perfectly placed pieces harden and solidify his premises as black didn't found a way to exploit his structure.

28.) Rf1, Qe6
29.) Bf4, Rde8
30.) Rh6, Bxf4

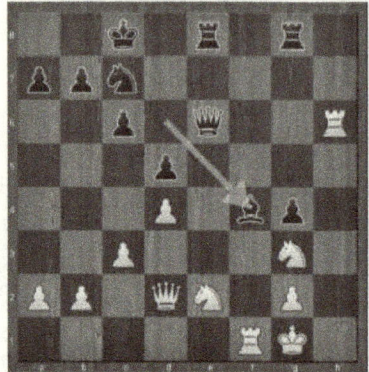

Move 30: Bxf4

One of the classic lessons in the game of chess, "If you're ahead, simplify; if you're behind, complicate.", and this is what Fischer is doing in this moment. Slowly and surely, after the exchanges, white will be lead to a winning position in the endgame afterwards.

31.) Qxf4, Qe7
32.) Rf6, Ne6
33.) Qe5, Ng5

Continuing his plan, white are provoking the trades preserving his position and forcing black to enter the endgame and exchange the pieces as black can't find a way to complicate the set up.

34.) Qxe7, Rxe7
35.) Rf8+, Rxf8
36.) Rxf8+ (1-0)

In any of the way possible, black can't escape the losing endgame, as white is threatening to play Rg8 and win.

Game 49
The Power of Activity

Robert J. Fischer – Edwin Bhend
Zurich (1959)

Move 20: Rxe7

Fischer's favorite opening to tame is the Sicilian Variation. Here, he immediately dominated the game and crushingly beat black easily like a beginner. His activity is better than any other plays on the board controlling and diminishing black in the cleanest possible style.

    1.) e4, c5
    2.) Nf3, g6
    3.) d4, cxd4

This is the Hungarian variation; we can see an early g6 on the board instead of Nc6 of the Dragon line, a refutable opening based on how Fischer manages to counter play black's movement until toward the middle phase of the game.

    4.) Nxd4, Nf6
    5.) Nc3, Bg7
    6.) e5, Ng8

White at an early stage, already controlled and dominated the center; the f6 knight is forced to retreat to g8 square instead of Nh5 preventing the deadly g4 cornering the piece, black at this moment, wasted several tempo and is already behind in development. Due to this, white would be so easy to continue the initiative.

    7.) Bf4, Nc6
    8.) Nxc6, bxc6
    9.) Bc4, f6

Move 9: f6

The move f6 is just out of sense for black as it opens a file for the white bishop to control and greatly weaken black's kingside structure. Black may continue to play Nh6 to safely hold the match.

    1.) Bc4, Nh6
    2.) Qf3, 0-0
    3.) 0-0-0, Qb6
This is a better way to make space for the king and to castle safely as possible.

    10.) e6, dxe6
    11.) Qf3, Qb6
    12.) 0-0, Nh6

Fischer may consider playing Qf3 instead of e6 at 10th move, holding the position and keeping the open diagonal for the bishop instead of closing black's structure. An interesting line would be:

    1.) Bc4, f6
    2.) Qf3, fxe5
    3.) Bxe5, Nf6
    4.) 0-0-0, Rf8
Black king will stay at the center exposed from attacks; a more dominative line in favor for white.

Game 49
The Power of Activity

13.) Na4, Qd4
14.) Bxh6, Bxh6
15.) Qxc6+, Kf7

Move 15: Kf7

Black is willing to sacrifice his c6 pawn as this is already defenseless and isolated just to use this as a tempo in driving his king in its safe square. Bhend escaped the threats and his king now is already protected at least for some time.

16.) Rae1, Rb8
17.) Bxe6+, Kg7
18.) Bd5, Bg5

It's funny to think that Fischer wants to complicate things more, instead of ending the game in a simpler way. In this moment in time, white could continue taking the rook but chose to add pressures on the e6 square. However, the match may end obviously as shown below:

1.) Qxc6+, Kf7
2.) Qxa8, Qxc4
3.) Qxa7, Qxc2
4.) Nb6, Qxb2
5.) a4, Bf4

Black's pieces are just wandering the board for no clear reasons while white is working a greater threat of promoting the a4 pawn. It is a clear winning line for white but Fischer want to continue more.

19.) Re4, Qd2
20.) Rxe7+, Kh6
21.) Rxa7, Bf5

White is demolishing the board; the pawn structure falls down and the black queen was drove in a very exposed square. At this instance, the activity and initiative is fully on white while black will continue defending after several moves.

22.) c4, Rbd8
23.) Nc5, Rhe8
24.) Ne6, Bxe6

Move 24: Bxe6

Black is trying to control the center files as he is behind in development, but can't prevent to trade pieces and simplify the position toward a losing endgame. Slowly and surely, white is grabbing the winning bar; the three passed pawns are so immensely strong and the endgame in favor of white is near to happen.

25.) Bxe6, Be3
26.) Rd7, Bxf2+
27.) Rxf2, Qe1+

In the middle of the trades, black had found a way to slightly even the match as the bishop on e6 will be attacked twice after the check. After several moves, the board will simplify but white will be left with several promoting pawns.

Game 49
The Power of Activity

28.) Rf1, Qe3+
29.) Kh1, Rxe6
30.) Rxh7+, Kxh7

Move 30: Kxh7

Out of simple rook position, Fischer found a way again to get another free pawn as he can take the d8 rook after Qc7+. White's isolated pawns are still intact and free to march toward the last square.

31.) Qc7+, Kh6
32.) Qxd8, Qe2
33.) Qd1, Qxb2

Black had sneaked a pawn but Fischer unstoppably wants to exchange queens to simplify the board toward his winning endgame. Once the queens were eliminated, it will be an easy game for white to continue his promoting plans.

34.) Qc1+, Qxc1
35.) Rxc1, Re2
36.) a3, Ra2

This is an easy endgame for white. The position is clear without a doubt that black is losing. Only after a few continuations that Bhend decided to resign the game.

37.) c5, Rxa3
38.) c6, Ra8
39.) c7, Rc8
40.) Kg1, Kg5 (1-0)

An endgame we don't want to play.

Continuing the situation, black will be hopeless to defend the c7 pawn and stop the white king from participating. The black rook is locked on the c8 square while the other can roam on the c-file. The position may continue as shown on the following lines:

1.) Kg1, Kg5
2.) Kf2, Kf4
3.) Rc6, Ke5
4.) Kg3, Kd5
5.) Rxf6, Rxc7
6.) Rxg6, Ke5

Playing the rook endgame with another two pawns on the side clearly wins the game in favor of Fischer.

The game easily went on to favor Fischer's position as early in the opening. The early g6 doesn't control any of the center squares followed by its Nf6 provoking white to play e5; the retreat of the knight doesn't gain anything. The Hungarian variation of the Sicilian line doesn't lead to a stronger position in the middle game and wasted several tempos in which white exploited and his advantages multiplied. However, in all of the Sicilian variations, e6 is a stronger reply to block the e5 pawn from infiltrations. The activity on the board, the control on the center and the participation of the pieces are the factors of winning this match. Fischer is famous in doing all of these that's why he delivered a winning line neatly as it seems.

Game 50
Aggressive Approach

Robert J. Fischer – Anthony Saidy
US Championship (1966)

Move 18: Rae1

Considered by many as one of the aggressive players in his time, Bobby Fischer hasn't lost his tempo since the opening and continued to play his winning advantage. In this game, black is defending all his resources until the very end just to keep his premises intact, and still, losing the game.

1.) e4, c5
2.) Nf3, Nc6
3.) d4, cxd4

This is the typical Sicilian game, a complicated line that houses several variations of combinations in which Fischer mastered to play. After several moves, the initiative will be on white and black will be forever defending.

4.) Nxd4, Nf6
5.) Nc3, d6
6.) Bc4, Qb6

As early as 6th move, black developed his queen which is not a clear continuation of the typical Sicilian. The better line is Bd7 or simply e6. As of this moment, white is ready to castle and create a masterpiece on the center.

7.) Nb3, e6
8.) 0-0, Be7
9.) Be3, Qc7

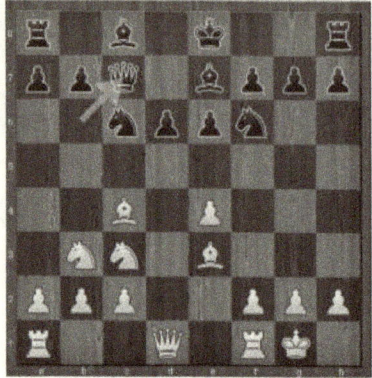

Move 9: Qc7

Black had lost one tempo of development as his queen was forced to retreat to c7 square. We can see that white's pieces are more active and dynamic compare to black's as this is the typical set up of this opening. Black must try to hold and keep his premises intact until the middle game; this is the time he can even the initiatives and counter attack.

10.) f4, 0-0
11.) Bd3, a6
12.) g4, b5

At this stage, white decided to stream on to black's kingside as his bishops are eyeing. In response, Saidy opened the diagonal of his b7 fianchetto exploiting the open spaces of the white king. But based on several games we had studied, black must defend the incoming pawn swarm rather than developing on the other side of the board before its getting too late to prevent the demolition.

13.) g5, Ne8
14.) Qh5, g6
15.) Qh6, f5

Game 50
Aggressive Approach

Black may try Nd7 at 13th move sparing some spaces for the rook and king to escape if necessary but Ne8 is not that really a bad response as it's keeping the bishop's diagonal opened for the defense. Saidy may respond f6 if he wants to create a more dynamic and complicated set up that may lead to the following position;

    1.) Qh5, g6
    2.) Qh6, f6
    3.) f5, Ne5
    4.) fxg6, Nxg6
    5.) Nd4, Ne5
    6.) Kh1, Ng4
    7.) Qh3, Nxe3
    8.) Qxe3, fxg5

As there are several pieces on the board defending the threats, white can still keep his intact premises, or at least for some time.

    16.) exf5, gxf5
    17.) Nd4, Nd8
    18.) Rae1, Ng7

Move 18: Ng7

White's pieces are slowly creeping through black's kingside, gradually infiltrating the position. But the knight pair is so flexible and can protect important squares against threats. Black is doing a great job in defending

the attack; he must keep holding this until the beginning of the endgame where he can now tear up the center for his counter play.

    19.) Rf3, Nf7
    20.) Qh4, Nh8
    21.) Rh3, h5

Move 21: h5

At close position, the knight is clearly better than the bishop, Saidy had managed to create a stronghold in his premises, locking the structure and keeping the weak squares protected. Black is literally a good defender here, essential when playing an aggressive classical player like Fischer.

    22.) Be2, Ng6
    23.) Qf2, b4
    24.) Nd1, e5

Somewhat somehow, instead of Be2, there is another way to tear up the defense. The move Nxf5, a provoking continuation giving white in the edge of winning as shown;

    1.) Nxf5, exf5
    2.) Nd5, Qb7
    3.) Nf6+, Kf7
    4.) Nxh5, Ng6
    5.) Qg3, Qd5
    6.) Nxg7, Kxg7
    7.) c3, Bb7
    8.) Bd4+, Kf7

Game 50
Aggressive Approach

9.) Rh7+, Ke8
10.) Rg7, Rh8
11.) Rxe7+, Nxe7
12.) Bxh8, Kd7
13.) Bd4, Rf8

White controls the situation but the fianchetto bishop on b7 is too risky to ignore. Maybe the Nxf5 combination is not that ripe to do as there are still loopholes in the position. Due to this, Fischer chose the silent but deadly Be2.

25.) Bxh5, Nxh5
26.) Rxh5, exd4
27.) Bxd4, Bb7

Move 27: Bb7

Black can manage and hold the situation with his teaming resources and until the time that there will be few minor pieces in the end, black can do the counter play as he has the strong bishop pair. White must do something to prove and keep his aggressiveness; sacrificing his knight for two pawns to control and access the e-file, risking a piece for positional play is a typical Fischer mindset. But there are safer choices to continue the match without risking the knight, as shown below;

1.) Nd1, e5
2.) Nb3, Bb7
3.) Qc1, h4

4.) c3, a5
5.) Nc1, Ne6

White will be forced to defend as black is slowly gaining back his lost hope to even the initiatives. From this viewpoint, trading the knight with two pawns, the h5 and d4 pawn, is worth to play.

28.) Rh6, Kf7
29.) Qe2, Be4
30.) Qh5, Rg8

Move 30: Rg8

This is the most demolishing part of the game where the black king will be driven away from his premises. White's piece sacrifice will be regained as the g6 knight will then fall after several continuations. All of the pieces of white are actively participating while there are still undeveloped rook on black's a8 square. This is not surprising on every match of Fischer, his dynamic movement and incredible wit to tackle and sneak into the position matches no one in his prime.

31.) Rxg6, Rxg6
32.) Qh7+, Ke8
33.) Qxg6+, Kd7

Now the plan was worth the risk. White is two pawns up but black's bishops were still a threat to the open

Game 50
Aggressive Approach

kingside. Both kings are in their awkward square so it's early to decide which color had the better position.

35.) Nf2, Qc4
35.) Nxe4, Qxd4+
36.) Nf2, Qxf4

Move 36: Qxf4

At 36th move, instead of taking the f4 pawn, black should play safely like Qd5 saving the bishop from the threat of white's Qe6+. This could be the more simplified way to approach the endgame as shown in the following continuation;

1.) Nf2, Qd5
2.) Rd1, Qe6
3.) Qxe6+, Kxe6
4.) Kg2, Bf8
5.) h4, Bg7

As long as there are no queens on the board, black can hold longer and even the initiatives from positional plays.

37.) Qe6+, Kc6
38.) Qxe7, Rg8
39.) Qe3, Rxg5+
40.) Kh1 (1-0)

The consequences of giving up the bishop really hit black in the face. The only compensation; the white king is cornered and subject for mating threat but as long as its pieces are defending the weak squares, black can do nothing but to wait. Once the queens were traded, it will be an easy win for white to continue the game. The match may continue as shown below;

1.) Qe3, Rxg5+
2.) Kh1, Qh4
3.) h3, Rg3
4.) Qe2, Kb6
5.) Rg1, a5
6.) Rxg3, Qxg3
7.) Qf1, Qf3+
8.) Qg2, Qe3
9.) Nd3, Qh6

The rooks were traded and the black queen can't have the support to infiltrate the king's position. As long as white defended its premises and not hasting to attack the black king, the endgame would be in his favor. The only thing that black must prevent is the trade of his pieces which is difficult to do in the future several moves as his king is slightly open for exploitations.

White ended the game with a piece up against his opponent but his king's position is subject for attack that must be carefully defended until the chance of trading the pieces exists on the board. This is a very risky and aggressive approach to tame the Sicilian, as we can see on white's early moves. All in all, the dynamic of white's pieces and its participation in unison is clearly the factor in winning this match. By the way, it is now in the 18th of July year 2021, and I'm hoping that you've learned several things from the 50 chess games. Good luck and enjoy your journey towards a more competitive future!

www.ingramcontent.com/pod-product-compliance
Lightning Source LLC
LaVergne TN
LVHW092303030125
800400LV00003B/627